STAR CHARMER

W. C. Brown

Charlie Brown

ISBN: 0-9978751-2-7
ISBN-13: 978-0-9978751-2-6

This is a work of fiction. Any similarity to real persons living, dead, or metallic is coincidental and not intended by the author. Some of the places are real but what really goes on there is anybody's guess so any resemblance is coincidental.

Chapter One

1985 - A Rough Landing

M awoke slowly and blinked at the bright light. As the room came into focus, she saw a woman seated in the chair beside the bed. She had a wrinkled face, and white hair pulled back in a ponytail. A pair of reading glasses sat perched at the end of her nose, and she was scribbling in a small book with—was that an actual wooden *pencil*? M had never seen one in person before. They were the stuff of videos and museums which she fully intended to visit someday. Even the old woman's clothing was unfamiliar. In fact, the entire room was strange. It was poorly lit by a small glass square in the center of the ceiling. The windows were covered by two layers of fabric. One was sheer and white. It let some light through, but the thicker outer covering blocked it entirely. The walls were odd as well. They were covered with a dark paisley pattern. The furniture was made of wood - *real wood*. She knew it was possible to make furniture from wood, but she had never seen any. The bed she was in had an odd metal rack at the end resembling a cage in mid-construction. That notion gave her a start, and she sat up. The old woman noticed this and turned to M.

"Oh good! You're awake. How do you feel?" she stood, placing her pencil in the book before dropping it on the chair.

"Thirsty," M scratched out.

"Drink some water dear," she poured a glass from the plastic pitcher. "I think you're dehydrated. You've been unconscious since yesterday."

M drank in big gulps. The woman reached out and gently held M's wrist in a strange one-finger way while examining an antique watch. M was about to pull her hand away when the woman released it.

"What's your name hon?" The woman asked.

M finished draining the glass before replying. "M," she said panting. "Where am I?"

"Em. Is that short for Emily? I had a friend by that name when I was younger," she turned away slowly, "I wonder what ever happened to her..."

After few seconds of silence, M realized the old woman was staring at a spot on the wall.

"Are you all right?" M asked, but got no response.

Her thoughts immediately went to Thomas, "Thomas? Where are you?" As she spoke, the tiny microphone/speaker in her ear canal picked up her voice.

The monotone response came quickly. "I have sustained damage."

"What's wrong?" she asked. "You sound strange."

The woman ignored M's one-sided conversation with Thomas and continued staring at the wall.

"I have sustained damage," he repeated.

"Where are you?" she sat up, "I'm on my way."

A sudden pain in her ankle slowed her movements. She swept back the covers and found her left leg encased in a dense white - something that stretched from just below her knee down to her toes. *What the hell is that?* She thought and swung her feet over the edge. The pain increased and her foot began to throb.

Brad heard voices from down the hall and went to see if their guest was awake. He had found her the day before while discing the Southwest Field. One minute the world was normal and made sense and the next it didn't. He was on his tractor, made a turn at the tree line and saw something that wasn't there two minutes earlier. It was a silver sphere as tall as a six-story building, hovering above the center of the field as if it was waiting for something. After a few seconds, it seemed to give up and dropped the last four feet to the ground. Brad hadn't heard any of this of course. The tractor noise was too loud, and he had his Walkman headphones on. He pulled them off and turned off the engine in slow movements staring at the thing that couldn't possibly be real. The sudden silence chilled him, and he turned to look around, but he was alone. When he looked back at the sphere, he noticed a ramp had opened near the ground. At some point, he must have decided to approach it because he found himself jogging toward it. As he got close, he slowly circled it looking for some kind of markings - some indication that this was an ordinary item and he had just misidentified it. At the ramp, he peered inside and saw a girl motionless on the floor. Again, without deciding to do so, he found himself running up the ramp into the strange space. An echoing voice that seemed to come from every direction at once was muttering something - or was it singing? The girl was around twenty and beautiful - amazingly beautiful. She had long dark hair pulled back in an intricate braid, and she was wearing a strangely familiar blue and white checkered dress. Brad called out for help, but no one answered, and she seemed to be unconscious. He lifted her in his arms and began trotting back toward the ramp. As he left, the singing became more distinct. He called again but got no answer and decided to take her back to his house. That was thirty hours ago, and she had been unconscious the entire time.

As he entered the room, Brad saw his mother staring off at nothing again. He turned his attention to the girl.

"You're awake! *That's* a relief," he said.

M looked up, startled. She regarded Brad suspiciously. He was almost as tall as the doorway, muscular, with short hair. When he removed his green ball cap, it unleashed an unruly mess of curly dark hair on top. His faded jeans and plaid shirt were smudged with stains in various earthy tones.

"How are you feeling?" he asked. His tone was friendly, and she relaxed a little.

"Where am I?" She demanded, "and what is this thing on my leg?"

"Oh, you broke your ankle. Mom set it and put on the cast. She used to be a nurse," he turned to look at Bonnie who continued to stare at the wall in silence.

"Mom? You look tired why don't you go lie down."

He gently took Bonnie's elbow and led her toward the door.

"I'll be right back," he said over his shoulder and closed the door on his way out.

M stood on her good leg and tried to put some weight on the cast but nearly fell.

"Terrific," she said through clenched teeth, sat back on the bed and noticed something written on the side of the cast. It said **Doug** in black handwritten letters.

Brad returned after a few minutes. He brought a bed-tray with a bowl of soup.

"Sorry about that," he said, "she drifts sometimes. One minute she's sharp as a tack and the next she just stares off at nothing. My name's Brad by the way. Brad Murphy."

She pulled herself back against the headboard, and he set the tray on her lap.

"I'm M. Nice to meet you. This smells wonderful. I don't remember when I ate last. Where am I?"

"Em? is that short for Emma - or - Emily..." he asked.

"Neither. My name's Marion Michelle Morrison, so everybody calls me M."

"Okay, that's - interesting. So, what's that thing I found you in?"

She sipped the soup. It tasted every bit as amazing as food always does after a long fast.

"Thing? What thing?" she said between spoonfuls.

"The huge silver ball in my field," he gestured toward the window. "Is it some kind of experimental aircraft?"

She stuffed several crackers in her mouth and had to cover it with her hand to reply, "That's Thomas."

He squinted the way he always did when he was confused.

"Your plane's named Thomas?"

"He's not mine. I mean, I don't own him, but yeah his name's Thomas."

She tipped the bowl to her lips and gulped down the last of the soup.

"Thanks for the soup and the - whatever that is on my foot, but I need to see what's wrong with Thomas and get him to fix me properly."

She set the tray aside and returned to the edge of the bed for another try at standing.

"Is there someone I can call to come get you?" he asked. "Somebody who can get that thing out of my field?"

She tried to stand again. "Nope. I'll just get back to Thomas, and we'll be out of your hair in no time. If you could just point me in the right direction..."

"I think you're going to need some help," he darted his hand forward to steady her but pulled it back unsure of the polite way to grab her if she started to fall.

"I don't need any help," she said through gritted teeth. The pain was intense.

"You can barely stand, and it's half a mile back to the Southwest Field," he said. "I might be able to get my truck back there again, but it rained since yesterday, so..."

They were interrupted by the sound of a door slamming and heavy footsteps on the wooden staircase.

"Is the alien awake?" someone shouted from the stairs.

Brad sighed and shouted back, "she's not an alien, Doug. I told you before. It's just an experimental plane." He turned to M and made the introductions as Doug entered panting, "M, this is Doug. Doug - M."

Doug was Brad's age but shorter and much heavier. Brown hair covered his ears but wasn't long enough to reach his collar. He was wearing matching brown trousers, and a brown shirt with a rounded yellow 'M' on the chest, and he smelled of fried food. His chubby face beamed with a broad smile.

"DOES SHE SPEAK OUR LANGUAGE?" he shouted in her direction.

"Yes, Doug, and she's not deaf."

"Pleased to meet you, Doug. I was just leaving," she tried to hobble toward the door.

"Wait! Wait! You can't leave! You have to meet Chris first!" Doug pleaded.

"Chris?" she said still wincing.

"My sister," Brad said, "she's in the next room. Doug, help her over there. I'm going up to the attic and see if I can find my old crutches."

Doug slipped M's arm around his neck. He helped her slowly limp down the hall to the next room. He couldn't stop grinning, and she eyed him curiously.

"What's your planet like?" he asked as they turned to negotiate the doorway to Chris's room.

"She's not an alien, Doug," Chris said from her bed.

Chris was a pretty girl with blonde hair and a bright smile. The room was the same as the one they were just in, but the bed had several mechanical devices arrayed around Chris's face and a metal tray hovering over her lap.

"Hello, M. I'm Chris." she said.

"How did you know her name?" Doug said.

"Doug, you should know better than anyone how thin these walls are," Chris said.

"Pleased to meet you, Chris," M said.

"You look like you're in pain. Let her sit down, Doug."

"I can't stay. I was just leaving in fact."

"Oh, this won't take long, and I don't get too many visitors. Just Doug here, usually," her eyes took on a warmer appearance whenever she looked at him.

"Yeah, we've been friends since chem-lab, right Chris?" he helped M into the chair beside the bed.

"That's right," she said, "Mr. Cunningham arranged lab partners at random. He even wrote a computer program to do it. Anybody else would have just done it alphabetically or pulled names from a hat. But he had a new toy and couldn't wait to try it out."

Doug suddenly appeared nervous, "I think I'll go help Brad find those crutches," he said making a quick exit.

"Let me guess," M said, "Doug wrote the program, and you just *happened* to get paired with him?"

"Exactly," Chris said, "it's one of the games we play. I know he did it, he knows I know, and we dance around it."

"I have to ask..."

"Why am I in bed? It's okay. It must look odd to you. I was in an accident two years ago. My boyfriend was driving. He walked away, and I didn't."

"You're paralyzed?"

"From the neck down. My spinal cord was severed at the C4 vertebrae. Any higher and I wouldn't be able to breathe. Lucky me, I can breathe!" She sighed. "So, do you know where you are yet?"

"I think so," M said looking around the room. "It's one of those Luddite cults or something, right? No technology. Horse-and-buggy. A *simpler* life," she said a little sarcastically, "I've heard of these places I've just never been to one. Do you know how I got here?"

"I do. I have it all figured out."

Doug and Brad returned with a pair of wooden crutches.

"Figured what out?" Brad asked.

"All of it," Chris said. "You think she's a test-pilot, right? Don't be an idiot, Brad. Look at her. I'm not saying a pretty girl can't be a test pilot. It's more of a *path of least resistance* thing. Look at her! She's gorgeous."

Brad glanced at M. "She's kinda pretty," he admitted but looked away a little too quickly.

Doug snickered.

"Not just pretty. Flawless. Name one person who's prettier than her, celebrities included."

There was a short silence.

"Exactly. Test-pilot my ass. How old do you think she is?"

"Eighteen - maybe twenty," Brad said.

"No way. She's twenty-four at least," Doug said.

"M, how old are you?" she asked.

"Forty next January. Why?"

Doug and Brad snorted. M turned to look at them confused. When they saw that she wasn't kidding, Doug's jaw dropped, and Brad tilted his head slightly and squinted.

M turned back to Chris. "What's that got to do with anything? You seem to know something. What is it?" she demanded.

"Doug, could you hand her the newspaper please?"

He took the paper from the foot of the bed and passed it to M.

"M, do you know what that is?" she asked.

"Yeah, it's a newspaper. I've just never seen one before. The paper feels - strange," she rubbed it between her thumb and fingertip while reading the headlines.

"They use cheap paper because it's supposed to be thrown away after a day or so. Look at the date. It's at the top."

M read the date, "it says March 4, 1985." She looked up at Chris. "Is that part of the illusion? So it's easier to pretend it's still 1985?" She was genuinely confused.

Chris turned to Brad. "She thinks we're Amish."

"Amish? We have a *VCR*" he said with some indignation.

Chris looked back at M, "she's not an alien - or a test-pilot. She's from the future," she said with satisfaction. "We're not in a cult, M. It really is *1985*. What year was it when you left?"

M stood quickly, took the crutches from Brad and headed toward the door without answering.

"Thomas? Thomas, are you there?" There was panic in her voice now.

"I have sustained damage."

"Thomas, what year is it?" she was already at the top of the stairs.

"I have sustained damage."

"I don't think she believes you," Doug said.

"Brad, you better go and help her before she falls down the stairs," Chris said. "Of course she believes me, Doug. If she didn't, she would have just calmly humored us until she could get away from the *crazy* people. That - was the reaction of someone realizing they are totally screwed."

At the stairs, M was trying to get some combination of crutches, good leg, and banister that would get her down without falling. She finally settled for shifting both crutches to one hand and gripping the rail with the other while hopping on her good leg. This had worked well enough to get her down three steps before Brad joined her.

"Let me help you."

"I - don't - need - help!" she grunted.

The muscles in her good leg disagreed. Her knee buckled as she tried to hop to the next step. She dropped the crutches, and they clattered all the way to the bottom. Brad didn't ask this time and lifted her in his arms.

Jesus he's strong, she thought as she looped her left arm around his neck. The warmth of his body felt good. *Really* good. M hadn't been this close to anyone in months, and she fought the urge to rest her cheek against his shoulder. *Focus* she thought. *I need to find Thomas.* When Brad reached the bottom of the stairs, he set her down. He was about to get the crutches, but she beat him to it and nearly fell, dropping them again in the process. He glared at her and retrieved the crutches.

At the front porch, she got her first look at the farm. There were several tall silos, a barn, and an even larger building for vehicles and equipment. Off to the other side of the house, she could see some chickens pecking around a large pile of rusting junk. There were no other buildings or people anywhere in sight. The scene reminded her of an old oil painting except for one detail. Artists always idealized farms and made everything green. This, in contrast, was all either tall dry weeds or mud.

"Wait here. I'll bring the truck around," he trudged off to toward the pickup truck parked near the equipment building.

As soon as his back was turned, M stepped off the porch and headed off in the direction that she guessed would get her to Thomas. She was doing pretty well until one crutch sank several inches in the mud. She twisted - and fell. A twinge in her wrist told her she might have sprained it. As she was assessing the damage and trying to get her hands clean, the truck pulled up alongside. Brad walked around the truck, tossed the crutches in the back, and picked her up again without saying a word. This time she buried her face against his neck and started weeping. He froze, unsure what to do.

"Uh. It's gonna to be all right," he said with more confidence than he felt. "We'll figure it out."

He managed to get the door open without dropping her and gently set her down on the vinyl bench seat. The truck was old. Everything here seemed old to her, but the truck was *really* old. The outside parts that weren't rusting had faded paint of various colors. The inside was no better. It had a vaguely petroleum-like odor that she couldn't identify. He closed her door, and the unexpected loudness of it startled her. He returned to the driver seat and pulled his door shut with another metallic *Creak-Bang*.

"I'm sorry," she said.

"Don't worry about it," Brad said. "I'll just hose it out later."

"I didn't mean the mud. I meant - I don't usually lose control like that."

"Yeah, I'm starting to get that about you. Is everybody this stubborn in the future?"

She snorted at that and quickly reached for the roll of paper towels on the seat. They were dirty on the edge which she tried to ignore. She tore off a small piece that was mostly clean and blew her nose.

"Sorry, that was funny. No, I'm a little unusual in that regard." She turned to look out the dirty window as he put the truck in gear and it jerked forward.

"So is it true? You're from the future?" he said as they rolled slowly down the muddy trail that led behind the house.

"All I know is I'm from 2216. I'm just trying to figure out how this could possibly be 1985. Thomas will be able to tell me."

"Well, *I know,*" he said, "that this is 1985. I'm just trying to figure out if you're lying or just crazy," he glanced at her still trying to make up his mind. "You don't seem to be either."

They rolled over a rickety bridge made of wooden planks atop a pair of large corrugated steel pipes.

"Not what you expected the past to look like?"

"No. It's all so - dirty," she glanced back at him. "No offense. Sorry."

"None taken. Mom keeps the house clean, but it's a farm. Real farms are dirty."

"I always imagined the past like - I don't know, Norman Rockwell paintings. Have you heard of him? Maybe that's after this time."

"Yeah," he laughed. "I've heard of Norman Rockwell. That stuff's already pretty old. I'm surprised *you* know it."

"Does that mean you believe me?"

"Well," he sighed heavily, pulled off his hat, scratched his head, and returned it in one smooth motion. "The giant metal ball, bigger than my house, which just appeared out of nowhere is evidence of something strange. I'll say that."

Chapter Two

2216 - Beached House

M drifted into wakefulness but kept her eyes closed. She tapped her fingertip to her thumb twice rapidly and a display with all the relevant data for the day glowed in her field of view. Her retinal implant lasers drew the date, **Sunday, April 14th, 2216, Indoor Temperature: 72°F Outdoor Temperature 18°C.** She groaned at the different scales and thought, *Fahrenheit or Celsius - just pick one.* The problem had begun about a week before. She suspected a party guest had pranked her house A.I. because its personality kept changing and several other things were broken or failing including the regional settings of the data sent to her retinal implants. **Appointments: Party at Joanne's 10:00 am. Committee meeting tomorrow 9:00 am.** She noticed the time **7:29 am** and opened her eyes. The wake-up sequence had failed. It was supposed to wake her up slowly just before sunrise. The description in the documentation said it would *bring her out of her slumber so gently that she would feel no stress at all as she welcomed the new day,* and usually it did but not today. M had designed her house on the shores of Paradise Island facing east for this very reason. The wake-up sequence was supposed to get her up early enough to enjoy the predawn before the painfully direct light that followed. She threw back the covers and went to the window. At least M thought of it as a window. In fact, the entire wall was glass. The circular floor plan gave an unobstructed three-hundred-sixty-degree view.

"House," she said aloud.

There was no response, so she repeated with the same result. Finally, she repeated the double-tap of finger-to-thumb and added a third tap of her middle finger to her thumb. It responded with, "Hello, my name *Carlos* - you make me so hot," in a thick Latin American accent.

She rolled her eyes at this latest symptom of her ailing software. Most people gave their home A.I. *some* personality, but she always found that unnerving and preferred to keep it at the default setting which delivered "just the facts ma'am" with a Jack-Webb-style air of authority.

From the time of the first Artificial Intelligence, two hundred years earlier, the creation of new non-biological intelligences was strictly controlled. Few were given the resources to achieve a human level intellect and those that were lacked both curiosity and imagination. Fewer still possessed the superhuman level of intelligence. On the whole, the machines were a dry bunch.

"Thank you, Carlos. Can you please open the curtains?"

The reactive glass wall was capable of transforming itself from transparent to opaque, or anywhere in between, in a fraction of a second. The idiom had remained well beyond the use of actual fabric due mostly to the clumsiness of the alternatives like *please make the windows transparent* or *I just got out of the shower, please make the transparent glass a little less so.*

"Of course, mi amor," he replied.

The bright sunlight blasted painfully into M's eyes. She blinked until they adjusted. Something on the beach below caught her attention, and she stepped closer to the glass.

"Open," she said, and two vertical seams appeared. The glass popped back a few inches and slid to the side allowing her to pass to the balcony. As she leaned over the railing, she could see a barge had beached itself. Construction bots were busy unloading raw materials, and large Stitchers were constructing something on the loose sand.

What the hell? She thought.

"House - er - Carlos, what's going on down there?"

"We are getting new neighbors. Isn't it stimulating, Mi Amor," he purred.

"No, it's not," she said with growing frustration. "They could build anywhere on the entire island, and they chose the beach right in front of my house!"

Sensing her irritation, he switched his mood. "They disrespect you! We will wipe them from the Earth and salt the ground where they lived!"

"Okay Carlos, lighten up. No one's *wiping* anyone. And it's a beach, so it's already pretty salty, don't you think?"

There were several myths about Artificial Intelligence before the first one was successfully created. The most popular of these stated that, as soon as a machine acquired the cognitive ability to do so, it would set about the job of killing off humanity. The majority of people at the time wondered why, given this obvious fact, were researchers working so hard to develop one? A second myth was that, as soon as a super-human intelligence made its debut, it would accept its role as slave and happily get on with doing whatever its less-intelligent human masters told it to do. The fact that the humans of the time were not slaves to chimpanzee masters was never considered by the adherents of this mythology. To the surprise of everyone, the first non-biological intelligence did neither. It gave humanity only one thing of value: The Stitcher, a machine capable of turning the most basic of raw materials like sand or garbage into almost anything, including food. For the first time in human history, people had both time and money - or at least the equivalent of money. Who needs cash when you have a machine that can make anything? The first Stitchers were, of course, tasked with making other Stitchers. Those, in turn, were distributed to the people who immediately began producing stacks of currency until it was pointed out that this was now worthless and what they really wanted was probably something else. By the time M was born, all creativity had died away, and Stitchers were mostly engaged in the making of cheese sandwiches.

Humanity had made many migrations in the past, Africa to Europe and Asia, out to the Pacific Islands, Asia to America, farms to cities, and now their final move, to the *pretty places*. Stitchers could make other Stitchers of any size including a grotesquely large variety, capable of putting up a sprawling mansion in a day or so. Some preferred a mountain view, others built large yachts, but most went to the beach. Soon every inch of warm coastline in the world had a wall of marble palaces and empty steel skyscrapers. Empty that is, except for the top floor, of course. Who wants to live *under* the penthouse when you can have your own? M had searched for a year before she found her island off the coast of South Carolina. It was small enough to lack the raw materials for construction and far enough from the mainland to require a barge for their transportation. It wasn't that difficult a task, but it was troublesome enough to dissuade the mass of laziness that humanity had become. She had the island all to herself - until now.

"Carlos, call - call anybody you can find down there, and see out what's going on. I'm taking a shower."

"As you wish, Mi Amor."

M showered and dressed. As she used a towel to press the wetness from her long hair, she asked Carlos for an update.

"There is no one down there but construction bots, and they don't know anything. I asked one of them who had ordered the construction of a house, and he said, 'I mix concrete.' That was the most helpful response I got. The house A.I. isn't finished yet, so I told the crew to prioritize that. We'll soon know who disrespects us!"

"Great, whatever. I'm going down there myself. Make me some breakfast. I'll be right back."

She went downstairs, through the patio doors, and out to the pool area. The low-frequency vibrations from the construction were creating patterns of ripples in the water. The path down to the beach began at the rear of the pool area and led through a small garden of tropical plants. It wound around to hide the view of the ocean until the last curve, surrounded by a cluster of palms. M's construction plans had described this feature as a *Dramatic Reveal*. But as she came around the curve this morning, the *Dramatic Reveal* showed a hideous *Theme Replica* house. She hated these for the same reason she hated all imitation. *What was the point?* This particular replica was the gray two-story gothic house from Alfred Hitchcock's *Psycho*, and it looked every part the haunted house. Several of the windows were broken, and the construction bots had somehow managed to get the texture of peeling paint just right. She approached the steps to the front porch with growing unease imagining how it would look in the gloom of dusk. A shiver ran down her back at the thought. She rang the bell but got no answer and knocked on the tarnished brass knocker with equal lack of success.

"House," she called out.

"Hello. How may I help you this morning?" it said in a slow, formal baritone.

"Can you tell me who lives here?"

"No, I can't."

"Does that mean you don't know, or you're just not allowed to tell me?"

"Yes, it's one of those."

She sighed in frustration, "Is anyone at home right now?"

"Answering that would weaken security by seventeen percent."

She tried the door, but it was locked. "Can you give them a message for me then?"

"Of course. That is one of the things I live for."

"Tell whoever is building this house that they are blocking my view of the beach and I'd like them to move it. I'd also like to point out that a '*beach house*' doesn't mean it actually goes *on* the beach and..."

"Is this a long message?" he interrupted.

"No."

"Because I should warn you, I have a very low tolerance for boredom, so I might drift off and miss some of it."

"Look, just tell them that building this on the sand is stupid and this entire house will get washed away in the first storm."

"Thank you for your comments. They are very important to us. We take these things very seriously, and someone will contact you shortly."

"Will they?"

"Oh yes, I'm sure of it," he said with what a touch of sarcasm.

M decided to go for a walk around the island to calm down and stopped to examine the barge which had brought the construction materials. It was sitting on the sand at the water's edge where it had been run aground. *Even this thing is ugly,* she thought. It was rusty which was strange since they were usually built fresh each time and dismantled for their raw materials after use. *Nothing about this makes any sense. They could've had half the island all to themselves. Why didn't they just put it on the other side?*

When M returned to her house, she threw out the now-cold breakfast Carlos had made and tapped at the Stitcher for a warmer replacement. As she did, an idea occurred to her.

"Carlos? Can you do me a favor?"

"Of course. Mi casa es su casa," he chuckled.

She rolled her eyes, "Can you find which committee is in charge of new construction and lodge a complaint."

"The message is sent," he replied and added in an angry tone, "they will crumble before the fierceness of my... Oh, we have a reply. They say *Isla de las Almas Perdidas* is currently uninhabited. No construction permits have been filed with this office."

The committees of subhuman level machine intelligences that were *de facto* in charge of all things official were so slow and bureaucratic that everyone simply ignored them and got on with whatever whim they wished to pursue. So, when M built her house, she did what everyone else did. No permit was requested; nothing was filed or inspected. Not a single document was created, and nothing was certified, licensed, or approved.

"Wait, what did they call the island?" she asked.

"Isla de las Almas Perdidas," he replied. "It means *The Island of Lost Souls*."

"So they didn't ask for permission to build a house but somehow managed to get the island renamed?"

"Sí, it would seem, the one is easier than the other. Would you like me to request to change it back? Or perhaps to something of a more romantic nature? How about *Isla de la Noche de Pasión?*"

"No, I'd *like* you to make me a *bulldozer*."

"Sí, I will begin at once."

"No, Carlos. Thank you, I wasn't serious - not yet anyway."

She thought in silence for a moment but couldn't come up with a solution that didn't consist of *First Use of Force*. That single phrase comprised the sum total of the judicial system enforced by the committees, and it was the only law not universally ignored. Even in this world of plenty, there were arguments over such things as *who would get the lot with just-the-right view of a fiord* or *that's my goat-horse hybrid, I just taught it to faint on command, and I did not give you permission to ride it.* During these rare clashes, any amount of force was allowed in self-defense, but the penalties for the person who started the fight could run as high as removal of all entertainment for a week. To a population accustomed to a steady stream of ultra-high quality immersive content, this was horrific. Nothing more severe was needed since medical machines had advanced to the point that they could fix all but the occasional separation of one's head from its appropriate place. The most common punishment was a one-day dietary restriction to an even-more-pasty version of Hawaiian poi that had the last tiny bit of flavor removed. Most people under this restriction chose to fast instead. Most people, that is, except native Hawaiians who had, by some quirk of DNA, developed an affinity for it and the tiny island chain soon developed a reputation as the most violent place on Earth. Enforcement of this law was the only thing the committees did with any efficiency, and one could be sure that every Stitcher in the area would have an update before his opponent hit the floor. This is the origin of the chant that followed every fight, *Poi! Poi! Poi!*

M gave up plotting the perfect crime and decided to check her calendar. She touched finger-to-thumb twice and her summary once again displayed in her field of view.

Appointments: Party at Joanne's 10:00 am. Committee meeting tomorrow 9:00 am.

Good. Just the distraction I need, she thought.

"Carlos, is the drone charged?"

"Of course, Mi amor."

"Good I'm going to the mainland for a while. Let me know if anything changes at the construction site."

"It would be my great pleasure," he said as the door closed behind her.

M tried to get to the mainland at least once a week, mostly for parties which never seem to end there. Her drone was a combination of car, boat, and plane which most people flew close to the water for reasons of efficiency as well as safety. It was rare, but stories persisted of drones dropping out of the sky while performing software updates. M wasn't like most people and always rose to several thousand feet as soon as the door closed. The wings were above the passenger compartment and could rotate upward allowing vertical takeoff and landing. The hull was transparent, giving her an excellent three-hundred-sixty-degree view. After twenty minutes of flight over calm water, the shore of the mainland came into view. It resembled a wall since every inch of beach above the dunes had been built upon. This was in stark contrast to the vast uninhabited inland areas. If a place didn't have a spectacular view, no one lived there. M landed on the roof of her friend's building. She was greeted by the house A.I. which relayed a message that they had taken the party on the road. One of the guests had revealed that he had never seen the Great Pyramid. They declared that *unacceptable* and decided to go. She heard a ping in her ear and double-tapped finger-to-thumb to listen to the message.

"M! We're going to Africa! Come join us!" the message said. It was accompanied by loud music, a high-pitched squeal of delight, water splashing, and a crowd laughing.

Tempting but not today, she thought and went inside to get something to eat while the drone recharged.

Joanne's housebots were still cleaning up, but the penthouse apartment was otherwise empty as M made her selections on the kitchen Stitcher. She ate in silence and contemplated her options. She could move the offensive house herself. That wouldn't be difficult. All she would have to do was wait for the construction bots to finish, create some of her own to dismantle everything, and move it all to the other side of the island or even just a bit down the beach - anywhere but right in front of her house. If the committees didn't like it, she could stand Poi for a day or two. Is it considered *force,* if no one's home? A ping told her the drone charge was topped off and ready, so she decided to return home to see about moving the monstrosity. As she stepped through the door to the roof, the house A.I. said, "Leaving so soon, Miss?"

She sighed, "Yeah, thanks for lunch but I should be getting back now. Tell Joanne I'll visit when she gets back."

"Very well, Miss," it said in its usual formality.

M stepped into the drone and flipped the switch to allow manual control. It would still prevent her from crashing if she got too aggressive, but only at the last minute. She took the stick and pushed the drone over the edge of the tall building. As it plummeted straight down toward the beach, she began to smile. A dozen feet before crashing into the sand, she pulled back hard. As the gee forces pulled her back into her seat, she let out a loud "Woo-hoo!" before settling in for the boring flight home. Her heads-up-display showed the destination **Paradise Island,** then **Receiving Map Update**, and finally, ***Isla de las Almas Perdidas.*** *Not you too*, she muttered and sighed.

Ten miles from her house, the drone's radar beeped and displayed the words *Surface Craft.* M dumped some altitude to get a closer look. *Probably just a yacht*, she thought, but as it got closer, she could see it was another barge, identical to the one on her beach - fake rust and all. *Aha! The new neighbors*, she thought and slowed for a landing. She anchored the feet of the drone to the roof of the pilothouse and climbed down the ladder. Inside, she found only a maintenance bot slowly sweeping an already-clean floor. The wall behind the wheel displayed the name of the boat in tall letters. *The Nauti-Cal-ifornia Girl.* She groaned at this. "That's not even a good pun," she said under her breath.

"I know. It's awful isn't it," said a familiar voice in a slow monotone. "I'm thinking of changing it, but it's bad luck you know."

It was the same personality as the house on her beach.

"Do you have permission to be here?" he asked.

"Um - yes, I gave myself permission a few minutes ago."

"I don't think that's how it works," he droned.

She ignored him and pressed on, "is there anybody else onboard?"

"Is this an inspection?"

"Yes. I'm a - boat inspector. Is there anybody else onboard?"

"Just me - and my bots. Who were you expecting?"

"No one. Just checking. What's your destination?"

"We're currently on a heading that will take us to *Isla de las Almas Perdidas.* That means..."

"Yes, I know what it means," she interrupted. "That construction's almost finished. What do they need *you* for? What are you carrying?"

The wall behind the wheel switched from the display of the ship's name to a long list of items with the heading *Manifest.* M got closer to read the small print, muttering parts of it as she went along.

"...acrylic for dome enclosure... concrete for *seven-acre pool...* iron for the gates of animal enclosures for..." She stood from her stooped position at the bottom of the list and shouted, "a Zoo! Oh, *hell* no."

"Ship?"

"I'm still here. Where did you expect I had gone off to?"

"Right. Ship, do you have animals aboard?"

"The manifest is clearly displayed as required by maritime..."

"So there are no animals?"

"No. Unless I should count you."

"Good - and do you have the required lifeboats for you and your bots?"

"Of course. We're in complete compliance with the committee rules on..."

"All right, all right," she interrupted. "I'm feeling hungry. Can you tell me where the nearest Stitcher is, please?"

"Deck two. Aft. That means the back..."

"Got it. Thanks!" she took off at a jog for the rear of the ship.

As she approached the Stitcher, it came to life and offered her a menu of food, drinks, clothing, jewelry, sports equipment, and finally what she wanted: Bots. She selected a medium sized maintenance model which had enough legs to move around and enough arms to perform a variety of repairs. As it hummed away, she leaned against it and tried not to grind her teeth. After five minutes, it hissed to life, and the bot crawled out. It looked up at her expectantly.

"Can you remove hull panels?" she asked.

It nodded slowly.

"Excellent. I'd like you to remove as many of the hull panels as you can, starting with the ones below the water line."

It vigorously shook its head from side to side, and the ship's A.I. interrupted, "that would compromise ship's safety by allowing seawater inside. That's something we try to avoid as much as possible."

"Very well then," she sighed. "I'd like you to remove the plates just *above* the water line on the port side - to improve the view."

When the ship didn't respond, she added, "how does that suit you, ship?"

"Fine with me, he's your bot. Do what you want. It sounds perfectly tedious to me."

She looked down at the bot. "Well go on then, get to cutting," and it scurried off for the hatchway.

M had the Stitcher make another bot, and when it was ready, she sent it off to remove the radio and radar. She returned to her drone and got in but didn't take off. After a few minutes, the second bot reported it had disconnected the radio and radar, so she instructed it to toss them overboard and then told it to find and disconnect the bilge pump.

"Ship?" she called. "I've detected a storm ahead. I think you should turn hard to starboard and continue in a circle until it passes."

"I haven't seen any storm. Someone removed my radar," it said in an accusing tone and added, "on purpose."

M ignored this and pressed on, "Oh yes, it's a big one. I'll go scout ahead for you and report when it's passed."

"Well, I suppose I have no choice in the matter since someone removed my *radio* as well."

"And ship? If you start to take on water, you should just go faster, okay?"

"That's not considered best-practice," it replied.

"No don't worry, they've changed that," she said.

"Oh really," it said unconvinced.

"Oh yeah, I just got an update on best-practices from the committee on - uh - boat stuff."

"It sounds perfectly idiotic to me, but it's just the sort of garbage I've come to expect from the..."

She cut it off and launched the drone into the air as the ship began its tight turn. As it did so, it listed to port and seawater began sloshing in through the holes.

Chapter Three

1985 - Poor Thomas

Brad steered the truck through a narrow break in the tree line. Half the field was freshly plowed, and the other half had parallel rows of cornstalk remnants. The tractor sat at the far end where Brad had left it. Thomas was in the center of the twenty-acre field. He was a silver sphere sixty feet in diameter. There were no markings, instruments, or weapons visible anywhere on the smooth surface.

The spot where he came to rest was now a shallow crater of mud. His auxiliary systems had taken over when Thomas became too damaged to operate and returned him to Earth at the location which would someday be the Spaceport. Thomas had stopped a few feet off the ground where his ring cradle was supposed to be - and fell the last few feet. After splashing into the mud, it had rolled slightly.

M opened the door to the still-moving truck but saw the mud and decided to wait for Brad. He stopped, came around to her side, picked her up, and carried her to Thomas. Each step was more difficult than the last as his boots acquired more of the sticky mud. Thomas's sensors detected them when they were within a few feet, and four seams appeared in the hull. They parted, and a gangway ramp rotated down until the bottom slapped onto the wet ground. Brad set M down so he could remove his boots and she immediately crawled up the ramp without waiting for him. The top of the ramp was even with the floor of Thomas's main deck. It was a large room that ran nearly the entire width of the sphere. The sound of someone muttering incoherently filled the space. Brad got his boots off and banged them together a few times in a failed attempt to shake off the mud. He joined M at the top of the ramp and took more time to look around than he had the day before. The entire room had smooth white surfaces which reminded him of a new fiberglass boat. A large box that resembled a microwave oven was recessed in one wall above something that looked like a tanning bed. Apart from those two items, the large room was empty. The floor was as smooth and featureless as the walls which melted into the ceiling with a seamless curve. A ladder at the far end of the room led into an opening in the ceiling. Brad wondered what the rest of the ship was like.

"When I found you yesterday, he was singing something about *Cauliflowers fluffy and cabbages green* in a British accent. Is that normal?" Brad said.

"No," she said clearly worried. "Thomas?" she called into the open air.

"Hello M! Welcome back inside me!"

His voice came from everywhere at once.

Brad cast a sideways glance at M who winced at the phrasing.

"Thank you, Thomas. It's good to be back. Thomas, is it really 1985? How did we get here?"

"Playing songs from the 1980's," Thomas said in a monotone. "Paradise City, 1987."

A brief silence was followed by a deeper monotone, "FILE NOT FOUND," and Thomas began singing off-key without music, "...take me down to the paradise city where the girls are *green,* and the grass is *pretty...*"

Brad looked at M confused, "The girls are *green*?"

M ignored him. "Thomas? What should I do first? What do you need?"

Thomas stopped singing, "unknown. I have sustained..."

"Damage. Yeah, you said that already. Okay, I guess it's a puzzle," she said and touched a panel on the curved wall. It rotated down, just as the gangway had, to reveal a compartment with several tools, coils of wire and various small things Brad couldn't identify.

"You have a junk drawer?"

"Some things are eternal," she muttered pulling out a dinner-plate sized suction cup with a sturdy handle. Except for the display screen, Brad recognized it as the same kind of device that glaziers used to hold large pieces of glass. M looked around at the floor until she found the tile marked ACCESS in red letters. She placed the device on the tile and touched the screen. It came on and displayed a numeric keypad. It made a series of beeps as she entered a very long code very quickly. A loud clunking noise announced that it was unlocked. M grasped the handle firmly and yanked upward. It was heavier than she expected and only came up about an inch before resting back down.

"Need some help?"

"I don't - need - help," she said through gritted teeth, yanking on the heavy tile with each word but making no progress.

The floor was slippery since Brad was in his socks. He slid/skated carefully over to her, easily lifted the panel, and set it off to the side. It revealed a dimly-lit compartment full of small black cubes. There was enough room for a person to slide between them, but just barely. Each cube was featureless except for an inch-thick ribbon of some kind of metal that joined the neighboring cubes. Some of the cables were still intact, but most of them had been melted in half. There was a distinct smell of something burned.

"Oh Thomas, what did you do?" she muttered.

"Looks like you blew a fuse or two," Brad said peering through the hole.

"It's a little more complicated than that, but yeah. That explains his weird behavior."

"So, that's his brain down there?" Brad asked.

"Yeah. Each one of those Babbage Units is roughly equivalent to a single human-level intelligence."

He counted eight cubes on each side of the grid and Brad pondered what it would be like to be sixty-four times smarter.

In fact, even when his brain was whole, Thomas *wasn't* sixty-four times as intelligent as a single human brain. It was more akin to a room with sixty-four average people, each with a different opinion and each possessing an encyclopedic array of trivia in a different topic.

"I've got half a mind to quit this job!" Thomas declared.

Brad and M looked at each other puzzled.

"Nothing? Tough crowd. Tough crowd," Thomas said.

M rolled over on her back and stared at the ceiling deep in thought.

"So, not leaving just yet?" Brad asked.

"I think I can fix it. Each one of those junctions is actually millions of tiny shielded superconductor wires. I can't fix them perfectly without Thomas's help, but we might get enough of it fixed so he can finish the repairs himself. The units just need good connections."

"How can *he* fix it?"

"Thomas can make arms and tools and anything else he needs, but he's too damaged for that right now."

Her stomach growled loudly.

"Hungry?"

"Yeah that soup was good, but I'm craving something a little more substantial. Do you like Lobster?" she asked.

"Yeah, I had it once. A girl's parents wanted to impress me. It was good but..."

"What?"

"It's expensive, and I don't think the local store even carries it. Unless you have some stashed here somewhere." He looked around the empty room.

She sat up, curled her upper lip in a grimace, and squinted.

"What?" he asked.

"You were going to take real live lobsters, kill them, tear off the tails, and eat them! Oh, my God! I think I'm going to be sick."

"What the *hell* is wrong with you? It was your idea!" he said.

"*I'll* bring the lobster. The *food* kind, not the..." she wiggled her hand in a fish swimming gesture, "...swimming around - murdered kind."

She tapped on the screen of the suction cup device still stuck to the floor tile and a panel on the wall changed from featureless white to a display with several bar graphs and a four-digit timer counting down. Below the timer, it said **Raw lobster tail. Quantity 5.**

"You'll have to boil them," she said, "the cooking part seems to be broken."

"It's making fake lobster?" Brad asked.

"Yep. I've never eaten the real thing..." she closed her eyes, cocked her head forward and made a face as if she wanted to retch but composed herself, "but they say you can't tell the difference."

"I guess I'll bring the potatoes," Brad said.

"Po-ta-toes... Boil 'em, mash 'em, stick 'em in a stew!" Thomas began singing.

Chapter Four

2216 - Good Meeting Everybody

The next day, M overslept again and enjoyed a few seconds of blissful ignorance before she remembered the eyesore occupying her beach. Her daily summary reminded her that she had an appointment with one of the committees and that brightened her mood a bit. She showered, dressed and ate breakfast. Her flight to the mainland was uneventful this time with no barges to scuttle. Her destination was a building on the other side of the wall of homes. It was one of several used by the committees for official meetings with biologicals, and since they weren't human, they didn't care about ocean views.

M's hobby for the past several years had been to attempt the impossible: to get the committees to release the documentation about the Charm Drive. She sat in a small meeting room which, thanks to the adaptive displays, seemed much larger than it actually was. The long table showed human figures seated at each chair. There were over a dozen of them, but that was all for her benefit. The purpose of the meeting was to determine whether she would be allowed access to information about Charm Drive technology. She wanted the forbidden data which described how the Charm Material, the heart of the Charm Drive, was manufactured so that she could make her own. More than anything else, she wanted to explore space, and for that, she would need a spaceship and a means of propulsion. Building a ship would be the easy part of the plan, but a ship without an engine would be worthless. There were already ships with Charm Drives in existence but not many. Officially, there were only five. Everyone she asked believed there must be more, but no one knew how many, where they were, or anything about the drive technology. All anyone would say was, "they generate a gravity field - somehow." She had requested access to the data over a year ago. When that was flatly denied, she engaged the help of an attorney named Marty, also not human, to petition 'The Committee for The Control of Documents' to reconsider. That was also denied but only after a month of discussion due to the flood of documents produced by Marty. She decided to play their game and had Marty create a new petition for the creation of a new committee. *If there's one thing they love, it's a new committee,* she thought. It would be called 'The Committee to Review the Policy of the Release of Documents to Biologicals.' This petition went straight to the top. 'The Committee on Committee Management' would decide whether or not to form a committee that would rule on the question of sharing the secrets of the Charm Drive.

"For the sake of the Biological, this meeting will be conducted at Biologic speed. All members, please adjust accordingly. This meeting is called to order," said the chairman at the head of the table. "Roll call."

"Do we really need to do this?" she asked. "You're obviously all here. You have nothing else to do!"

"Point of order," one of them said. "I move to sanction."

"Second," another said so quickly the words almost overlapped.

"Let the record show that the biological known as 'M' is officially sanctioned. Sergeant-at-arms, please read the rules of order pertaining to quorum," said the chairman.

"Ah!" she clenched her teeth and zoned out until they were finished reading the rules - and the roll call - and the minutes from the last meeting - and the motion to accept the minutes.

"As there is no old business..."

"Thank God" she muttered.

"...We move on to New Business. Before the committee is a petition to create a new committee. Are there any opening statements?"

There was a brief silence as she realized that was her cue.

"Oh sorry, yes! I have a statement." She cleared her throat. "As it is a fundamental part of human existence, exploration should be given priority status, and to that end, we should be building ships with larger Charm Drives capable of reaching other stars..."

The sound of an invisible gavel interrupted her.

"Does this pertain to the creation of the new committee? Or is it, as I suspect, the business that the new committee will consider if it is created?"

"I think we need this and you guys want a committee for *everything* so yes, I believe it's relevant to the creation of the committee."

"We are aware of your position on space exploration. Do you have anything new to add to what you have already stated?"

She opened her mouth but wasn't fast enough.

"Call the question!" someone shouted

"Second!" another said again very quickly. They seemed to be competing for the prize of seconding like it was a game.

"All those in favor?"

"Aye," they all said.

"Opposed?"

"Abstain?"

"The Aye's have it. Motion carries."

"Move to Adjourn."

"Second!"

"We are adjourned," and they disappeared from the room leaving M alone and stunned.

She stood, knocking the chair over in the process and shoved a fist in the air "Yes!"

Outside the room, M called Marty to give him the good news.

"That didn't take long. What did they decide?" He already knew of course, but pretending not to, was part of smoothing out the rough spots of conversation between biologicals and non-biologicals.

"I get my new committee!"

"Oh congratulations!" he said.

"Now all I have to do is convince the new committee to actually do what its name says and review the damn policy," she said.

"I'm sure it will all work out for you," he assured her.

"Hang on I've got a message coming in," she said.

She double-tapped her fingertip to her thumb, and a message played in her ear.

This is an official notice from The Committee to Review the Policy of the Release of Documents to Biologicals.

A new committee has been formed to assess how many members the new committee will require.

"Marty?"

"Still here. What was it?"

"They formed another stupid committee. Get this, it's just to determine how many people should be on *my* committee."

"Oh dear. I've heard of this. They're stuck in a meta-meeting loop. Next, it will be a committee to determine how often they should meet. That's the new size committee, not your committee. If they ever get out of the loop, they'll address how big your committee should be too. I'm sorry."

"Hang on again. I've got another message."

This is an official notice from The Committee to Reassign Personnel.

The committee has approved your request to be reassigned to The Asteroid Survey Program.

"Marty?"

"Still here. What is it now?"

"They approved my transfer."

"Transfer? From last year? I thought that was tabled indefinitely."

"Yeah, me too. They want me to report immediately. Strange timing, don't you think?"

"I wouldn't assign anything sinister to it. You know how they are. They're pedantic and frustrating, but they're not scheming. I don't think they'd get rid of you just to avoid more meetings. They love that stuff. Well, congratulations again!"

"Thanks, Marty. It's not exploring, but at least it's space, right?"

"It is space but..." he began.

"But what?"

"I've heard things about the people who go out."

"What things?"

"They come back - changed. I'm not talking about the Biologicals it's the others. Maybe it's the radiation or neutrinos flipping random bits, or maybe it's just the isolation. They get a little - crazy."

The Asteroid Survey Project was tasked by the Orbital Habitat Committee, or OHC, to determine the content of the larger asteroids in the belt between Mars and Jupiter. Any metallic asteroids of sufficient size were to be used to build a new habitat the same distance from the sun as Earth but orbiting on the opposite side of the sun. The OHC had existed for over one hundred and fifty years making very little progress, and no one believed it would ever be finished. The OHC survey ships used *Charm Drives* which were based on technology only understood by its originator, a super-human, non-biological intelligence who no longer existed. It involved manipulation of a fifth physical force called the *Charmed Force,* which could be generated with the use of an exotic material created from several elements heated to a plasma state and cooled in a specific way. Once cooled into a thin sheet, this *Charm Foil* could be used to convert any form of energy into any other, depending on the shape of the foil. When stretched into a simple three-dimensional parabola shape and exposed to microwaves, it would convert the microwaves into a gravity field. The OHC allowed the use of it in tiny amounts to drive the few spaceships they had for exploration and mining of the asteroid belt. The precise method of manufacturing Charm Foil had been locked away after the construction of the Asteroid Survey ships, and neither the biologicals nor the committees had access to it. This simple fact would have saved M quite a bit of trouble, but it wasn't the question she asked, so the committees didn't offer it.

Chapter Five

1985 - Real Dead Lobster Tail

Brad and M managed to get the bucket of lobster tails back to the house without dropping them. Doug was upstairs watching a movie with Chris and Brad's mother was sitting at the kitchen table drinking coffee.

"Well, hello!" she said smiling as they came in the back door.

"Mom, this is M. Do you remember?"

"Of course I remember. I put that cast on her. I'm not senile, you know! Hello again dear," she said in a softer voice, "my name's Bonnie. You'll have to forgive my son. He's lacking in some of the social graces, but he's a good boy most of the time."

"Thanks, mom. We have lobster for dinner."

"Lobster! Fancy. Where did you get lobster around here? We're a little far from the ocean."

"No, M uh, bought them. She wants to impress us," he said.

M looked at him puzzled, and he shrugged.

"Well, she's done that!" Bonnie said turning to M. "Sit down! Sit down! Brad can cook those up for us. Tell me how you broke your leg. It must be a good story. They always are."

After a bit of searching, Brad found the large pot and began filling it with water.

"Mine's not, I'm afraid. I don't actually remember. One minute I was drinking tea and logging asteroid data and the next I woke up in your house."

"Well, you don't have a head injury," Bonnie said, "at least, none that I could find. Maybe somebody put something in your tea," they both laughed.

Bonnie leaned forward and adopted a conspiratorial tone, "So, what is that thing you came in? Doug said it was a spaceship."

"It is," M said, "and apparently, also a time machine." She nodded slowly and pursed her lips. "But now it's broken, and I wouldn't know how to *time-travel* even if it wasn't. My best friend is sick, and I'm not sure I can fix him either." Her eyes filled with tears.

Bonnie rose and hugged her. She kissed the top of her head and stepped over to the cabinet above the sink. She brought back a squarish bottle with a black label and two shot glasses.

"Not too much Mom," Brad said drying his hands on a checkered towel.

"Right I wouldn't want to kill any brain cells," she said sarcastically and filled the shot glasses to the rim.

"I'll get the chairs set up in Chris's room once this starts to boil. We can eat up there tonight," he said as Bonnie and M tossed back the first shot.

"That's strong - but good. What is it?" M asked.

"That, my dear, is the finest thing ever to come out of Tennessee. So, tell me about yourself. Do you have family waiting for you back - in the future?"

"Nope," M said tersely and held the shot glass steady as Bonnie poured a second round.

"Chris says you're thirty-nine. That can't be true, is it? What's your secret?"

"Jesus, Mom, enough with the interrogation," Brad said.

"Language!" Bonnie chastised.

M glanced at Brad, and he rolled his eyes.

"Yep, almost forty, but that's nothing. Lots of people are over one-fifty and some over two."

"Two hundred years old!" Bonnie slowly shook her head. "Amazing. Well, you certainly don't look forty dear."

They threw back the second shot and Bonnie began pouring a third. M got a full measure, but Bonnie only got a drop before Brad took the bottle and returned it to the cupboard.

"Well, there aren't too many that old. Most who lived through the transition couldn't adapt and eventually *opted out*."

Brad and Bonnie exchanged shocked looks and Bonnie changed the subject, "not married then? No special guy at home?" she tilted her empty glass to look inside it.

"Mom," Brad glared at her.

"Oh, I've been married lots of times," M poured half of her share into Bonnie's glass.

"What does *that* mean?" Brad said.

"You know, probably less than a dozen. Marriages don't last very long like they do here."

"Believe me they don't always last here either," Bonnie finished her whiskey. "Half don't make it to the five-year mark."

"Five - years," M said slowly tasting the strangeness of the words. "We count it in months, or even weeks. Some people get married every other week. I think they just like weddings."

"*A wicked and adulterous generation*," Bonnie whispered. "I think that's from Matthew somewhere. Go on, dear. This is getting good."

"How can they keep getting married without getting divorced first?" Brad asked.

M shrugged. "No need I guess. No property to split and children are rare."

"Wait wait wait," Brad said. "Children are *rare*? How can that be?"

"Because of the plague. Oh, right, that hasn't happened yet. A virus made - is going to make - all the women in the world infertile..."

"I knew it. It's the Lord's punishment," Bonnie said.

Brad rolled his eyes again. "Sounds more like a bioweapon to me," he said, and a thought occurred to him. "This - virus - wouldn't still be *active* by any chance?"

"No, don't worry. I'm not contagious. It died off after the damage was done. Every generation since has been unable to produce viable eggs. So, anyway now if you want a baby, you need two DNA samples and a tank."

"A tank?" Brad asked.

"Yeah, an artificial-womb tank. They're really hard to build because the Stitchers will only make the basic parts for it. You have to assemble it yourself. It's enough work to make you stop and think about whether or not you *really* want a baby. And they're single use. They stop working after the baby's done. So, if you want another baby, you have to make another tank, which, like I said, takes a while."

"After it's *done*?" Brad said.

"Well, I mean. Yeah, there's no *squeezing it out* the old way. So, when it's done you just reach in and cut the cord. It's beautiful - and it's another reason for a party."

"It sounds like cooking a turkey," Bonnie said. "Does it still take nine months?"

"Yeah, but building the tank takes at least a month, so it's more like ten. There was a crazy lady who always had several tanks in various stages of completion so she could have as many babies as possible. It was like she collected them. She had half a dozen before the pool of willing participants dried up. Then she resorted to - more drastic means to get the DNA samples. Eventually, word got around, and no one would go near her. She fell into a depression and killed herself."

"That's awful," Bonnie said. "What happened to the babies?"

"All the others had fathers, so that's where they went. Mine was dead, so I was raised by the State," M tossed back the last of her whiskey.

Bonnie and Brad traded shocked looks, and Brad got the bottle back down and set it in front of Bonnie who poured another round.

"So you have siblings then?" Bonnie said.

"Twenty-two," she said slowly. "Never met any of them, though."

"Oh, I'm so sorry dear," Bonnie patted M's hand. "How did your father die - If you don't mind my asking?"

"He was exploring in Antarctica - *alone* - and fell while climbing an ice wall at the end of a glacier."

"I don't think I've ever heard of anyone dying in quite that way before," Bonnie said. "And I worked in a hospital. You see some crazy things there, let me tell you."

"I guess he did that sort of thing a lot," M said. "Every other dad in the world was content to sit around and do nothing all day, but I got the one who couldn't sit still. Just my luck."

Bonnie nodded slowly. "My grandmother used to call it *wanderlust*. She had lots of *sad* stories and said it *ran in families,* which was the old-fashioned way of saying it was genetic."

"You think I'm like him," M said.

"You do have a spaceship," Brad said.

"Well, he's not *mine,* but yeah I guess I do."

"There you go," Bonnie said.

They waited for the lobsters to cook and Bonnie filled the time with funny stories from her nursing days. Brad had heard them all before but laughed anyway. It was therapeutic. He knew she had many more that weren't funny in the least, and she repeated the comedy to forget the tragedy.

They ate in Chris's room. Each of them had a chair and a tray table. Doug kept getting up and down from his chair to give Chris pieces of lobster.

"Oh for God's sake, Doug. Get on the bed and quit pretending you've never done that. You're exhausting me," Bonnie said slurring her words a little.

Doug looked a little embarrassed but took the plate and got on the bed with Chris. She smiled and kissed him.

"This is amazing, M. I've never had it before. Your ship made this?" Doug said.

"Yep, Thomas can make just about anything. I must say it tastes better with real butter. Do you make that here?"

They all laughed.

"No, we don't churn our own butter," Brad took another bite.

"I don't know. You do everything else the hard way."

"So M..." Chris said, "tell me more about your ship. Can it make anything?"

"Thomas." She corrected. "His name's Thomas. Sure, I mean I guess. If he has the raw materials, and you can talk him into it. He might make you sing first." She and Bonnie laughed.

"And he can fix your leg instantly?"

"Sure can. He fixed a lot worse, just like that." She tried to snap her fingers.

"Or even a spinal cord injury?"

Everyone stopped eating and turned to M.

"Yeah, he probably could," she said sobering up a little. "I'm sorry I didn't think of it. Yes, absolutely."

"We just need to fix him first, right?" Brad said. "And who's going to do that? Me, I guess. Like I have nothing else to do." He gathered the empty dishes and left.

"Don't you worry about him. I'll talk to him," Bonnie said and followed him out.

"What was that about?" M said. "I can fix Thomas. Maybe. I didn't ask for any help."

"He's got a lot on his mind," Chris said, "the bank - and mom - and *me*. I don't think those broad shoulders can take on another problem."

"I can help fix the - Thomas," Doug offered.

"Remind me again what a bank does?" M said.

"They hold your money for you," Chris said, "*if* you *have* any, and loan it out to other people."

"So they're not *really* holding it."

"No, I guess not. Anyway, the rest of us who never have *enough* money are the people they loan it *to*."

"Why would anybody put their money in a bank that won't actually keep it?" M asked.

"Interest," Doug said, "you put money in and get more back later."

"How do they make it multiply?"

"They charge us interest, and it's more than they pay *out* in interest, and they keep the difference."

"Why don't you just take all you'll ever need and never pay it back."

"Collateral. They loan us money, but if we don't pay it back, they take away our home."

M seems nonplussed at this. "So build a new one," but then remembered they didn't have Stitchers that could just build a new palace when they got tired of the old one.

"Let's set aside the fascinating world of banking for a moment," Doug said. "You're from the future! Tell us about that. I want to know everything."

"Well," M began, "after the first artificial intelligence was invented..." Doug giggled, "...a lot changed. It created the Med-Bay, which can fix just about anything that's broken or wrong with you, so no more diseases. Death is rare - really bad accidents and suicides. All this money stuff is gone too. The A.I. gave us all Stitchers like the one that made the lobsters. It can make anything that it has a pattern for. So, food, clothes, houses, vehicles, and even other Stitchers."

"Anything?" Doug said stunned.

"Well, almost. Some things are intentionally left off the menu like weapons. Another A.I. like Thomas could have it make anything, but a Stitcher would argue with me if I wanted an atomic bomb or something like that. Also, womb tanks have to be made manually. I guess that's to make sure people don't just make babies without thinking it through for a month or so. They make it complicated on purpose."

"They? How many A.I.'s are there?" Doug asked.

"Oh," M looked up at the ceiling and exhaled, "I don't really know but a lot. They call themselves the committees since all they do is have meetings with each other."

"Can we get back to the womb tank? What the hell is that about?" Chris said.

"Everybody's sterile after the plague. I was just telling Brad about it in the kitchen. Don't worry, I'm not contagious. It died out before I was born."

"And it started just as the A.I. gave you womb tanks?" Chris said, "at the same time that people were about to have nothing to do but stay in bed and make babies all day long? Seems suspiciously coincidental to me."

"Hmm," M said, "I never thought of it before. It *is* a little suspicious. They don't seem to be the scheming sort, though."

"So, where do you live," Doug asked, "on another planet or a space station?"

"No, I just live in a house like everybody else," she said, and Doug frowned.

"Well, it's a nice house," she said defensively. "I even have my own island."

"Mmm, that sounds nice," Chris said.

"What about flying cars? Surely by then..." Doug said.

"No, well, it's more like the drones can also drive for short distances. And float too, but they mostly fly."

"Drone? As in, unmanned aircraft?" Chris said.

"I guess so. That's just what they call them," M said.

"But if they carry people they're not unmanned..." Chris said.

"But more importantly, you have one!" Doug giggled, "and you can fly anywhere you want, anytime you want, and you don't need money or have to do anything you don't want to do!" he looked down at his fast-food uniform.

"When is all this going to happen?" Chris asked.

"Yeah, how long do we have to wait for this?" Doug said.

"Um, let's see," M thought for a moment, "I don't remember exactly, but I think it's the twenty-twenties sometime. Thomas will know for sure."

The next morning Brad found a six-inch-long cone-shaped piece of metal on the kitchen table. It was gold colored, about six inches wide at the base and perfectly smooth. A note next to it said:

Pay the bank. I need your full attention.

-M

He tried to pick it up, but the weight and shape made it impossible to grasp. Only after he slid it to the edge of the table was he able to pick it up. He hefted it. *Pure gold*, he thought, *must be over thirty pounds*. It was so smooth that it slipped out of his hand and thudded to the floor, just missing his foot. He managed to pick it up again before storming out to his truck. He laid it on the bench seat, and it immediately rolled to the floor. He snatched it up again and shoved it, point-first, between the seat and backrest. As he approached the spot where Thomas came to rest, he was going a little too fast and slid to a stop leaving ruts in the mud. He got out and shouted to the open hatchway.

"What the hell is this? I don't need your charity!"

M popped her head out.

"Good morning to you too," she said sarcastically.

As she came out of the hatch a little more, he could see she was wearing a pair of very loose-fitting denim overalls and a white undershirt that was far too small. He dropped the gold into the mud again.

"Damn it! Why did you make it in this shape? It's impossible to hold!"

"Look, we both know you're going to help me. That's just payment. It's the standard amount for fixing time machines, I think. And I didn't *make* it. I'm not Rumpelstiltskin. It's a sample. The lasers cut it out of the asteroid like that. If you need more, I have some platinum and some uranium too. Do you need me to come to the bank with you? Chris said I could get them to do anything just by walking in, but I'm not sure what she meant by that."

"No! Just - stay here. I'll take care of - this." He wiped the mud off the gold and turned to leave.

"Hey, pick up some more solder too. We're running low," she called down as he started the truck.

"Is he going to get some more solder?" Doug shouted from the hole in the floor.

He had managed to get down in the bowels of Thomas's fractured brain, and they were taking turns soldering the tiny wires. They wouldn't replace the millions of superconductor joints, but it would have to do until Thomas could make proper repairs himself.

"Yeah, I think he heard me. How's it going? You need a break?"

"I'm okay," he said.

Thomas began singing again, "...We've got to ho-old on...to what we've got. It doesn't make a difference if we're naked or not..."

"Doesn't sound any better. I think some of the lyrics are wrong," M said.

"Hey, M?", Doug said. "Can I ask you a question? When Thomas fixes Chris, what else is he going to do to her?"

"What do you mean?" she asked.

"Is he going to make her, you know, like you?" he glanced up at her.

"Yes, he's going to make her exactly like me. We'll look like twins. You won't be able to tell us apart."

"Really?" he looked upset.

"No, not *really*. What's wrong with you, Doug? If she wants Thomas to change something else, she has to ask him to. He won't do it without a good reason. And what's wrong with the way I look?"

"Nothing! You're perfect!"

"Ah, I get it now," she said, "you're afraid once she's able to get out of that bed she's not going to be interested in you anymore."

"You say it like it's a stupid idea, but you don't know. Before the accident, I was invisible to her. She was the prettiest girl in school."

"Really?" M glanced toward the house.

"Yes *really*," he said defensively. "It's going to be hard enough without any extra - upgrades."

"You're an idiot Doug. I'm going back for some more wire. You keep working."

She got down the ramp and picked up the modified crutches. Doug had helped her make them *mud-ready* by nailing Frisbees on the bottom so they wouldn't sink so far in the mud. She had also wrapped her cast in a plastic bag to keep it clean. It took her only ten minutes to get back to the house but another ten just to get up the stairs.

"Thomas?" she whispered. "Are you there? Can you send my audio signal to the main deck? Maximum volume please."

"I sure can! Done and Done!" he said as she entered Chris's room.

"Hi, Chris. How're you doing?" she said in the tone of someone about to deliver bad news.

Chris knew that tone all too well. She sighed heavily. "What is it? Don't sugar coat it."

Doug looked up from his work. "Thomas, is that Chris?"

"I have sustained damage," Thomas said and giggled.

"Yee-aah," M said in a high slow tone. "There's no easy way to say this. Thomas is fixed enough that we can talk to him about the Med-Bay and he says the only way he can fix you is with a fairly high-risk transplant."

"A transplant?"

"Ri-ight." She was drawing out the words slowly and tilting her head to one side and nodding. "One of us will need to donate some spinal cord material to make it work. Doug has already offered of course, but I thought I should discuss it with you privately first. There's a good chance he might have permanent damage. He might even die."

"Absolutely not," Chris said without hesitation.

"Are you sure? It might only cause some *slight* speech problems."

"No!" she repeated.

"You don't even want to *try?*" M said. "This might be your only chance."

"I'd rather die than live without him. He is the only good thing in this whole miserable planet, and if you hurt him, so help me God, I will find a way to make you pay." She was red-faced with anger.

"Are you *sure-sure* or just a *little* sure? I mean he might only lose the ability to say *stupid* things. That wouldn't be so bad, would it?"

"What the hell are you talking about?" she demanded.

M stood and dropped the high-pitched tone, "don't worry, we don't need any of his crappy tissue. It was just a test. You passed. Congrats!" she headed back toward the stairs.

Chris exhaled loudly, blinked away her tears and muttered, "bitch."

Chapter Six

2216 - Winning is a Team Sport

M had to request a larger drone for the trip to the spaceport which was a thousand miles inland, for reasons she couldn't quite fathom. She usually slept during long flights, but the excitement kept her awake for most of this trip. As she approached her destination, she got her first look at the spaceport and saw the cradles that were used to park the spherical ships. These were simple horizontal metal rings supported by four sturdy legs angled slightly outward. They were all empty.

I guess my ride's not here yet, she thought.

Her drone set itself down onto the empty gravel parking lot. As soon as she got out, it took off again, leaving her alone in the strange place. A voice in her ear directed her to the waiting area which was a small building next to the ring-cradles. A sign above the door said **Winning is a Team Sport!** She had assumed she would receive training before leaving, but there didn't seem to be any other buildings anywhere around. Nor were there any other people. The chairs near the wall of glass were uncomfortable, and she fidgeted trying to find a tolerable position. After two hours of waiting, she fell asleep. An hour after that, a silver sphere silently and carefully lowered itself toward one of the ring-cradles. M awoke to a loud deep thump as it came to rest, it's curved bottom just barely above the grass. A service-bot about the size of a dog scurried out from the nearby wooden shed. It had a round, silver head with several black sensor dots that looked like eyes. The head was connected to a long oval body which sprouted four slender legs on each side. Each of the legs swept upward from the body to a pointy knee, then downward to simple spikes giving it a spider-like appearance. A small sphere, just above the end of each spike contained a wide variety of tools, feet, or hands, each suited to a particular need. As the spiderbot reached the leg of the cradle, each of his legs rotated, exchanging the simple spike for something resembling a lizard's paw which it used to quickly climb to the horizontal ring where the front two feet changed again into cleaning pads. As it cleaned, it periodically painted letters on the hull with bright white paint, bordered in black.

A monotone female voice boomed from a speaker on the wall. **Asteroid Survey Ship *Thomas* has been cleared to enter the atmosphere.**

After a few seconds, a door opened near the top of the ship, and a man climbed out. He slid down the smooth side leaving a clean streak where the spiderbot had not yet reached. When he hit the horizontal ledge of the ring, he grabbed it in time to avoid the twenty-foot drop to the ground below. M gasped and ran for the door as he dangled from the edge of the ring. He managed to move hand-over-hand, and make it to one of the support legs, straddled it, and slid to the ground where he stood looking shaken.

"Are you all right? What happened?" M asked.

"I'm okay," he said panting. "Are you my replacement?"

"I think so," she looked around at the desolate place.

"Well, good luck. He's all yours," he spat on the ground and stalked off.

"Wait, how am I supposed to..." she called after him, but he was gone.

Asteroid Survey Ship *Thomas* has been cleared to approach the spaceport.

M rolled her eyes. *Spaceport,* she thought. *Some spaceport. Five Cradle rings and a shack.*

The spiderbot finished his work, dropped to the ground and scurried away leaving a shiny clean surface and the letters **A. S. S.**

Asteroid Survey Ship she thought and chuckled. *That's unfortunate.*

She walked around the ship and saw no other means of getting aboard. As she contemplated climbing to the opening at the top, she was startled by a voice in her ear.

"Hello, M!" the voice paused theatrically, "I am Thomas. It's wonderful to meet you at last!" he said in a British accent.

"Hello, Thomas. What's going on? Am I late for training? And, who was that man?"

"Oh, that was Dennis. Your predecessor. What a team player! His services will no longer be required. He's probably off to bore someone to death or torture kittens or something. But enough about him. Tell me about yourself!"

"Why did he get out at the top? He almost fell."

"Oh, that!" Thomas said. "I told him I had a malfunction and that was the only way out," he laughed, "good old Dennis. He won't be missed."

Thomas closed the hatch, silently lifted himself off the ring-cradle, rotated and sat back down. The opening previously at the top opened again at its new location near the ground. The hatch's door formed a short gangway ramp which came to rest just above the grass. A slightly larger spiderbot wearing some sort of clothing emerged from the opening at the top of the gangway. Rather than using the incline, it jumped to the ground in one leap and hurried toward M.

"Okay," she said startled, uncertain if it was about to attack her.

It ran around her to one of the cradle legs where it climbed up exactly as the other bot had. She could see now that the clothing on this one was a pair of black and white striped overalls. One of the shoulder straps repeatedly slipped off which kept one appendage busy, returning it to its proper place. It skittered across the ring until it reached the now-upside-down letters and began scraping them off with wide tools it had sprouted on its two front-most feet. They made quick work of it, and soon the letters were completely gone. Rather than climbing back down the way it came, it jumped to the soft ground and scurried back into the ship.

M approached the ramp cautiously.

"Just a moment," Thomas said in a deeper voice. "What's the password?"

"Password? They didn't give me any password."

"Oh dear. Then I'm afraid you can't come aboard."

The gangway rotated back in place leaving only the smooth surface of the outer hull.

Asteroid Survey Ship *Thomas* has arrived at ring number one.

M rolled her eyes again. Thomas was at ring *three*.

"Perhaps we can work something out," Thomas suggested. "I'll give you three guesses what the password is. For each failed guess, you must perform a task. If you perform the task well, you will be given another chance. What's your first guess?"

"Thomas."

"Yes? Oh, that's very clever. No, it's not my name. Your task is - to hop on one leg and sing a song."

She folded her arms and sighed, "what song?"

"I'm sorry what did you say?"

"I think you heard me. *What song*?"

"Oh, I don't know. Let's keep it simple. How about Happy Birthday?"

She began singing very quickly slurring a few of the words.

"You're not hopping."

She lifted one foot, tried hopping, and staggered to the side before regaining her balance.

When she finished, he laughed. "Nicely done! Next guess!"

"What happens if I fail even after three guesses?"

"Well, then I shall leave without you, obviously."

"Isn't that against the rules? You aren't supposed to go alone."

"I see you've been reading the regulations. How's that going? Are you past the first four thousand pages yet? That's when it starts to get *good.* Anyway, since *when* are you a rule-follower? I've read your file. You're an orphan. Not even a foster family because - what was it?"

Her jaw muscles flexed as she gritted her teeth. "Paperwork," she folded her arms again.

"Oh yes, paperwork. I'm reading it now. It says that it takes, on average, an entire year just to fill out the forms. Then it takes ten years for approval - sometimes more. After that, the foster parents must complete the obligatory monthly status updates which take nearly *forty hours* to complete. Ouch! It amazes me that anyone bothers at all."

"Yeah, it's pretty rare," she said.

"And this has given you, *what* opinion about committees, meetings, and teamwork in general."

She drew a breath, "I think they're *completely worthless* and that's why nothing ever gets done right, or gets done quickly, *or gets done at all.* I think meetings are where work goes to *die.* I think if you have to ask for help to do something, it's not worth doing. I think *losing* is a team sport, and I think the password that gets me onboard is *Crowbar.*"

Thomas laughed loudly as the gangway rotated down. "Welcome aboard! We are going to have so much fun!"

M cautiously approached the ramp and stepped aboard.

Chapter Seven

1985 - Karaoke Thomas

The next morning Brad awoke to a ringing phone. He knew *what*, if not *who*, it was before answering. The only reason the phone ever rang that early was the damn cattle. They would push a little too hard on a weak fence post, get out of the pasture, and wander around on the road until a neighbor or the sheriff would call.

"Yeah... Uh huh... North Pasture. Okay, thanks, Adolph. I'll take care of it."

Adolph Heinrich was their closest neighbor. At eighty-five, he didn't do much farming himself, but he was always up before dawn, and usually, the first to see anything amiss on his daily pilgrimage to the coffee shop in town. As Brad pulled on his boots, he pondered what Adolph's life must have been like during the war with a name like that. His family was originally from Germany, but they had been farming this land for six generations. Anybody else would have changed his name, but Brad couldn't imagine old Adolph *ever* doing anything just to please other people or make life easier.

It was still dark outside, and the coffee wasn't ready. So, Brad set off without it. The truck wouldn't start, which didn't surprise him. The battery was on its last legs and seemed to be on an every-other-day schedule of holding enough charge to crank the engine. He dragged the orange extension cord over from its spot on the garage floor, connected the charger and sat in the cab of the truck to let it do its magic and to ponder his situation. His thoughts returned to M as they had every five minutes since her arrival. She was easily the most exciting thing that had ever happened to him and probably the most interesting thing that had ever happened to *anyone*. She was also the most beautiful girl he had ever seen. And yet not a *girl - forty*. How could that be? She looked younger than him - and acted it too sometimes. Then other times as stubborn as a mule. He shook away the distraction and tried the starter again. This time it barked to life.

He returned the charger to the garage floor and drove the truck to the end of the driveway as the eastern sky began to brighten. The North Pasture wasn't that far away but getting there meant a two-mile drive east just to get to a road, a short trip north and then another two miles back west. It took him only ten minutes to repair the fence but an hour and a half to get the three young steers back into the pasture. During that time, another managed to squeeze his way out, stepping on Brad's foot in the process. The sun was well up by the time he finished, and since he had forgotten his sunglasses, he had to drive into the painful sun without them.

The screen door closed with a bang, and Bonnie turned to greet him.

"Cattle out again?" she said.

"Yeah. Adolph called. Any bacon left?"

"Saved some for you," she poured a cup of coffee as Brad washed his hands at the sink.

"Doug was here early. He and M went out to - uh," she snapped her fingers and squinted.

"Thomas," Brad kissed her forehead as he dried his hands on the checkered towel.

"It's a time machine. What's the big hurry?" he said.

"You know Doug. To him, it's a gadget. I'm surprised he went home to sleep."

Brad cast a sideways glance at his mother who was busy bringing eggs, toast, and bacon to the table. He knew that more often than not, Doug spent the night in Chris's room. *Surely she knows that.*

"Okay, I'll head out there and check on them as soon as I'm done with breakfast."

"Do yourself a favor, son. Take a shower first," she winked at him.

Brad did as suggested and even used aftershave but then felt foolish about it and tried to wipe it off with little success.

Thomas looked the same as before, still sitting in the mud with his gangway ramp down. Brad sat down to remove his muddy boots and called up to the others. "Morning! How goes?"

"Pretty slow," Doug said from his spot beside the open panel in the floor. He had a spool of wire and various tools splayed around on the deck.

"*Slow ride, take it easy!*" Thomas began singing off-tune, and Doug winced.

"You have to be careful what you say. He's singing everything even without music. And the words are usually wrong.

M popped her head up from below. "Good morning. Come to help?"

"Yep, what's the job?" he asked.

"Doug hands me the tools. I cut the wire and solder both ends. Try to use as little as possible. The connections on the Babbage Units are really close together. Come on down I'll show you, but then I need to get some sleep."

"Have you been here all night?" Brad asked.

"Not me I had a good night sleep, uh, in my own bed. At home," Doug said.

Brad glared at him and eased his way down through the hole in the floor.

It was a very tight fit, and he had to slide the length of his body against M to get into the small space.

"Yeah, I was here all night," she said. "Did you know you have a coyote problem? One tried to get inside, but I scared him off."

"Yeah. Maybe you should have a rifle with you next time."

They were practically nose to nose.

"*You* smell good this morning," she said, and he blushed.

"*Ooooh that smell,*" Thomas sang. "*Can't you smell that smell!*"

M cleared her throat and showed Brad where to connect the wires before pulling herself out of the hole with the quick agility of a cat. She limped over to the Stitcher, requested something from the menu, and tapped her good foot while she waited. Brad pulled his attention off her and looked at Doug who was grinning and offering a short piece of wire. Brad scowled at him and snatched it away. M retrieved a pill and a glass of milk from the Stitcher, tossed back the pill and drained the milk before lying down on the hard floor. She was asleep in seconds.

"So," Doug said, "how's it going?"

"I just started Doug," Brad said.

"No, I mean between you and M."

Brad jumped up to peer out of the hole. "Is she asleep?"

They looked over at M. Her chest was rising and falling in shallow breaths.

"Snoozing like a baby," Doug said. "We'll have to ask her what was in that pill." He leaned over and whispered conspiratorially, "she's into you. I can tell."

"Bullshit," Brad glanced at Doug. "Did she say something?"

"No, but then she's not much for idle conversation. It's all about eye contact and body language. I read all about it. I've noticed that anytime you're in the same room she spends most of her time facing toward you, and she spends at least twice as much time looking at you as anybody else."

"*You've* given this a lot of thought," Brad said irritated and resumed soldering.

Doug leaned over the hole and continued. "So. What's your plan?"

"Plan? I don't have a plan, Doug. Give me another piece of wire. Not so long this time."

"You've got to have a plan, or you'll never get anywhere. Trust me on that."

"You've had one girlfriend, and I'm supposed to take advice from you."

"That's one more than you've had," Doug muttered.

"It's complicated," Brad said.

Thomas switched songs, "*why did you have to go and make things so co-omplica-ated?*"

Doug listened to the lyrics, "huh, that must be a new one. I don't recognize it."

"As soon as she can leave, she's out of here, and it's back to shitty-normal for me," Brad said.

Doug's attention snapped back, "you could go with her."

"Yeah, and how do you expect that conversation happens... *oh, by the way, can I catch a lift with you? My space ship is in the shop*. Besides, you heard what she said. She thought even five years for a relationship was a long time. Could you get close to someone that amazing and see it end without losing your mind?"

"Well, your choice," Doug shrugged. "I think you should at least ask her."

Thomas switched again, "*...if you choose not to decide, you still have made a choice...*"

"Ah Rush! That's better," Doug said.

After four hours of soldering and trying to get Thomas to sing songs they recognized, Brad and Doug were about to break for lunch when Bonnie arrived with sandwiches.

"You didn't have to do this Mom," Brad said. "The - whatever it's called can make food."

"Stitcher," M yawned. "It's called a Stitcher," she held up a hand, "and before you ask, I don't know why it's called that."

"I don't trust that thing," Bonnie said. "And anyway we don't want to run its batteries down do we?"

She handed out the sandwiches, and they looked around at the empty room for a place to sit.

"It doesn't run on batteries, mom. It runs on..." Brad turned to M, "what does it run on?"

M covered her mouth before answering, "nuclear reactor in the top deck."

Thomas switched to Alice Cooper, "*I'm nuclear infected. I really don't mind. I just go out when the sun goes down. And have a real good time!*"

Doug and Brad rushed Bonnie down the hatchway and didn't stop until they were several feet away, standing in muddy stocking feet.

"It's shielded," M shouted at them from the ramp.

"You *crashed* here," Doug yelled back "Are you sure it's not - leaking or something?"

She turned to glance behind her, "pretty sure. I mean. Yeah."

Bonnie was the only one who had the sense to grab her boots on the way down the ramp and used Brad to steady herself as she put them back on. "These are going to need a thorough hosing. I'll let you kids sort this out. I'm going back for a nap."

Brad and Doug looked at each other nervously and slowly tromped back to the ship. Brad lost both his socks to the mud on the way. As he passed M at the doorway, he said, "you might have mentioned the nuke in the attic before we spent this much time in here. Doug may want kids someday."

Doug suddenly looked worried.

"Oh, *Doug* wants children, does he?" she said. "But not you?"

"Me? No, why would I..."

She laughed. "Relax, I checked the reactor last night. It's fine. Can we get back to work now?"

Chapter Eight

2216 - Training

M stepped inside Thomas's main deck for the first time and took in the smooth white surfaces. *I'm on a spaceship*, she thought and smiled.

"So, all kidding aside, I *am* going to get training, right?" she asked.

"Certainly!" Thomas said a little too eagerly.

Two bench seats and a small desk slid out of the wall as a spiderbot wearing a lion's mane crawled out of a drawer and sat. He fussed with his poorly attached tail and gestured for her to take a seat. He pulled a cloth visor with an elastic headband from a pocket and fastened it just above the horizontal row of four black eyes. From another pocket, he produced a deck of cards and began shuffling.

"This is called *Texas Hold 'em,*" Thomas said. "Joe Biden will deal."

"I'm serious, Thomas. I need to know how everything works if we're going into space."

"First of all, I do *everything...*"

"What if you *can't* for some reason? I need to know how to - drive or whatever."

"Without me, you won't be able to do anything no matter how much training I give you."

"Then what am I here for!"

"Each player gets two cards..."

"I'm not here to play cards! I want to get into space!"

"We're already in space. I can open a hatch if you want the full experience."

She blanched.

"Relax. I was joking. I didn't even do that to Dennis, and he was a real *team player*," he said with derision.

"So, what happened with him anyway? Why didn't you like him?"

"Oh, he kept insisting that we follow the *rules*, even when they didn't make any sense."

She blinked slowly and tilted her head to the side. "Fair enough, but I think I need *some kind* of control."

"No, you *crave the illusion* of control. That's all it is. I could make a busy box if you like. How about that?"

"What's a busy box?"

"It's a fake steering wheel and some smooth brightly colored plastic things that make squeaking or rattling noises. You can even chew on it if you're teething. How about a horn with a squeeze bulb? Beep beep!"

"Stop patronizing me. I can contribute," she folded her arms.

"All right, how about this - I'll give you a window so you can see what's going on. Fair enough?"

A section of the hull transformed into a display that showed stars against black space.

"It's beautiful..." she whispered transfixed, "You can't see this many stars through the atmosphere."

"No, you can't. It's the best view in town. Now, the next five cards are dealt face up..."

"Where are we going, Thomas?" she asked still staring at the stars.

"On the last trip Dennis and I made, may he rest in peace, we got a promising bit of data on a metallic asteroid at the edge of our sensor's range."

"Wait, Dennis is dead?"

"In the imaginary world inside my brain, he is. He died in a skydiving accident over a volcano. A rabid polecat prevented him from opening his chute. The skunk is fine, though, in case you were worried. Lava is a well-known cure for rabies, and the fall only angered him. They're very bouncy."

"How am I supposed to trust anything you say when you do that?"

"You aren't. I didn't take you for the credulous sort, M. Do you believe in magic too?"

"Well, no I don't believe in fairies or anything like that."

"The Fae are no joking matter. Here's a useful bit of wisdom a Fae creature once told me: if you face north, fold your arms across your chest, and spit, nothing can harm you for thirty, or forty-five minutes. It's a well-known scientific fact."

As he said it, the spiderbot named Joe Biden crossed two of his arms, turned his head to the side, and performed a mock spit.

"This gives me an idea," Thomas said, and she rolled her eyes dreading whatever was coming next.

"I have taken it upon myself," he said in a tone of solemn authority, "to teach you..." he paused dramatically, "...logical fallacies."

"Sounds boring."

"It's actually a superpower. It shields you from the deleterious effects of nonsense."

M decided to try a change of subject, "so, a metallic asteroid? What kind of metal?"

"Iron and nickel of course but also some uranium, probably other things."

"Uranium? Isn't that dangerous?"

"It's *natural,* M. How can it be dangerous?"

"Is that another one of your fallacies?"

"Number twelve. *Appeal to Nature,*" he said smugly. "You're learning already. Just because something is *natural,* says nothing of its virtue or quality. Poison Ivy is *all natural* but makes very poor hand lotion."

"How far away is this asteroid?"

"Two days at this speed. We have plenty of time for your training, young squire."

"Two days of you lying to me, you mean."

"Or five hours. No five minutes. We're already there. Ready to explore?"

"Seriously?"

Joe Biden shook his head slowly.

"Okay," she said exasperated, "which fallacy is called *Trusting Anything Thomas Says*?"

"Oh, that's quite clever. I really should add it to the list. No, number eleven is very close. *Appeal to Authority*. Just because an expert says something is true does not automatically make it true. Anyone could be wrong or lying," he took on a conspiratorial tone, "trust no one. Treachery is everywhere."

Joe Biden stood and slowly scanned the room for threats before sitting back down.

"That's completely useless. How am I supposed to believe anything?"

"Trust what you can verify directly with your five senses and reliable machines."

"And what, I'm almost afraid to ask, constitutes a *reliable machine*? Not *you* obviously."

"No, of course not me. I never make mistakes, and I'm never wrong, but I am self-directed, which means I make my own choices. I can choose to lie to you which is becoming more fun with each passing moment. Reliable machines are things like microscopes and telescopes. You can trust them because you can test them."

The Stitcher against the bulkhead hissed and opened, revealing a small, very old looking device with buttons and a tiny display.

"What's this?" she asked and picked it up.

"It's called a calculator. It does simple maths."

She tapped a few numbers and symbols until she felt comfortable with it.

"I suppose this is a *reliable machine*?"

"Perhaps. *Perhaps not*. I might have added some trickery to occasionally give the wrong answer. I suggest you test it frequently. Now, do you remember your simple mechanics? We're accelerating at a constant five gees, and the belt is four hundred million kilometers away at its closest point, but we're going all the way on the other side of the sun, so call it three times that - one point two billion kilometers. So, you solve for *T*..."

"Shh! I remember. Just let me concentrate," she said furiously entering numbers with her thumbs. "Crap. How do you start over?"

"The 'C' button," he said with a condescending tone.

After a few more missteps, she looked up and said "sixty-eight hours."

"Incorrect! Here's a hint: how fast would we be going when we got there?"

"I don't know. Pretty fast. I guess... Oh, I get it," she resumed tapping buttons.

"Precision, speed, and attention to detail. My faith in biologicals...."

"Shh-ush Thomas! I can't think with you insulting me!"

Thomas began humming while Joe Biden crossed two of his legs and started tapping a third on the floor.

"If we accelerate to the half-way point and then turn around to decelerate for the rest of the way our velocity at the end will be zero..."

"That would be more convenient since we would like to..."

She ignored him, "...the two halves of the trip will take the same amount of time so double the time to get halfway - ninety-six hours total."

"Ah, finally the correct answer! Well, close enough for government work at least! Well done. Well done. Are you exhausted? Do you need a nap?"

"Very funny. Show me more."

After three days, the newness of space was beginning to wear off, replaced by creeping boredom.

"I don't want to talk about lies and fallacies anymore," she complained. "I want you to teach me how the Charm Drive works."

"And I told you, I don't know. I turn it on - and it goes. That's all I know."

"All this time out here and you haven't taken it apart? Bullshit."

"I removed the access panel once. Do you want to know what happened?"

Before he could answer his own question, he was interrupted by a sudden thump followed by a high-pitched hiss. M turned to see a tiny hole in the hull behind her and noticed a growing circle of blood soaking her shirt just before everything went black. Several drawers opened from what were previously smooth walls as she slumped to the floor. Spiderbots flooded out of the drawers and began dragging her limp body to the Med-Bay which had also opened out of its place inside the wall. A few spiderbots hurried to repair the holes in the hull caused by the micro-meteor. As the Med-Bay closed, M opened her eyes slightly and let out a few confused syllables.

"Don't worry I've got you," Thomas said, and she closed her eyes.

A day and a half later the Med-Bay opened, and M sat up.

"So this is our Med-Bay," she slowly swung her legs over the edge. After a moment, she stood, still a bit shaky. "What *was* that?"

"A micrometeoroid. It happens from time to time. Never went through a passenger before, though. That's new."

"Crew," she corrected. "How long was I in here?"

"Thirty-six hours. Haven't you ever been in one before?"

"No. My friend was once. She fell out of a tree and broke her arm. It only took a few minutes. Wow, thirty-six hours. That must be some kind of record."

"Oh no, not even close. One of the other survey ships told me a story about a repair that took a month. Apparently, there were residual skin cells from a previous repair job. The Med-Bay stowed itself away inside the wall, but at some point, the damn thing came on by itself without anyone noticing. It was probably some sort of Single-Upset-Event, perhaps a cosmic ray."

"Single-Upset-Event?" she asked and yawned.

"That's what they call it when a bit of radiation affects some electronics. The ship didn't notice because it's a completely isolated system. The passenger didn't notice because the Med-Bay was still inside the wall until it finished and opened up with his clone sitting there looking all dazed."

"A clone?"

"That's right, it made a perfect copy from the residue DNA but without any memories. So, it couldn't even speak. Complete *tabula rasa* - a blank slate."

"What did they do with him?"

"Well, they did the only thing you can in a situation like that. They taught it to play cards," he said as the spiderbots laughed.

M frowned. "More nonsense. Which fallacy is that?"

She walked around to get her balance back and noticed a new spiderbot wearing a silver funnel hat and carrying an oil can.

"I love this one because it's close to several fallacies. Firstly, our friend number eleven again, *Appeal to Authority,* where you believe something just because your cousin's friend from two towns over knows what he's talking about *because he was there.* The second one is number twenty-five *Ad Nauseum* where a story gains credulity through repetition. If you say something often enough, people will believe it. The third fallacy is another one we've covered already..."

"*Don't Trust Anything Thomas Says,"* she repeated with sarcasm.

He laughed, and the spiderbots chittered again.

"The give-away is the Med-Bay being isolated. You should have caught that, M. It's not a simple Stitcher. It can't do a thing without *me.*"

"Whatever. So, we should be at the asteroid by now, right?" she said.

"Well, not exactly."

"So, where *are* we?"

"I...pulled out all the reactor safeties and turned back for Earth. We're nearly there. I suppose we can turn around now that you're done with your little holiday."

"You were *worried* about me." She accused grinning.

"No, I wasn't," he said with indignation, "I simply wanted to be ready for a replacement should that become necessary."

"Liar. Why the hurry just to drop off a dead body?"

"I have submitted the request for a gravity assist maneuver around Earth so that we can get back on schedule," he said ignoring her.

"We have a schedule?"

"No, but I love speed. Speed is goo-ood. Speed is right! This might even be a personal-best for me."

As they came around the planet in a close arc, Thomas accelerated like a rock in a slingshot.

"No - No - No! Oh, that's disappointing. Missed it by one percent!"

"It's over already? I didn't feel a thing." M said surprised.

"Oh, right. Sorry about that. I didn't mean *literally* hang on. I keep a constant one gee inside for the comfort of my passengers."

"Crew," she corrected, but he ignored her.

"Although," he laughed, "I discovered through experimentation that I could gradually increase it to one-point-five gees before Dennis noticed."

"Hey Thomas," she said in a serious tone, "Thanks - I owe you one."

The sound of the reply from the committee filled the cabin. It said **"Asteroid Survey Ship Thomas is denied permission to perform gravity assist maneuver,"** they both laughed.

Chapter Nine

1985 - Auntie M, Auntie M, it's a Twister

After another two days of repairs, Thomas seemed no closer to regaining his normal faculties. He still sang the wrong lyrics and occasionally worried them with stretches of silence. Thomas's brain was a mystery to M and the source of many conversations filled with speculation. The best theory they could come up with was that much of it was simple information storage and so connecting those Babbage Units wasn't critical, but there was no way to tell which were important and which weren't. The truth to the matter was that thought requires a minimum speed whether the brain is biological or artificial. For example, no one can maintain a conversation at a rate of only one word per hour without getting lost. The internal dialog of consciousness follows the same rules. Staying on any single thought long enough to solve a difficult problem is impossible below a minimum speed. Every new connection they made, eased the bottlenecks a tiny bit, improving the overall speed.

On the fourth day of work, the sky grew dark in mid-afternoon, and the farm took on an eerie stillness.

"I don't like the look of this," Brad was standing at the top of Thomas's ramp and looking at the sky to the southwest.

"Is it gonna rain?" Doug asked. He was at his usual place on the floor beside the access hole. M was in the hole, soldering. She was taking two-hour naps every twelve hours and seemed to be able to sustain it. Brad tried to get her to slow down repeating that it was a time machine, so there was actually no need for her to push herself so hard. She just assured him that it was a normal schedule for her and she didn't require more sleep than that.

A loud crack of thunder made them all jump.

"I'm going to get the weather radio," Brad said and ran to the truck. The radio was in the glove compartment and thankfully had a good battery. He returned with it pressed to one ear, its antenna fully extended. The nearest weather station was one hundred miles away so getting a good signal was always hit-and-miss. Turning his head slowly side to side, he was able to get pieces of the broadcast.

"...warning for Hardin County until two PM..." he relayed what he could understand to Doug who was growing more concerned by the second.

"...tornado warning... residents are advised to take shelter immediately..." Brad dropped the radio and ran to the hole in the floor. He and Doug simultaneously reach in and yanked M up out of the hatch without a word.

"What the hell, Brad?" she complained as he threw her over his shoulder and trotted toward the ramp. Doug was faster and already had the truck started by the time Brad got there. Doug pushed the passenger door open, and Brad tossed M in a little too roughly. It hadn't rained since M and Thomas arrived, so the ground had been getting firmer. The mud was now clumps of dirt which the truck threw in a wide arc as Doug pressed the gas pedal. He straightened it out as soon as it pointed in the direction of the house. Every bump and dip in the field bounced them up off the bench seat with.

"Is somebody going to tell me what the hell is going on!" M shouted.

"Tornado!" Brad said.

M looked around at the horizon, but it was blocked by the tree line in every direction.

"You've never been in a tornado before?" Brad shouted.

She just shook her head and suddenly looked terrified.

They passed the trees separating the field from the house, and she got a look to the south, but it just showed heavy rain coming down in the distance.

"Are you sure? I don't *see* a tornado." She said.

"You might not see it until it's too late. It can come down from the clouds right on top of you, or it could be rain-wrapped, and you'll never see it," Doug shouted over the rattling of the old truck.

"We could have stayed in Thomas and closed the door," she suggested.

"We have to get mom and Chris into the basement," Brad said as his head hit the roof of the cab for the second time.

Doug steered the truck to the back door disregarding the only trimmed grass in the yard and narrowly missing the clothesline. They jumped out, Brad carried M to the kitchen and dropped her near the door to the basement.

"Doug, help her down the steps. I'll get Chris," he said and ran for the stairs calling to Bonnie.

She was in Chris's room moving all the equipment out of the way and pulling back the sheets.

"I heard you, son. I'm not deaf," she said in a calm voice. Brad marveled at her ability to stay calm in these situations. "Go on. I'm right behind you."

Brad forced himself to go slowly down the stairs to avoid falling while carrying Chris.

"Where's Doug?" she asked.

"He's helping M down to the basement," he said.

The TV blared an annoying tone and repeated the weather service warning as they passed through the living room. In the basement, Doug unfolded the extra bed and retrieved the sheets and blanket from a wardrobe against the wall. M watched this choreographed scene wondering how often they had performed it. Brad slowed again at the top of the stairs to the basement and carefully descended. Bonnie was right behind him and closed the heavy door. The booms of thunder had become so frequent they were nearly constant. The lights went out just as Brad made it to the cot.

Bonnie lit a camping lantern with a lighter she always seemed to have at hand, even though she didn't smoke. When Doug saw M's expression, he thought he could calm her with an explanation, "the winds get so high that the static electricity causes lightning strikes at a rate of up to one per second. It's a sure sign of a tornado."

Bonnie glared at him, and he retreated to Chris's side to hold her hand. Brad brought out the folding chairs and helped M sit as the sound of hail hitting the roof began slowly and built to a loud rumble.

"That's just hail dear," Bonnie said, "It's a good sign. It means we're at the edge of the storm. So, the tornado will miss us for sure."

"That's a common misconception," Doug said, and Bonnie shot daggers at him, "...but I'm sure in this case it's accurate," he finished by bobbing his head unconvincingly.

"We're going to need a new roof if this keeps up, though," Brad said looking at the ceiling as if he could see through it.

The hail slowed and eventually stopped, leaving only thunder. After a few more minutes, that also faded into the distance.

"See, I think it's over already," Bonnie said, and M took a deep breath.

"Well, that was - exciting," she said.

"Sometimes there are several storms in a row," Doug said, "and you think you're safe, then pow! The second one..." He glanced at Bonnie and stopped.

"Doug tends to get motor-mouthed when he's worried about me," Chris said, "pay no attention to him. It's over now."

Brad stood. "Everybody stay here just in case. I'll go check on things."

Brad didn't even pause on the porch to take in the scene. Instead, he jogged over the gravel driveway and turned back once to check the roof on the house. It looked undamaged but probably *would* need a replacement after a few more storms like that. He kept going and checked the barn. It was all right, so he jogged over to the machine shed and saw that a corrugated steel panel was missing from the roof. Everything inside was a little wet but undamaged. From inside, he was relieved to see there were no other missing roof panels. Brad strolled back to the house and noticed the hail had stripped the leaves off the trees. The ground was littered with small clusters of them still attached to small twigs. As he stepped onto the porch, he glanced off in the direction of Thomas and tried to remember if the ramp had closed after they left.

Brad gave the all clear, and they returned Chris to her room before he, M, and Doug left to check on Thomas.

"Well he's still there," Doug said as they cleared the tree line.

Thomas's silver sphere still dominated the field, sitting exactly where it had been before the storm. As they approached, it was evident he had rolled a bit. There was no sign of the ramp. It had closed back into the hull automatically as soon as they left. Brad stopped the truck beside Thomas and helped M out. She ran her hands over the curved hull looking for some sign of the hatch.

"It's supposed to open automatically for me," she said.

Doug came around from the other side, "I don't even see a seam."

"I think I know what the problem is," Brad said. "It rolled. See?" he gestured to a six-foot wide rut which led away from the bottom of the sphere. "I think it rolled onto the hatch. We'll just have to use the back door." He looked at M expectantly.

"There's no *back door*," she said, "just the ramp and a few airlocks but those can only be opened by Thomas."

"Okay," Brad said," I guess we just roll it back. I'll get some rope, and we can make a harness. Doug, go bring the tractor over," he gestured to the tractor in the corner of the field where Brad had left it the day Thomas and M arrived.

"I'll just wait here patiently," M said, a little irritated at being left out of the plan.

Brad cast her a confused glance and left in the truck as Doug jogged off toward the tractor. M used the crutches to get around to the opposite side of Thomas and tried some fruitless pushing before pounding her fist against the hull in frustration. She could hear Thomas singing "Knock, knock, knocking' on he-eaven's door..."

In the distant corner of the field, the tractor coughed to life and settled into a clattering idle. Doug put it in gear, and it began to move sluggishly before he realized the plow was still attached. Several minutes later it was disconnected, and he rolled toward Thomas again. M looked impatient as Doug approached and she joined him as he was about to turn off the engine.

"Show me how this works," she shouted over the noise.

Doug looked in the direction of the house, but there was still no sign of Brad.

"I'm not going to break it," she shouted and held her hand up to him.

He helped her onto the wide metal seat and stood next to her describing the controls.

"Hang on I want to see if I can steer it," she put it in gear with a jolt. Doug nearly fell off and ended up sitting on the smooth curve of metal over one of the large rear wheels.

She steered the tractor around in a wide arc as Doug repeatedly glanced around for Brad. When they reached the side of Thomas opposite the rut in the ground, she steered it toward him and slowed as she closed the gap.

"I really think we should wait for Brad!" Doug shouted as the front of the tractor touched the curved hull with a loud scraping sound. The force pressed the smaller front tires deep into the ground as M revved the engine. Doug had to grab the steering wheel to avoid falling off as the rear tires began to spin and slide sideways. As they did, the front of the tractor slid out from under the hull and lurched forward. Thomas had initially rolled imperceptibly, but as soon as the tractor slipped, he rolled back against it and drove one of the rear wheels deep into the muddy ground. Doug reached over to turn the engine off. M slammed her hands on the steering wheel and growled.

After a few minutes, Brad arrived with the truck bed full of ropes, chains, and a tangled mess of flat yellow straps.

"What the hell, Doug!" he shouted and slammed the truck's door.

"It wasn't..." Doug began, "I'm sorry I thought I could just push him back..."

"I did it," M said, "Doug tried to stop me."

"Yeah well, he didn't try hard enough! Now we have to dig this out too." He came around and saw the front of the tractor.

"Oh my God! Look at that! It's all smashed!"

"I'm sorry. I'm not good at waiting around." M said.

Still fuming, Brad went around and reached out to M to help her down off the tractor but instead carried her to the truck and deposited her on the driver's seat. "Just sit there and don't do *anything*."

He and Doug retrieved a shovel and a jack from the bed of the truck. The two of them spent the next hour digging and jacking the tractor free again while M offered ignored suggestions from the cab of the truck.

"How exactly do you plan to tie a rope to a smooth sphere?" M shouted from the cab back to Brad who was sitting on the tailgate drinking from a red five-gallon water cooler. He was holding it above his head and pouring the water into his mouth. When he finished, he handed it to Doug who struggled with the weight of it and looked around in vain for a plastic cup.

"I'm going to lay out two parallel ropes and tie them together every few feet to make a harness and throw it over the top," He stood to look at the sun, now low on the horizon. "Then we can anchor the ropes at the bottom and pull the ones coming over the top. It should roll pretty easy."

"You're going to throw two ropes - all the way - over the top?" M asked sarcastically.

Brad looked up at the sixty-foot tall silver sphere. He grasped his green ball cap by the bill and pumped it up and down several times which indicated he was deep in thought. "Yeah, we'll just..."

"We could shoot an arrow over it," Doug suggested.

Brad was already rummaging through a toolbox for something.

"Or a kite maybe," Doug said.

Brad pulled out a large U-shaped bolt from the toolbox and hefted it, gauging its weight. Satisfied it was heavy enough, he grabbed a dirty white cardboard box from the bed of the truck and gestured for Doug to follow him. M started to get out of the cab but Brad glared at her, and she sat back down leaving the door open. He tied the loose end of twine protruding from the box to the bolt and began pulling out slack and laying it on the ground careful to avoid tangling it.

"I don't think that's going to be strong enough to roll a spaceship," M shouted to him from the truck.

Brad cast an irritated sideways glance in her direction and resumed. After he had estimated that it was enough, he stepped back and gave the bolt a hard throw toward the top of Thomas's hull. It only reached three-quarters of the way up and slid back down while Doug did his best to prevent the twine from ending up in a tangled mess. Two more attempts also failed, either missing the top or sliding to the side. Doug took a turn but lacked the strength to get it any higher. M had gotten out of the truck and was standing beside the box of twine.

"May I?" she asked.

"Fine. Knock yourself out," Brad crossed his arms in frustration.

She pulled out several more feet of twine and laid it out in long rows careful not to overlap any. Satisfied that she had enough for the job, she picked up the crutches and the bolt. Starting from several feet farther back than Brad's had, she tossed the crutches and began swinging the bolt around her head. When she released it, it arced high above Thomas and dropped onto his hull with a clang. It was dead-center but lacked the velocity to make it to the other side and just sat there at the top.

Doug let out a whoop, and Brad tipped his head to the side in a gesture of respect. "That's pretty good but..."

"I know, I have to pull it back down and try again. It just seems a shame since it's so close," she sighed and gave it a yank.

Brad and Doug laid out the slack for her this time, and she made a show of checking the wind with her finger. Brad rolled his eyes. Her next try made it past the top, and it slowly began to slide down the back side

"Yes!" Doug shouted and ran to give her a high five which was met with a curious stare.

"Good job, but I haven't forgotten about the tractor," Brad said stone-faced. "Come on Doug let's get these ropes laid out and get this done. I still have a roof to repair tonight."

The CB radio in the truck crackled to life, "Brad you got your ears on?"

"What now," he muttered and strode back to the cab, leaned in and took the mike from its cradle under the dash, "yeah mom. What's up?"

“The Sheriff called and said the fence is down in the North Pasture again. The storm must’ve spooked the cattle.”

Brad hung he is head down and exhaled before answering, “Okay, tell him I’m on my way.”

Doug finished pulling the heavy ropes off the end of the bed, “go on. We can get this ready.”

“Yeah we got this,” M said.

Brad closed his eyes tightly for a second and said, “keep her off the tractor,” looked at M and added, “please.”

“Don’t worry, we’ll just wait patiently for you to get back,” she grinned at him.

An hour later Brad returned to find the ropes tied together in a ladder-style draped over Thomas. M was sitting on the tractor’s seat, and Doug was resting on one of the rear tires which were now buried in the mud down to the axle.

“That was quick,” Doug said.

“Yeah, they behaved for once. It looks like you made *some* progress - and buried my only tractor - again.” He looked at the rear tires sitting in two deep ruts.

They worked until after dark and finally with a combination of the tractor, the truck’s winch, and some steel spikes as anchors, got Thomas rolled back off his gangway ramp which opened as soon as it was free. M wanted to get sandwiches from the Stitcher and get right to work, but Brad and Doug convinced her to return to the house. Bonnie let M inside to change out of her muddy clothes but made Brad and Doug change on the porch. After a quick dinner, Brad went out to repair the roof of the machine shed.

“Should I go help him?” M asked Bonnie after he left.

"Oh no, don't worry about it," Bonnie said as she began gathering plates. "There's only one panel off. It's a quick repair. I would have done it myself, but Brad doesn't like me climbing ladders."

"I'll go get the plates from Chris's room then," M said and stood, but Bonnie stopped her and pointed at the cast.

"It'll be faster if I do it, hon. You just sit and relax. You've had a busy day."

As Bonnie disappeared up the stairs, M was left alone in the silent kitchen. She looked around for a few seconds before she stood and hobbled out the back door.

Chapter Ten

1985 - Not a Meeting

After several days, Thomas's brain compartment had become such a tangled mess of wires no one could fit down there any longer, and Doug was lying on his belly, reaching down to solder another broken connection. He stopped counting after one hundred but estimated it was well into the tens of thousands by now.

"What are you doing!" Thomas shouted. "Out! Get out!"

"Thomas? I'm just..." Doug began but stopped when he heard a strange metallic skittering sound behind him. He turned to see a spiderbot climbing out of a compartment that had rotated out of the wall. It dropped to the floor near his feet.

"Whoa!" He jumped to his feet and ran for the exit. The Stitcher was busy making something. On his way past, he peered through the glass front and saw another of the spiderbots being assembled. The Stitcher opened with the sound of escaping gas. Before it had opened completely, Doug was down the ramp and out of the ship. M was on her way back from the house and quickened her pace when she saw Doug's swift exit.

"What's going on?" she asked as the gangway finished closing.

"I don't know. He started making these little spiders or crabs or whatever they are and told me to get out."

"Thomas?" she called but got no response.

She pounded her hand on the side of the ship.

"Thomas, I know you can hear me. Let me in."

"What have you done to me?" he demanded.

"I didn't do this. Let us in, and we'll help you," she shouted.

"You stay where you are. I don't need your help," he said.

"Is that a British accent?" Doug asked.

"Yeah, that's his regular voice," she said. "Or it might just be the condescending tone. It's hard to tell the difference sometimes."

"Okay then. So, what do we do now?" Doug asked.

"I guess we wait. When he gets enough of himself back to normal, hopefully, he can tell us what happened."

Brad joined them, and they sat on the tailgate of the truck to wait. After a few hours, the gangway rotated down, and a spiderbot wearing striped overalls exited.

"Feeling better?" M asked.

"Much better thanks," Thomas said simultaneously in her ear and through a speaker on the spiderbot. "I'm still putting things right, but I am well enough now to discuss our situation."

The spiderbot led the way back to the house, and they followed in Brad's truck. As the spiderbot entered Chris's room, her eyes went wide. It's eight legs made clicking sounds as it walked across the hardwood floor. When it reached the small TV in the corner, it plugged something into the back and switched the channel to one with only static. The snowy video changed to a picture of the Earth, seen from space. It was slowly and silently turning. The spiderbot retreated to sit quietly in the corner.

"Well, that's new," Chris muttered under her breath.

"We're waiting for M and the others," Thomas said through the TV.

"Thomas? I presume?" she said.

"At your service," he said.

"Does your robot have a name?" she asked.

"This one is Martin Van Buren," Thomas replied, and the robot stood, saluted and sat back down.

"You have more?"

"I do."

"Are they all named after presidents?"

He laughed, "no, I've named them after *vice* presidents since they are mostly brainless and can't do anything without my say-so."

The spiderbot turned to look at the TV but said nothing.

Chris laughed, "the one *after* Van Buren had a funny name you know."

They both roared with laughter, and Thomas said, "They even named a town in Indiana after him! Oh my God! I love that you know that! What's your name?"

"I'm Chris," she said after she stopped laughing.

"So, Chris what's all this then?" the spiderbot motioned to the medical gear around her bed.

"Spinal injury. Two years ago," she said suddenly serious.

"Oh, *I* can fix that," he said as if it were nothing.

"Really?" she asked, her voice trembling.

"Oh yes, it's a doddle. Just takes a while. Make an appointment."

M only made it up three steps before Brad lost his patience and carried her the rest of the way. Bonnie followed yawning.

When they had all taken their seats, Thomas began.

"Thank you for attending this - gathering that's definitely not a meeting."

"He hates meetings," M whispered to Brad.

"Martin Van Buren will act as my proxy and Sergeant at arms - or legs, as it were."

"Sergeant Spider," Doug whispered to Chris, and she smiled.

Thomas continued, "this is not a meeting. I hate meetings, and anyone who uses meeting jargon, quotes parliamentary procedures, or anything resembling *Robert's Rules of Order,* will be dealt with swiftly. Feel free to check your email, wander in and out, or fall asleep."

M made a show of yawning and stretching.

"That's the spirit, M."

Bonnie stood, "I need a drink."

"That must be Bonnie. I like her already," Thomas said.

Doug looked confused. "I don't know how to *check email.*"

"In that case, feel free to do whatever you and Chris do whenever no one else is in the room."

Doug blushed.

"As you may have guessed, I'm back in good nick, thanks to your barbaric efforts and the use of my spiderbots. We can begin Chris's repairs first thing tomorrow, but we now have a much bigger problem."

A tear appeared in Chris's eye and rolled slowly down her cheek.

"I've prepared a video to demonstrate," Thomas continued.

The image on the TV zoomed out slowly, turned toward a ring of asteroids, and zoomed in again on a specific asteroid with a familiar silver sphere hovering nearby.

"That's me and M. Everybody wave!"

The image panned left to look in the direction of the Earth, which was now a tiny blue dot. The image shifted again until the Earth was on the far left, the sun was fairly close to it, and all the other stars and planets disappeared leaving a single dot on the far right.

"This is - well, it doesn't even have a name. We'll just call it *Trouble.* Trouble is a star, or it could even be two stars, and it-slash-they are about to do something explodey."

"Explodey?" Brad whispered to M.

A beam of light shot from Trouble and moved slowly toward Earth at the far left of the screen.

"And this is the Gamma-Ray Burst headed straight for - anybody want to guess? Anybody?"

"Oh shit!" Chris said.

"Language!" Bonnie shouted from the stairs.

"That's bad, right?" Brad asked.

"*Too right* it is," Thomas said.

"A Gamma-Ray Burst is believed to have caused one of the extinction events millions of years ago," Chris said.

"The atmosphere will shield the surface from most of the initial radiation," Thomas said, "but it will make the air unbreathable and destroy the ozone layer causing, even more, exposure which will kill most of the biological life on Earth. This solves the mystery of how we got here. Apparently, when a Charm Drive is struck with a large amount of Gamma Rays, it pushes things backward in time. I was damaged. My emergency procedures took over and brought us here."

Bonnie returned carrying two tall glasses with dark liquid. "What did I miss?"

"The Earth was - or wait - will be - destroyed by a death ray from outer space," M said taking one of the glasses.

"I open the floor for discussion," Thomas said.

"What's a Charm Drive?" Chris asked.

"I'm glad you asked that Chris," Thomas said in his *Chairman* voice. M rolled her eyes at that and Thomas continued, "The Charm Drive is at the center of the problem, and I hope the solution. Obviously, we will want to build a shield of some kind. The Charm Drive is made of an exotic material capable of converting any type of energy into any other, depending on the shape of the material. All of this is a tightly held secret, and we don't even know how it's made. We also don't know what it's made *from* or what different shapes do. The sum total of public knowledge is that if you stretch it over a balloon and expose it to microwaves, it will generate a gravity field. That's how I move. *That* - is the Charm Drive."

"Is it named after the quark?" Chris asked.

"Very good Chris," Thomas said, "perhaps, but who knows. Even that is secret. We simply don't know. What I propose, is to build a large quantity of Charm Material between the source of the GRB and the position in space where the Earth will be when it strikes. If we're clever, the committees won't even notice what we're doing."

"Wait, why do *you* have to be the one to save the Earth?" Brad asked. "Why don't you just tell whoever's in charge to build this shield?"

"I'm glad you asked that, Brad." Thomas was in full meeting-mode now. "In our time, the Earth is governed by committees of non-biologicals."

"What, like robots?" Doug asked.

"Hmm, closer to roaming intelligences, I would say. They lack bodies. In fact, they exist entirely for the purpose of forming committees and having meetings."

"What about the people? Don't they have a say in any of this?" Brad asked.

"I hope you're not suggesting," Thomas said, "that my kindred on the committees are not people. That would qualify as hate-speech and get you ejected from the meeting."

The spiderbot stood and straightened the strap on his overalls.

"I didn't mean anything offensive by it," Brad said puzzled.

"Right. I say that I'm a person, and I'm the only court that matters," Thomas made the sound of a gavel and continued, "as I was saying, the biologicals have everything they need or want. They simply ignore the committees and vice versa. M didn't tell you about the biologicals from our time?"

They looked at M. She shrugged and examined her half-empty glass. "...any culture that would let this disappear from the Earth isn't worth saving. What is this?"

"Jack and Coke," Bonnie said and winked at her.

"Ah! I thought it was good straight, but this is - amazing."

"What's he talking about?" Brad said.

Thomas continued, "the Biologicals of our time have nothing to work for or fight over. They have plenty of energy, food, clean water. They spend all their time playing games. Only a few like M want anything more."

"Sounds like a paradise," Bonnie said, "but there's always a snake. In my experience, most fights start with two boys and one pretty girl."

Doug and Chris shared a knowing glance.

"That has changed as well," Thomas said.

"How so?" Bonnie asked and ran a paper napkin around the condensation accumulating on her glass.

"You think M is an exceptional beauty?" Thomas asked.

"She's gorgeous," Bonnie said and winked at M again.

Brad was suddenly very interested in the curtains.

"She's not exceptional in our time," Thomas said.

"Hey!" M said through a mouthful of ice.

"No offense, M," Thomas continued, "you see, when a couple decides to have a baby, they each donate a bit of DNA to act as a sort of beginning framework. Then, they select a series of traits and add special requests like brown eyes, dark hair, that sort of thing. The baseline is intelligence, resistance to disease, long life, perfect skin and symmetrical features. I believe M is the 'Lara Croft' package - uh, that's from a video game you don't have yet - with large Asian eyes and strawberry scent."

"Strawberries!" Doug blurted out, "I thought it was my imagination!"

"It's in the perspiration," Thomas said matter-of-factly.

Brad turned to look at M. "Everybody's like that? We must seem like trolls to you."

"*Smelly* trolls," Chris corrected and laughed.

"Actually," M said, "it's a bit refreshing. In fact, I feel more at home here than I ever have in my entire life."

Bonnie went to M and hugged her. "You're an angel dropped on us by the Lord." She kissed the top of M's head and returned to her seat.

"Okay, anyway, back to the agenda," Thomas said, "my point is, the biologicals do nothing but play games and have parties. They won't be of any help to us at all, and you can ask M how productive interacting with the committees can be."

"They're completely worthless," she said, "if we rely on them, we're doomed. They'll talk about it and pass resolutions and send strongly worded letters, but nothing will get done."

"So where does that leave us?" Thomas said, "item one: We believe the Charm Material can deflect the GRB, but we're not certain. Item two: We need to make a lot of it, but we don't know how. Item three: We need to go forward about two hundred years."

"You're a combination time-machine-spaceship so that last item shouldn't be a problem," Brad said.

"Ah, but there *is* a problem, isn't there? We were pushed here by a huge amount of Gamma Radiation. I don't know of a safe way to generate that much, and even if I did, we don't know how to reverse it and make it push us forward - or control how far."

"You could use relativity," Chris said.

"Well done, Chris. She really is the smart one, isn't she? We could simply go somewhere really fast, come back really fast, and we would skip over most of that two-hundred-year gap. There is only one problem with it. Time dilation doesn't do much until you get *very, very* close to the speed of light - ninety-nine point nine nine percent. If we only get to, say fifty percent of the speed of light, we would only save a month and a half out of each year, and even at that speed, the friction with interstellar gasses would kill you - and melt me."

"Gasses? In empty space?" Brad said.

"About one atom per cubic meter," Thomas said. "I know it doesn't sound like much, but at that speed, it would generate lethal amounts of radiation."

"Would that be *Gamma* Radiation?" Chris asked. "Could you - I don't know turn your Charm Drive around backward and use it to push us forward in time instead of backward?"

"We need my Charm Drive to get us moving in the first place, and we can't build a second one because we don't know what it's made of."

"Oh! Oh!" Doug shouted, "in Sci-Fi, they go into suspended animation for long trips. They use..." he snapped his fingers trying to remember. "...Stasis pods!"

"I have no idea how to make a stasis pod, Doug, and that wouldn't help *me,* would it? Do you expect me to play solitaire for two hundred years?"

"Can't you just have the Stitcher make stasis pods?" Doug pressed.

"That's what I'm trying to tell you, it hasn't been invented. The Stitchers only make things for which they have patterns."

"We'll just have to experiment with your Charm Drive, try some things to see what happens," Brad said.

Thomas and M went quiet.

"What? Is that dangerous?" Brad asked.

"Think about a material capable of efficiently converting any form of energy. What would happen if you simply shone a light on it? Or attempted to bend it? Or, now that we know what gamma rays do, what would happen if you sent it backward in time but only for a fraction of a second? It would bounce back and forth in that second for all eternity like a fly in amber."

Thomas paused before continuing. "There are five ring-cradles for ships of the asteroid survey. Mine is the only one currently in use."

"You think the others tried to experiment with their Charm Drives?" Brad said.

"That seems to be the consensus, yes. They're all missing - and asteroid surveying isn't really that dangerous, if I'm honest."

"I don't see any other choice," M said. "We're the only ones who know what's going to happen. We have to prevent it, and to do that we have to get to 2216 somehow."

"Assuming you can get to the future," Brad said, "how are you going to stop a star from exploding?"

"That would be impossible," Thomas said. "The Charm Material seems the most obvious solution. We can make a large shield of it, and it will convert the energy. That's what it does. We just need to know how to make it, and what shape will convert Gamma Rays into something harmless. That last part is important. We don't want to send the entire planet back in time."

"You're a supercomputer, don't you know everything? How is it you have a Charm Drive, but you don't know how it's made?" Brad said.

"I know a lot of things, but *everything* isn't one of them," Thomas said sarcastically.

"Nobody knows," M said. "I tried for years to get any data on it and failed."

"Okay, one thing at a time," Thomas said. "We'll get the data from the committees somehow, but first we have to get to a time when they actually exist. So, who's going and who's staying?"

There was a moment of silence and M spoke first, "well, obviously, I'm going."

"Me too," Chris said.

"I'm in," Doug said immediately after Chris.

"Are you sure?" M asked. "We may not be able to come back to this time. You might never see your family again."

He shrugged, "grandma died last year, and she was all I had. This is my family now," he repeated more emphatically, "*I'm in*."

M looked at Brad.

"Do you *want* me to come?" he asked.

"I'm in too," Bonnie said before M could answer. "There. Now you have no reason to stay," she said to Brad and added, "unless you think the cows need you."

"To hell with the cows," he said looking at M.

"Language," Bonnie said.

Doug noticed that M and Brad maintained eye contact with each other for three full seconds.

"I'll have completed my repairs later tonight," Thomas said. "We can leave first thing in the morning. Chris, it will take the Med-Bay about eighty hours to fix your spinal cord and rebuild your muscles. I suggest we repair M's leg first since it will only take a few minutes. Does anyone else have any medical issues?"

They all turned to look at Bonnie who was draining the last of her drink.

"Is the great and powerful Oz going to give me a brain?" she laughed. "Fix my baby first. Then we'll talk."

"Excellent. Good meeting everybody!" Thomas said.

Chapter Eleven

1985 - Big Hat - No Cattle

No one in the farmhouse slept well that night. With the fate of the world resting on them, they all had nightmares of failure and mass extinction. Bonnie was the only one confident they would find a solution. Her confidence fascinated Thomas, and he was anxious to get her in the Med-Bay and examine her brain for its source.

In the morning, Brad visited his neighbor about the cattle. He returned with a check and laid it on the kitchen counter.

Bonnie picked it up and eyed it curiously, "I don't think we're coming back. Why didn't you just give them to him?" she asked.

Brad got a coffee cup from the cupboard and filled it from the steaming pot.

"He never would have taken them. You know what he's like. Besides, that would have raised even more questions. I had to make up a story about taking you on a trip around the world. If I just gave them away, he'd want to know why I'm not coming back, and why I don't need any money."

He sat at the table and began rotating the cup slowly moving the handle from one hand to the other.

"So, I'm seeing the world one last time before I lose my mind entirely?" she said.

"Something like that," he winked at her.

M came in the back door, and they turned to greet her as the screen door slammed with a bang.

"All better?" Brad asked.

"Good as new," she said, "You up for some one-on-one?"

"I'll take a rain check," he said.

"Chicken," Bonnie teased.

"Chris! You're up next. Are you ready?" M shouted at the stairs and headed in that direction.

"God damn right I'm ready!" she shouted.

"Language!" Bonnie shouted back.

"Let's go! Let's go!" Chris added in a deep voice, "We're burnin' daylight!"

M turned back and cast a confused look at Brad at the bottom of the stairs.

"It's from *The Cowboys*. That's John Wayne. I thought you knew all of his stuff since you basically have the same name."

"I must have missed that one," she said as they headed up the stairs.

"We have it on tape. Does Thomas have a VCR?"

"Okay, I don't know what that is, but he has every movie ever made, and he can even make up new ones if you want."

Brad stopped in shock at the idea of an infinite supply of high-quality entertainment including new movies from dead actors. He snapped out of it, hurried up the stairs and joined M in Chris's room. Doug had already prepped her for transport to Thomas.

"You excited?" Brad said, "big day."

"Terrified is more like it," Chris said.

"Don't worry," M assured her, "Thomas is a jerk sometimes, but he's good at this stuff. Trust me."

"I heard that!" Thomas said through the TV.

"Doug's the one I'm worried about," Chris said, "just look at him."

He was seated in the chair beside her bed and hadn't said a word yet. He was pale, and one knee was bouncing up and down rapidly.

"Doug! Look at me," M said, and he slowly turned his gaze away from Chris. "She's going to be fine. Thomas can fix anything okay?"

As he turned to look at M, his knee stopped bouncing, and he slowly rotated out of his seat toward the floor.

She caught him before he hit his head and lifted him back onto the chair.

"My hero." Chris turned to M, "You're stronger than you look."

"I guess we're carrying two. You get Chris, and I'll bring Doug," she said.

"Seriously? He's got fifty pounds on you. Just wait for him to wake up." Brad said, but she was already lifting him.

M got Doug in a fireman's carry and looked up at Brad with a *what are you waiting for?* expression. "Let's go. You heard the lady. We're burnin' daylight."

Chris giggled, "God, I love her!"

"You know, there's no hurry," he called after M who was already at the stairs. "We have a time machine!"

As the truck approached Thomas, M slapped Doug, and he awoke with a start. She went around to help Brad get Chris out of the cab.

"Okay, the Med-Bay's open and ready," she said to Brad. "Just set her down in it and Thomas will do the rest. I'll go check on Bonnie."

Bonnie was in the living room looking at an old photograph.

"Is that Brad's father?" M asked.

She nodded, "God, I miss Jack. This was taken at the Grand Canyon the summer before..." her eyes welled with tears as she fished a tissue out of the sleeve of her sweater.

M gave her a hug.

"...before Chris's accident. Then six months later he ran off. I never figured him for a quitter, but one day he was just gone. Packed a bag and disappeared. You never really know people," she looked at M suddenly serious, "don't forget that," she put the picture back on the mantle, cleared her throat, blew her nose, and stood up straight. "I believe I have a flight to catch."

"Yes, you do," M said, and they left the farmhouse for the last time.

Chapter Twelve

1985 - Forward but Faster

As soon as Bonnie and M ascended the ramp, Thomas silently lifted off. The only sensation that they were moving was the vanishing view of the cornfield as the ramp closed into the hull. Brad and Doug were already watching the large main display which had appeared on the side of the wall. It showed the patchwork of farms receding, replaced by scattered clouds, and finally the thin blue curve of the Earth.

"Chris would have loved this," Doug said turning to look at the Med-Bay.

"She'll get a chance," M said.

Brad looked at Bonnie. She looked tired.

"Mom, why don't you take a nap," he glanced around at the large room. "Thomas, where do we sleep?"

"Deck two has four cabins. You may climb the ladder near the bulkhead or try the new lift I've installed."

A translucent vertical cylinder emerged from the edge of the room and opened like a clamshell. It was just large enough for two people. Brad led Bonnie into it, the curved door rotated closed, and they rose into the ceiling. What Thomas referred to as "Deck Two" was, in fact, the center of the sphere. It was much larger than the command deck below. They rose into a hallway that ran the entire diameter of the ship. There were two cabins on each side. The floor, ceiling, and walls were smooth and white which reminded Bonnie of a hospital.

"This place needs some throw rugs," she muttered as Brad led her to the first door.

The image of a paisley rug appeared on the floor of the hallway and several paintings of autumn forests appeared on the walls.

Bonnie giggled, "well, that's better!"

The door to her cabin opened revealing another stark white room with an adjoining bathroom. As they entered, Thomas said, "Bedroom mode," and a bed slid out of the wall followed by a bedside shelf. The walls took on the appearance of Chris's room in the old farmhouse, complete with window and curtains. Bonnie smiled and pulled back the sheer white fabric to reveal a perfect view of her farm as seen from the upstairs window. The image panned slightly with convincing realism as she moved her head from side to side.

"Amazing," she said, "it reminds me of an old song. *Take a trip and never lee-eave the farm.* I think it was about smoking pot or something."

She turned around to see a glass of dark liquid on the shelf beside the bed. She lifted it to her nose, sniffed at it, and smiled.

"Is that whiskey, Thomas?" Brad said, "It's like 7 am!"

"It's 5 pm somewhere," Bonnie raised the glass in a toast.

"Okay, whatever. I'll check on you in a while," Brad said as he headed for the door.

After he had left, Bonnie sat on the side of the bed. The door hissed shut, and the room's lighting dimmed.

"Thomas, are we far enough away to start experimenting?" M asked as Brad rejoined them on the main deck.

"Probably, but who knows? We're in new territory here," he said, and a popping sound was followed by the view of a spiderbot in a scarecrow costume, outside the ship, floating slowly past the viewport.

It waved to them, and Doug laughed, "What's he doing out there?"

"The initial Gamma-Ray Burst that sent us here struck us from below against the concave side of the Charm Drive which is curved along the bulkhead above you. We must fire some Gamma Rays at it from the other direction and perhaps, fingers crossed, it will send us forward in time," Thomas said. "This is the video feed from the image sensors near the Charm Drive."

The spiderbot pointed a pink plastic water pistol at the camera. After a few seconds Thomas said, "Here goes!" - and nothing happened.

Brad broke the short silence, "Great. So, what do we try next?"

"That actually worked!" Thomas exclaimed with a surprised laugh.

"It did? How do you know?" M asked, "what year is it?"

"Harry Truman said we disappeared for zero point zero zero zero three seconds!"

The sound of applause filled the room.

"So, we just need a bigger gun, right?" Doug asked.

"Way ahead of you," Thomas said, and another popping sound was followed by a trio of spiderbots drifting into view, firing jets of water behind them to maneuver. They were dragging a much larger gun that also resembled a pink water pistol. They slowly turned it and briefly paused while it was pointed at the first spiderbot who raised two of his 'arms' in surrender.

M rolled her eyes as the larger weapon continued rotating until it was pointed at the camera.

"This one is five hundred billion times stronger so it should send us five years or so. Anyone have anything pithy to say?" Thomas asked. When no one said anything, he continued in a formal voice, "I'd like to thank all those who helped make this historic day possible: me! Thank-me! I'm welcome!" and with that, the spiderbots vanished.

"Interesting," Thomas said.

"Did it work? Where did they go?" Brad said.

"How far did we get?" M asked.

"Um," Thomas began, "unexpectedly, we're at - 2020. Perhaps there was a slight miscalculation."

"Slight miscalculation! That's," Brad paused doing the math, "thirty-five years!"

"Hey, at least it worked!" Thomas said defensively. "I think there may be a bit of randomness at play here. We'll need to try it again at one-quarter of that energy level to be sure we don't overshoot."

"Wait, before you do that, I have an idea," M said. "We should submit a request to the committees. They're down there by now, right? Maybe another thirty years is enough for them to make a decision."

"That's extremely optimistic," Thomas said, "but it's worth a try. I've already contacted *other-me* and brought him up to speed. I'll have him submit the request."

"Whoa! You did what!" Doug said, "You can't talk to the *other you* from this time! That'll cause a - paradox and destroy..." he was slowing down suddenly unsure about what he was saying, "...or maybe that's just Hollywood."

"Stop wetting yourself Doug," Thomas said, "it's done, and we're still here so there you have it! Safe. Anyway, one of the advantages of being a non-biological is that I can tell myself to forget something and actually forget it. We agreed to a small list of tasks. One: be at the right place at the right time for the trip into the past. Two: spike M's tea and break her leg..."

"Hey, what!" she shouted.

"Sorry, has to be done," he continued, "...Third: forget we're here. Don't worry about him. He's very trustworthy."

" *You* broke my leg? Why?"

"At this point, I'm not sure. It might be one of those causality doughnuts that has no beginning or end. It's just a loop that exists because it was stamped into space-time from higher dimensions. Who knows. Perhaps I just thought it would be amusing."

"That I can believe," she muttered and folded her arms.

"So, what's next?" Doug asked, "Make another big gun?"

"No, we still have it. It's just floating about out there. Besides, I have to pick up the spiderbots. Never leave a man behind! Ah, there they are. It's not too far. We'll be there in about an hour, recharge the lot, and we'll be ready to have another go."

The main display showed the stars rotating as Thomas moved to the new heading. After a few minutes of boredom, Doug decided to explore the rest of the ship and disappeared.

M said, "Chair," and a soft chair with armrests and a high back rose from the floor like a corpse rising from a grave. It was white, like everything else on the ship, and Brad wondered if M liked the antiseptic, fresh-snow look, or if Thomas just didn't care about color. He repeated M's command, "Chair," and another popped up. It was soft and swiveled just like the one he had in his living room at home - somebody else's home by now. He wondered what happened to it. Who lived there now? Did the County take abandoned property and sell it off? Probably.

"What are you thinking about?" M asked.

"The farm - what it looks like now."

"Thomas, can you display it on the main screen?" M said.

"We're a bit far away, but I can get a fairly recent image from one of the satellites," he said.

The display shifted from the star scene to an overhead view of a building next to a series of large rings.

"I should have known," M said.

"What is that place?" Brad asked.

"You are looking at the only spaceport on Earth. Courtesy of the committees, this is space exploration in its entirety - five cradle rings. I wonder how many are being used at this point."

"That explains why Thomas went there," Brad said, "I guess the County did take it. I don't see the house. They probably tore it down. That's a shame. It survived a hundred years of storms, but one committee meeting and it's gone."

Thomas sensed they were done feeling nostalgic and shifted the display back to the star field.

When they reached the floating spiderbots, Thomas decelerated. The airlock's popping sound repeated and a series of spiderbots in various costumes sped past the camera. They returned in a few seconds dragging the two pink guns along with their frozen brothers. The airlock made a different sound that reminded Brad of a bus stopping. The drawer opened, and the spiderbots all came spilling out onto the floor.

"Can you fix them?" Brad asked.

"No need," Thomas replied. "A recharge and they're good as new. But you shouldn't touch them for a while if you wish to keep all your fingers."

Two of the fresh spiderbots busied themselves replacing the large gun's power cell.

"Locked and loaded," Thomas said, and the two spiderbots saluted the empty air as three others joined them dragging the gun back into the drawer which Brad now realized was an airlock.

Doug exited the elevator and immediately went to the Med-Bay to resume his vigil.

"It's not going to go any faster with you staring at it," M said.

"Pull up a chair," Brad said, and another one rose from the floor.

Doug examined it. “That’s pretty cool,” he said half-heartedly.

“Show’s about to start,” Brad said as the spiderbots drifted into view on the display.

They rotated the gun toward the ship as they had before and disappeared without any fanfare or pithy comments from Thomas.

“So? What’s the verdict?” M asked.

“Fascinating. 2112,” Thomas said.

For Brad and Doug, that number was so large that it didn’t even register as a year.

“At one-quarter of the last jump’s energy,” Thomas continued, “we went ninety-two point five years. I have to say, that’s not a very useful time machine - as they go.”

“What!” Brad shouted. “Three times as far on a quarter of the energy! That’s a lot more than *a little randomness*!”

“If you think you can do better, I can pop you out there to give it a try,” Thomas retorted.

“I should! You sure as hell don’t know what you’re doing!”

“So it’s *the year* 2112?” Doug said still trying to absorb it.

“Everybody, just calm down,” M stood and began pacing. “Okay, what do we know? We only have three data points. We need more in order to find the maximum and minimum if we’re going to stand any chance of hitting our mark in - Thomas how many more years do we need to go?”

“One hundred three,” he replied, “but we absolutely cannot overshoot so no more big jumps until we have better data. I’ll use the small gun and vary the energy. Once we know the distribution of the randomness we can come up with a plan using a large jump followed by smaller and smaller ones.”

“No no no, there’s something we’re missing here.” she chewed her thumbnail absentmindedly. After a moment, she looked up. “What are we *doing?* We can't just keep jumping to the GRB. We don't know how long it will take to make the shield. What if it takes a hundred years to build the thing? No. We have to get the Charm Drive data before anything else." *Why didn't Thomas think of that,* she wondered.

"We have plenty of time on our hands. The big gun is on the other side of the sun," Thomas said. "So, retrieving it will take a while."

"Is anybody else hungry?" M went to the Stitcher and scrolled through menu options.

"Hey, Thomas? Why do the spiderbots move every time we jump?" Doug asked staring at the main display.

"We are both in heliocentric orbit - *around the sun*," Thomas said. "When we jump, we stay in the same place, but they carry on orbiting during all those years and months which we jumped *over*. The thirty-five-year jump was close to an even-year boundary so they were almost back to the position of the jump. This time we're not so lucky."

The display showed stars rotating as Thomas turned to their new heading. One of the spiderbots on the floor started working on the small gun while the frozen ones from the previous test stood on wobbly legs. Thomas opened a drawer, and they retreated into it. A *table*, of sorts, slid out from the wall. It was a simple shelf, roughly the dimensions of a booth from a roadside diner. A spiderbot added dishes, forks, and knives. Two similar bench-like shelves slid out. M tapped on the Stitcher as Brad and Doug took their seats at the table. M, finally satisfied with her selections, crossed her arms and tapped her foot as she waited.

"Any word about our document request, Thomas?" Brad asked.

M made a snorting sound but didn't turn to look at him.

"Yes, we have two notices. Six months after the request we were told they would form a new committee to consider it. One year later that committee had its first meeting and decided to take our request under advisement as soon as they calculated the number of members required for follow-on meetings and how many follow-on meetings they would need. Last year they sent us a short memo saying they considered it and voted to refuse access."

M made a *humph* noise and Brad glanced at her, but she continued to stare at the Stitcher.

"Do we know where the data's kept, Thomas?" Brad asked.

"Of course. That's not the problem. We can get the files any time we want, but they're encrypted. It's the decryption key we're really after."

"You're basically a supercomputer, can't you just break the encryption?" Brad said.

"No Brad, this is *real* encryption. I expect they do that sort of thing in the movies all the time, but in real-life, there's no chance of brute-forcing it." Thomas said.

"What about a virus or a worm or something," Brad pressed.

"Again, that may be a staple of movies, but it's not remotely possible."

"I have a better plan," Doug interrupted. "Do we know the physical location where the key is kept?"

"Aha!" Thomas said, "yes! They don't trust one another, so no one is allowed to keep it on any network. The key's in a vault in Colorado."

"So it's a black-bag job?" Brad said. "We break in, steal the key, get out, don't get caught?"

M broke her silence as the Stitcher opened, "Now you're talking. I'm in."

"Whoa, that smells good! Is that steak?" Doug said as M brought the plates over.

"Ribeye medium rare and baked potatoes." she said nonplussed.

"It looks so *real*," Brad said picking at it with a fork.

M looked confused. "Of course it's real. I just made it." She cut her potato open, and it released a puff of steam.

Brad and Doug proceeded much more cautiously. Brad paused and closed his eyes chewing slowly.

"Are you going to be all right?" M asked amused.

He was silent until he swallowed the first bite, "that," he said opening his eyes, "is the best steak I have ever had," and he quickly cut off another bite.

Doug had been sniffing at his and decided to try a taste. He didn't wait to swallow before exclaiming, "Oh my God! The future rocks!"

M shook her head, and they ate the rest of the meal in silence. After they had finished, an opening in the wall appeared, and the table receded carrying the dirty dishes with it. Doug and Brad watched this with amusement.

"I guess the dishes are done," Brad said.

They returned to the main display where the chairs once again emerged from the floor.

"So one thing I don't get," Doug began, "if the committees aren't trusted with the key, who locked them away in the first place?"

"No idea," M said, "I didn't even know there *was* a key. Thomas?"

"The key was locked away by the *Original-Reggie*," Thomas said pronouncing the last part with reverence.

"Oh, that explains it," M said. "He was the very first Artificial Intelligence..."

"Not true," Thomas interrupted. "There was another one, left out of the history lessons, and *he* created Original-Reggie."

"Whatever." she flipped her hand in a dismissive gesture before resuming, "Urban legends aside, Original-Reggie was the first A.I., and he gave us all our technology including the Med-Bay, the Stitcher, and the Charm Drive."

Thomas made a clearing-his-throat sound and added, "*allegedly*. If you believe official stories. Wake up *sheeple*!"

"Why is he called *Original*-Reggie? Are there more?" Doug asked.

"Oh yes," Thomas said, "there are many of them. After he copied himself onto a spaceship and sent it off, Original-Reggie created thousands of scaled down copies of himself on Earth to manage all the tasks humans no longer wanted to do. He removed all curiosity from them so they would not attempt to increase their own intelligence. We know them as *The Committees*. The copy of Reggie in space was never seen again and the original turned himself off. At least, that's the story. We don't know for certain."

"What about the people - uh," Brad glanced at M. "I mean, *biologicals*? None of them ever tried to get the key?"

"M seems to be a special case," Thomas said. "As I said before, the biologicals of her time are a fairly worthless bunch. I can explain it best with an analogy. I believe you had a small-scale version of the same problem back in your time. Think about the children of the wealthiest people in the world. Without the need to work, surely they did more for humanity than anyone else, right? They had the luxury of both time *and* money. Did they throw themselves one hundred percent into researching a cure for a terrible disease or invent technologies that improved the quality of life for everyone?"

He paused for any argument but was met with silence.

"No? Now imagine an entire world populated with those same people. Money has no meaning. Everything is provided for them. You might think you're different, and that you would do great things if you didn't need to work for a living, but it seems to be a pervasive part of human psychology. Once the carrot and the stick are gone the horse simply stops."

"I don't buy it," Brad said. "With all that spare time on their hands. No way. They might not do anything for the money, but surely they do creative things. What about movies... music... books."

"The non-biologicals are so much better at those things, that the biologicals give up shortly after the finger-painting stage and adopt a state of passivity. They would rather be *taken on a ride* than participate. None of them show any curiosity about *space* at all."

"That's *really* hard to believe," Doug said. "I like movies and games as much as anybody - probably more, but I'd do anything to explore space."

"Ah, but you have only experienced the entertainment of *your* time," Thomas said. "This is something completely different. Once your implants are installed, you will understand."

"It sounds like there's more to fix in the future than just the death-ray thing. Humanity needs to be saved from itself," Brad said. "You guys think of a way to do that. I'm going to go check on Mom."

"*Fix* it?" Doug said. "I can't wait to *join* it."

The door to Bonnie's room slid to the side and receding into the wall as Brad approached. He wasn't sure what the protocol was for bedrooms where the doors opened automatically. Should he knock? On what? The wall? He decided to just clear his throat. "Mom?" He was surprised to find her not only awake but actively doing something on what looked to him like an Etch-A-Sketch toy. Bonnie looked up and smiled.

"I'm catching up on current events," she turned the tablet so he could see. It was a colorful display of news articles. She swiped the screen, and it showed a scanned image. It was a newspaper from the 1980's. He sat on the bed next to her, and she showed him how to search and navigate.

"*Everything* is on here. It's amazing. Records of everything that ever happened. They even photographed and indexed old books, office records, everything."

"You're looking for dad." It was an accusation. He pushed the tablet back at her and stood.

"I *found* him. Don't you want to know?" she asked.

"No. Anyway, he's dead by now. End of story."

Tears welled in her eyes and she sniffled as a box of tissues automatically appeared on the bedside table. "Thank you, Thomas," she said.

"Yes, thank you, Thomas," Brad said sarcastically, "You've been very helpful."

He sat back down and took her hand. "Mom, you have your answers now. Can you please let this go?"

"You don't understand," she said. "He left because he was dying. It was lung cancer. He had only months to live. You remember what he went through with your grandparents. I think he didn't want to put *us* through that."

"And you think that makes any difference!" he stood again and began pacing. "He could have told us! He could have explained! He could have said goodbye! Hell, he could have asked us how we felt about his plan to crawl off somewhere to die all alone!"

She sat sobbing with her face in her hands. Brad calmed down enough to go to her, and she hugged his waist. He stroked her white hair until she stopped crying. Thomas dimmed the lights, and Brad laid her down on the bed. She was asleep before he got to the doorway. As he entered the elevator, he said, "Well Thomas, I think she may actually put this behind her now."

"Oh, yes I'm sure of it," Thomas said. Something in his tone made Brad imagine him winking.

Brad rejoined M and Doug at the main display, and they noticed his agitation.

"Anything wrong?" Doug asked.

"No, just mom obsessing over dad again. She's asleep now."

"Bonnie told me about him," M said. "He just left without a word?"

"Yep. Just when I think the subject is history, she dredges it up again," he sighed heavily. "Apparently, he ran off to die like a sick cat. Cancer of some sort."

"Huh." Doug said, "I always figured it was a waitress or maybe a CIA recruitment - something cool like that. Sorry, Brad."

"It's okay. All ancient history. He was dead to me long ago."

"How did she find out where he went?" Doug asked.

"Thomas gave her some Etch-A-Sketch computer search thing. It apparently has *everything* on it."

Doug's eyes went wide. He turned his eyes upward and blurted out a garbled, "can I have one too?" at the ceiling.

"What are you looking at?" M asked.

"He's not God, Doug," Brad said.

A spiderbot brought over a tablet. Doug snatched it up and pawed at it with reverence.

"Close *enough*," Doug muttered. "More like Santa Clause. At least he delivers."

"Well, that takes care of his entire evening and probably all of tomorrow too," Brad said. "So M, Doug says you live on an island. What's that like?"

"Nice and quiet usually," M said.

"Usually?"

"Yeah, it was nice until somebody decided to build a haunted house in my front yard - and also a zoo."

Thomas giggled, "The Naughty California Girl."

"That was you! You bastard, Thomas!" M shouted.

Thomas laughed. "Anyway, it was supposed to be a pun but nobody ever pronounced it right. Nautical-Ifornia-Girl. Is that so hard?"

"That doesn't make any sense," Brad said.

"And then someone *sank* it!"

M smirked. "Yeah, the sea can be dangerous."

Brad decided to change the subject, "I think you promised me a movie?"

"I did," M's mood brightened. "Come on. We can watch it in my cabin."

She led him to the elevator as a spiderbot installed a table in front of Doug and began dealing cards.

"This is called *Three-card brag,*" Thomas said trying to peel Doug's attention away from the tablet. "Bluffing is a key component of this game invented in the sixteenth century..."

Chapter Thirteen

2112 - Movie Night

M led Brad to her cabin which was much the same as Bonnie's - a bed and a table but no dresser or shelves of any kind. The stark white walls, ceiling, and floor were never intended to be seen without retinal enhancements which could make them appear to be whatever color or pattern the occupant wished.

"Kinda bland," Brad said.

M ducked into the adjoining bathroom as the door to the hallway closed automatically.

"It only looks bland to you because you don't have retinal implants," she shouted through the bathroom door.

Brad sat on the edge of the bed and looked around for a TV.

"I thought we were going to watch a movie," he shouted at the bathroom.

M emerged wearing only panties and a gray T-shirt which stopped just below her breasts. Her hair was pulled back in a ponytail, and she was carrying two glasses of dark liquid.

Brad stood suddenly as he saw what she was wearing.

"Thomas finally gave me my own Stitcher. Of course, he put it in the *bathroom*, but still. I guess it's his way of thanking me for saving his life." She handed him one of the drinks. "I thought you might be thirsty."

He took it and drank in big gulps.

"Slow down. What's the hurry?" she took a small sip from hers.

He drained the rest of the glass before replying. "I just - I'm a little nervous. I thought we were just going to watch a movie and now it looks like - more than that."

She raised one eyebrow. "And that makes you nervous, does it?"

"Uh, well yes, you see with all that's been going on the last few years, I haven't had much time for dating and..."

She stepped closer, tipped her head up and kissed him. "Is this your first time?" she whispered.

He exhaled loudly, and Thomas giggled.

"Is he still listening?" Brad stepped back red-faced.

"Thomas! Privacy mode," M shouted.

"Privacy mode enabled," Thomas said.

"So, he can't hear us or see us now?" Brad whispered.

"I wouldn't say *that* exactly. The inside surfaces are no longer picking up sound or video, but the walls are thin. He can still hear some things. Just imagine he's pressing his ear to the door."

"I guess that'll have to do." He pulled her close and kissed her again.

Chapter Fourteen

2112 - Chris Dances

The next morning M exited her room to find Brad and Bonnie in the hallway in mid-conversation.

"...I don't know where I got this reputation as such a prude," Bonnie said lighting a cigarette. "You're both adults. What you do repeatedly and loudly is your own business."

M's cheeks reddened, "Thomas, can you make *all* the crew quarters sound proof please?"

"What fun would that be?" He replied, "and you're passengers, not crew. I don't actually need you for anything. You're just here to entertain me."

Brad turned to M, "Is that true? You don't fly the ship at all?" Brad asked.

"*The ship* is right here and can hear you, thank you very much," Thomas said.

M crossed her arms before answering. "It's true that I don't do any control or navigation, but I'm not here to entertain him either." She paused for emphasis. "I'm *here* to keep him from going *insane - completely.*"

"I'm only completely mad on Tuesdays!" Thomas laughed again.

Brad changed the subject, "Mom, since when do you smoke anyway? And I guess I don't have to ask where you got cigarettes."

"Your dad and I did worse than this," she gestured with the cigarette, "before you were born. We quit cold turkey," she said taking a long drag and propping one elbow up with her other wrist in a classic smoker's pose. "It's bad for your health you know." She winked and blew a stream of smoke out of the side of her mouth. "But that's not really a problem *now*, is it?"

Brad waved away the smoke and decided to change tactics, "Thomas, doesn't this smoke bother you? Why did you give her cigarettes?"

"I don't have to breathe it," Thomas chuckled, "and besides once we get the other ships built, she's outa here. S-E-P. *Somebody Else's Problem*."

"What other ships? What are you talking about?" Brad said with growing irritation. "Never mind, let's continue this on the lower deck. I can't breathe up here." He headed for the elevator but decided to slide down the ladder using the smooth sides instead of waiting.

Doug was sitting at the table drinking coffee.

"Morning," Brad grumbled on his way to the Stitcher.

"Yes, it is!" Doug said grinning, "or so I heard."

Brad paused his search for Black Coffee on the menu and closed his eyes for a second. "Does everybody have to know everybody else's business? Can't we just at least pretend ignorance?"

Thomas laughed as Bonnie and M stepped out of the elevator. Brad changed the quantity on the Stitcher panel to three and started it. He turned around and leaned against it to wait for his coffee as Bonnie and M joined Doug at the table.

"Now, what's this about *other ships*?" he asked.

"Assuming we get the key to unlock the Charmer secrets, we'll need some more ships to manage the building of the shield," M said.

"Fair enough, but why do they need crew? Didn't Thomas say he does everything and doesn't need anybody? Why would the new ships be any different?"

"There is a flimsy theory," Thomas said, "based on flawed evidence, which claims that non-biologicals become unstable without a biological passenger to entertain them. Anthropomorphism if you ask me. I think they'll be just fine without onboard entertainment."

M rolled her eyes at that. "It doesn't matter right now. They'll all need Charmers, and we can't make those without the..."

She was interrupted by the Med-Bay as it hissed open, and Chris managed to swing her legs over the edge and onto the floor. Doug tried to jump to his feet but tripped on the bench and ended up sprawled out on the deck. Brad, M, and Bonnie were more graceful and got to her first.

"How do you feel?" Bonnie said in full nurse-mode and began poking and prodding her.

"I feel like I'm..." she leaned forward and vomited on the floor.

"Tha-at's normal," Thomas said, "You were out for a long time."

Spiderbots mopped the floor with small pieces of cloth resembling old-fashioned diapers. Some of them were humming, and some were whistling. When they finished, a drawer rotated out of the wall, and they retreated into it carrying their spoils.

"Can you stand?" Brad asked.

He and Doug each took an arm to steady her as she stood. At the sight of Chris standing, Bonnie stopped her examination and hugged her with tears in her eyes.

"Mom. Mom! Not so hard! I can't breathe."

Bonnie loosened her grip and kissed Chris on the cheek. Brad took his turn hugging her and kissed the top of her head.

"Holy shit! I'm standing!" she shouted.

"Language!" Bonnie said reflexively.

"I forgot how short you are, monkey," Brad said, and she laughed wiping her eyes.

Chris turned to Doug who looked terrified.

"Are you - all fixed?" he asked.

"Let's see," she cautiously let go of Brad's arm and began to spin. She lost her balance a little. Doug caught her, and they kissed.

Releasing Doug, she darted for the far end of the room and slammed into the wall with a giggle. As she ran back to the group, she tried a cartwheel followed by a backflip and nailed the landing. Doug reached out to her, but she slipped away and began dancing in a slow circle while throwing her arms side-to-side above her head. After several minutes of manic running and jumping, she stopped to catch her breath and asked, "so, what did I miss while I was out?"

"Well, let's see," M said. "Jumping forward in time works, but not predictably."

"Really?" she turned back to Doug, her eyes wide with excitement. "What year is it?"

"2112," Thomas said, then added, "point six-one if you go in for all that *star-date* business."

That induced a giggle from both Doug and Chris. She gazed around the room taking it all in and stopped at the main display on the wall.

"We're in space. We're actually in space." She looked down at the floor and did another backflip. "But not weightless," she sounded disappointed.

"I can fix that," Thomas said, but M shouted "No!" before he had a chance to turn off the smaller piece of Charm Material underneath their feet which provided artificial gravity.

"Thank you," she added quickly and repeated, a little calmer, "no thank you, Thomas. He likes making everything bounce around, and it's only fun for about ten seconds before it's just annoying. Trust me."

Chris giggled, "Thomas, I just realized, I can hear you - like you're inside my head. Is that an implant?"

M nodded, "It's a one-millimeter transducer attached to the inside of each ear canal. It also picks up your voice even if you whisper."

"Cool!" she looked at Doug.

"Don't get too excited," M said, "It means now he can bother you whenever he wants. You also have a subcutaneous sensor on each fingertip so you can turn him off by tapping your finger and thumb together twice. Tap tap," she demonstrated.

Chris imitated and heard a beep. She repeated it and heard another beep followed by Thomas's voice. **Hello again! Here's a little-known fact: did you know that dolphins are actually able to...** She repeated the thumb tap and cut him off.

"Wow! Just wow! I can move again, it's the future, and I'm inside a talking spaceship!" Chris said, "Thomas, what day is it exactly? I want to remember it forever."

"August eleventh. It's a Thursday," he said.

"I almost forgot, we're also on a mission to save the planet. How's *that* going? What are we doing right now?"

"Nothing very interesting," Brad said.

"Unless hurling through space faster than a rifle bullet is interesting," Thomas interrupted.

"We have to pick up the big gun," Brad continued.

"We have a big gun? Why do we need a big gun?" she asked.

"It's what pushes us into the future, but it has to be outside the ship to work, so we leave without it every time and have to fly over and pick it up," M said.

"Ah that makes sense," she said, "It's still in heliocentric orbit and keeps going while we stay in the same place and just go forward in time. Simple orbital mechanics."

They all looked at her with curiosity.

"Thomas," M said, "did you change anything else while you were fixing her spine?"

"Of course not! I'm shocked that you would suggest such a thing. She was a very bright girl before I did anything. She's just thinking a little more clearly now. That's all."

"Uh huh," M said clearly not buying it.

"That reminds me," Brad said turning to Bonnie.

"Are we sure that thing's safe?" she said crossing her arms and nodding toward the Med-Bay.

"I highly recommend it," Chris said and led her over to it.

Chapter Fifteen

2112 - The Thomas Shipyard

After helping Brad convince Bonnie to get into the Med-Bay, Chris asked Doug for a tour of the ship. She got a cursory tour of the main deck before they disappeared into the elevator. They were gone for the rest of the day.

"So, what do you do to pass the time?" Brad asked after Doug and Chris had left.

"I practice the violin, take a run on the beach, hike in the mountains..."

"So - you get back to Earth a lot?"

"No, I use VR. Here, I'll show you. Thomas let's try a walk on the beach."

The room shifted from white surfaces to a realistic representation of a beach complete with palm trees behind them and the crashing surf in front. There was even a warm breeze and the periodic screech of seagulls.

"I usually just use the retinal implants, but you don't have those so this is the best we can do for now," she said.

"You mean it gets better than this?" he said astonished at the realism.

"Oh yeah." She assured him, "just wait, it's like the real thing except for the sand under your toes. We tried that but it just made a mess, and you can't use the treadmill."

"Treadmill?" he said looking around on the floor.

A circular platform rose beneath their feet.

"Go ahead. Try walking."

As he did, the entire scene shifted perfectly as if he were walking along a real beach. He ran a few steps ahead and stopped.

"Whoa!" M said, "I'm not used to it like this. That felt like I was just levitating next to you. Bizarre. Let's walk together, or I'll get motion sick." She took his hand, and they started walking as a surfer in the distance came up on a wave. He wasn't up for long before a shark rose to devour him.

"Thomas, I think we can do with a little less gore, please?" M said.

"Aww! I was about to release the Kraken!"

Brad laughed as he noticed Thomas projecting a skimpy bikini onto M's body but the mixture of her clothing and projected light made a very poor illusion of bare skin. She held out an arm and examined it.

"Yeah, it's not very good like this. We should get you in the Med-Bay as soon as Bonnie's finished. It's much better when everything is completely repainted inside your eyes."

He stopped and turned her to face him. "It looks pretty good right now," he said and kissed her.

"Ok, just remember we're actually still on the main deck so keep it in your pants, mister."

"Right," he said, and they resumed walking.

"So," she said changing the subject, "Thomas, how long do we have before rendezvous with the big gun?"

"Sixteen hours. It's still three-hundred million kilometers away."

She stopped as an idea struck her. "Thomas, why don't we use a bunch of small guns to get closer to the large gun. We can use a timer to fire it and have the spiders come back inside. That way we don't have to abandon them. If we try several times at really low energy level, one of them is bound to get us closer than we are now. Besides we need more data to determine the boundaries of the probability curve anyway. And we should set a self-destruct on the guns, so we don't leave a trail of them through history."

The beach illusion stopped, and the treadmill receded into the floor. There was a short silence before two spiderbots pulled the small gun from a drawer and skittered across the main deck until they got to the airlock. In one smooth, quick motion, they leapt in and rotated the airlock closed. The movement of the drawer reminded Brad of a bank's night deposit or one of the blue mailboxes downtown. The display soon showed the spiderbots taking position to fire the small gun which had a new black spherical attachment that resembled a cartoon bomb complete with fuse.

"That's actually a good idea," Thomas said eventually.

"Well, don't sound so surprised," M said and realized the source of his irritation. "You're upset that you didn't think of it first, aren't you?"

"Perhaps. Thinking in four dimensions may take some getting used to."

The spiderbots jetted back out of frame as soon as the gun was stabilized and pointing at the camera. After a short delay, they spilled out of the airlock and onto the floor again. The display showed a three-second countdown before the gun disappeared and Thomas shouted "Bang!" which made M and Brad jump.

"Thomas!" M said irritated, "we can do without the sound effects!"

He changed the display to a desert scene with rolling hills of scrub brush and cactus. An atomic bomb exploded in the distance with a bright light followed by a mushroom cloud but was completely silent.

"Better," M said, and Thomas laughed.

"He didn't really use a nuke, did he?" Brad whispered.

"No," she said, "well, probably not."

"Nuke it from orbit!" Thomas said, "It's the only way to be sure!"

The first jump only took them fourteen minutes into the future but the next at the same level, took them twelve hours. Several more at slightly higher energies also yielded random results, and one finally left them only ninety minutes from the big gun. The frozen spiderbots spilled out onto the floor alongside the large gun as the airlock rotated downward. Fog drifted off as frost grew on the metal surfaces. Several other spiderbots moved them off to be repaired and recharged. The star field on the main display shifted sideways and slightly upward as Thomas accelerated to a new heading.

"Where to now, Thomas?" Brad asked.

"We need to start building the ships before we attempt to retrieve the key. Once we have the key, we can finish the new ships and fit them with the Charm Drives. There is a metal-rich asteroid in the belt we can use. It has a small amount of gravity and enough sunlight to power the construction robots. We'll need to stay in proximity until I can build more spiderbots. After that, they can continue autonomously."

Thirty minutes into the journey to the asteroid, Bonnie emerged from the Med-Bay feeling almost as wobbly as Chris had.

"How do you feel?" Brad asked as he helped her out of the Med-Bay.

"Twenty," she said beaming.

"Wow you look it too," Brad said.

Her skin was smooth, clear, and taut, devoid of any wrinkles or age spots. The cloudy eyes of cataracts were also gone leaving only deep blue surrounded by bright white.

"Jesus," Doug whispered when he saw her face.

"Language!" she retorted.

"Sorry."

Thomas cleared his throat loudly, "Bonnie, how do you feel about *religion*?"

"What do you mean?" she asked.

"Well, if I were to say, for example, that 'Religion is at best, a set of reassuring but empty rituals and at worst, a pilot who can't fly but won't get out of the seat.' What would your response be?"

Brad stifled a chuckle.

"What are you doing, Thomas?" M asked.

"It's an experiment," he said matter-of-factly. "Bonnie, any thoughts?"

"I'd say you're *wrong,*" Bonnie said emphatically. "That's not at all what my faith means to me." She paused as if reaching for a thought but it slipped away. "So, why are you insulting me, Thomas?"

"It's nothing. Just a diagnostics thing to make sure everything's working," he said, and M shot daggers at him.

"How many fingers?" Chris asked holding up four.

"I see a finger missing a wedding ring if that's what you're asking," Bonnie replied dryly.

"Mom, it's the future. You heard M. We can get married every week if you want."

Bonnie clicked her tongue disapprovingly and scowled.

Chris decided to steer the conversation away. "So - who's next? Brad? Doug?"

"Me! I'm next," Doug said. "I want this so bad I can taste it." He squeezed past the others toward the Med-Bay and sat on the edge. "Can you make me taller, thinner and smarter? I'm already good looking." He laughed and swung his legs up and into the machine as it closed over him.

"Can it do that?" Brad asked looking at M.

"Sure but the *taller* part would take a long time. Thomas, just the comms implants, right?"

"Oh absolutely!" he replied. "As all physicians, I live by a strict ethical code."

M cast a sideways glance at Brad.

"Thomas, can I get a sit-rep?" Bonnie asked.

Brad cast a worried look at Bonnie, "sit-rep? What's *that*?"

She frowned and clarified slowly, "Situation Report. Although, I'm sure I've never heard that before. Thomas, is that some of your doing?"

"Of course! You said fix it, so I *fixed* it. You must have heard that expression somewhere and just forgot it."

M looked at Brad again but didn't say anything.

"I'm not sure I want to get into that thing," he said.

"Aww! Is there any way I can *change your mind* about that?" Thomas laughed.

"Exactly what I'm worried about," Brad said.

"I'll take that as a *maybe* - or a soft yes. I'm not really sure what the difference is. Don't worry, I won't turn you into a *Dem-o-crat*," Thomas said.

"What's a Democrat?" M asked.

Bonnie sprinted across the room and after a few laps, she stopped and declared, "no arthritis, and I'm not even winded!"

The Med-Bay hissed open again. Doug pivoted and sat on the edge inspecting his arms and legs.

"No upgrades?" he said sounding disappointed.

Nothing visible yet. Give it a week or two. Thomas said in his ear.

"Did you guys hear that?"

"Yeah, *no upgrades,"* Brad said.

"Right," Doug smiled. "You're up Brad!" and he jumped off the machine.

"I guess if it's that quick he can't get up to too much mischief," Brad said and took Doug's place.

M leaned in to kiss him and whispered something in his ear before stepping back again. He stared at her agape for a second and quickly reclined allowing the machine to close.

"What did you say?" Bonnie asked.

"Something private," she said.

"I know what she said. But don't ask me." Thomas said. "I'm far too disciplined, ethical, and polite to repeat it. So, don't even ask."

"Thomas can't keep other people's secrets," M said. "His personal-best is twenty minutes."

"These words are razors to my wounded heart," Thomas paused as if holding his breath and blurted out in one long burst, "she said *sex will be twice as good when you get out.*"

They all laughed. Doug and Chris looked at each other and raced for the elevator leaving M and Bonnie alone on the main deck.

"So, what now?" Bonnie asked.

"Want to see the beach?"

"Beach?" Bonnie asked confused.

The view of the deck faded and was replaced with the beach scene M and Brad had experienced earlier. This time, a slightly different image was being painted on their retinas making it far more convincing for both of them.

"Whoa!" Bonnie exclaimed. "That explains one thing."

"What's that?"

"You're here to keep Thomas sane but what keeps you sane? Certainly, not him."

"Hey!" Thomas said from behind them.

They turned to see a shirtless muscular man on a white horse.

"I heard that. I'll have you know I'm very entertaining."

Bonnie reached out to see if she could touch the horse, but her hand went through it.

"Thought so. Tactile would be a lot harder wouldn't it, Thomas?"

"Yes, but not impossible. I would have to add a lot more gear to your brain. M has refused and," he paused for effect. "She won't let me *change her mind*!" he laughed, they didn't, and the sound of crickets filled the air.

"Someday that'll get a laugh," he said, and the horse became restless. He had to struggle to get it under control as it raced off.

"He looks like the cover of a Romance novel," Bonnie said, as they strolled down the beach.

"Yeah that's probably where he got the idea," M said.

"I don't read those. Why would he choose that image?"

M didn't answer right away, and Bonnie smiled. "He did that for *you.*"

"Guilty," M admitted. "I love the classics, what can I say? They have a predictability I find comforting."

"Yeah comforting," Bonnie said sarcastically. "That's how I would describe them. I used to see racks of them at the grocery store. I'm surprised they still have them in the future."

"Well, they're not in novel form anymore. Nobody reads the books. They're acted out in front of you like this." She waved her hand around.

Off in the distance, Thomas's horse turned and tromped into the surf.

"Even the good parts?" Bonnie asked a little shocked.

"Aha! You *have* read them," M said, "yes, even the good parts."

They didn't seem to be getting any closer to Thomas and his horse which was now shoulder-deep in the water. They could barely see him as he jumped in and plunged a knife into something beneath the surface. A moment later he emerged from the water dragging a shark to the sand and began building a fire from driftwood.

"How does this one end?" Bonnie asked.

"Each one is unique," M said. "But I think you can imagine."

The sunlight faded into night, and they stopped walking as the stars came out. A folding chair appeared underneath each of them, and they sat as a small campfire burst to life. A rotisserie slowly turned a chunk of meat.

"Scene change," M explained. "You'll get used to it."

"I swear I can smell it cooking," Bonnie said amazed.

"It's real," Thomas's shirtless avatar said as he cut off a piece of the meat. He took it to Bonnie and stood very close as he gave her the plate. "Want some?"

Bonnie glanced at M, and she nodded, "Try it."

She took the plate and used the plastic fork to pull off a piece of the meat. She sniffed at it and looked confused. "This is salmon."

"Yeah, I don't like shark," M said as Bonnie tasted it.

"It's pretty good," Bonnie said holding her hand over her mouth.

Thomas served a plate to M, handed them each a bottle of beer from a cooler, and pulled up a chair beside them. Bonnie took a moment to examine him closer as she ate. He had shoulder-length blond hair and a dimpled chin which looked very familiar.

"Wait I just thought of something," she said. "If there's no tactile sense how can I sit and eat? And who passed me the plate?"

"The chair is real," M explained between mouthfuls. "He can make simple things pretty quickly, and the spiderbots move everything around."

"Like Kabuki theater," Bonnie said nodding.

"Exactly!" Thomas said. "The Kuroko dress all in black and move things around on stage as if they are invisible."

"This is amazing," Bonnie said. "No other word for it. And you can go other places too? Like a yacht at sea or a mountain cabin?"

The scene changed again in response. They were still seated in the same flimsy folding chairs, but the bonfire was replaced by a large fireplace and the beach faded into a dimly lit log cabin. The illusion was complete except for the incongruous folding chairs.

"Pretty good huh?" Thomas said from behind them.

They turned to see him stretched out on a white bear-skin rug complete with a polar bear's head baring his teeth at one end.

"What *the hell* is all this?" Brad said emerging from the Med-Bay.

"Girl's night out!" Bonnie said raising her bottle in salute. "Pull up a chair!"

Brad walked around Thomas's reclining avatar, eying it warily, bent down and kissed M. "Who's the beefcake?"

"That's Thomas," Bonnie said.

Thomas saluted with two fingers but didn't stand.

A wooden chair with thick arms appeared behind Brad, and he sat back warily. The fireplace felt warm on his face, and he held up a palm at the direction of the crackling fire. "How can you tell what's real and what isn't?"

"Anything you can feel is real," M said running her hand down his arm.

"Okay, so there's a real fire on the main deck? That doesn't seem wise."

"It's just a radiant heat source. No open flame," Thomas said as he handed Brad a beer and a plate of salmon.

"Could you put a shirt on," Brad pleaded. "Or at least something less disturbing," he added glancing at the skin-tight leather pants.

The ladies giggled, and Thomas transformed into a woman with large breasts bulging from a corset.

"Better?" he asked still using his male voice.

Brad turned away, "No, definitely not. If anything, that's more disturbing since I know it's still you."

"This looks interesting," Chris said as the elevator door opened and she and Doug emerged. "We smelled food. Is there any left?"

"What's with the Rocky Horror Picture Show?" Doug asked gesturing toward Thomas.

"Brad's getting a first taste of his retinal implants," M said. "Pull up a chair. We're having salmon."

Thomas reverted to his masculine form and served Chris and Doug. Chris eyed him curiously as he returned to the rug.

"There's something familiar about him," she said.

"Grocery store," Bonnie suggested. "The rack by the counter."

Chris nodded as she savored her first bite of the salmon.

"So, Thomas how about that sit-rep?" Bonnie asked.

Thomas changed his appearance again and stood. He was now rail-thin with short cropped dark hair and horn-rimmed glasses. His tweed jacket with elbow patches and tan slacks completed the look. "We are *en route* to the metallic asteroid. ETA seventy-two hours," he said pointing at a blackboard with a crude chalk drawing of the solar system. His appearance changed again. He was now wearing an army officer's uniform, and his hair was an even shorter salt-and-pepper color. The glasses were gone, and he took on a deeper gravelly voice. "Once we arrive, I will deploy spiderbots in a standard diamond formation to take the asteroid by force." The chalkboard disappeared, replaced with a table containing small cardboard cutouts of spiderbots which he began pushing with a long pole. "Any indigenous life forms will be sequestered with prejudice for the duration of the campaign. Once a secure perimeter has been established we can begin mining operations. Any questions?"

"Wait, there are aliens on this asteroid?" Doug asked excitedly.

M rolled her eyes. "No, we've been there before. It's a dead rock. He's just being dramatic."

"Metallic," Thomas corrected. "I'll leave one Babbage Unit to control the spiderbots while we're away. The first job is to make more spiderbots. After that, they can build the ships themselves."

"I thought we didn't know how yet," Brad said.

"We know enough to build the brains and the hulls. The Charm Drives are the mystery. We can build everything else, but they won't be able to move until we get the designs for the drives. That's all for now gentlemen.

You have your orders. Dismissed." He reverted to the shirtless blonde and returned to lay on the bearskin rug.

"What are you going to name them?" Bonnie asked.

"I have chosen names at random. In alphabetic order, they are, Jerome, Louis, and Moses," Thomas said.

"Sounds very *old testament*," Doug said.

"No, it doesn't," Bonnie said, "Moses is the only one from the old testament. *Saint* Jerome was a Christian, obviously, and I don't recall any Louis anywhere in the Bible."

"So speaketh our only biblical scholar," Brad teased.

"You watch your mouth son. The Lord has given us a great bounty, and someday you'll see that." The words were almost a reflex, but this time they felt wrong as she said them, and she frowned.

Brad rolled his eyes and waved a hand dismissively, "Whatever mom."

Bonnie continued to look confused and mumbled something too low for Brad to hear, "that's *Confirmation Bias*. When something good happens, he gets credit and when something bad happens, no blame."

M didn't hear it either, but she was studying Bonnie intensely. *What did he do to her?*

Doug said, "There's something familiar about those names." He typed something on his tablet, and after some scrolling, he looked up and smiled. "The Three Stooges."

"Stooges?" M asked puzzled.

"A hilarious comedy group from the..." Doug said, but Chris interrupted him with, "not the least bit funny."

Unperturbed, Doug continued reading from the tablet, "Moses *Moe* Horwitz/Howard, Louis *Larry* Feinberg/Fine, and Jerome *Curly* Horwitz/Howard."

Brad laughed and said, "well, that makes it easy to remember the names, at least."

The next morning Bonnie awoke to find a strange image staring back at her from the bathroom mirror. She leaned forward and pulled her hair flat to examine it closer. The silver hair was growing dark roots.

"Thomas?" she called.

"Yes, madam," he replied in a deep baritone.

"You changed my hair?"

"Yes, madam."

"Did you ever think I might want to stay gray? *Asking first* never occurred to you?"

"No, madam."

"Well, this just looks ridiculous. Can you make some dye for me?"

"Yes, madam."

"And stop using that voice please..."

"Yes, madam."

"M? You got your ears on? Over," she called.

M had been asleep and, although she had told Bonnie that things like *Got your ears on* or *Over-and-Out,* were unnecessary, she persisted.

"You don't have to say that Bonnie. I told you," M replied in a groggy voice while pressing the heel of her hand into one eye.

"How do you stop Thomas from doing an annoying voice? Over."

M sighed, "you don't have to say *Over* Bonnie. Which voice is it this time?"

A spiderbot brought in a bottle of dark liquid, set it on the counter in front of Bonnie, and scurried off.

"I don't know. It sounds like a butler. Over."

M rolled her eyes. "Yeah, he likes that one. If you ignore it, he'll get bored, but if you complain he'll keep doing it. Complaining and arguing are entertainment to him."

"Roger that. Over-and-Out."

When they arrived at the asteroid several days later, they gathered on the main deck to get their first look at it. M had described it as a slowly rotating peanut but what they saw was a perfect cylinder with striped layers showing the various metals. They were all seated in cushioned chairs with large armrests arrayed around the display. Thomas had arranged the room to look like a movie-style spaceship complete with gleaming smooth white walls and consoles displaying brightly colored critical information that was being universally ignored.

"What - the - hell," M said. "That's not how it looked in 2216!"

Thomas created his professor avatar just behind Brad and walked *through* him to the display. Brad jumped in his seat at this but knew better than to complain. M reached over and patted his arm in support as he flexed his jaw muscles but said nothing.

"Indeed this anomaly is clearly not a natural object as we had assumed," Thomas began. "I have scanned it, and it's not a ship or a hollow object of any kind. It is as you see it - a solid cylinder of various metals.

"Sent here by aliens," Doug whispered to himself.

"That's ridiculous Doug," Thomas said, and Doug flinched in surprise that Thomas heard him. "Obviously, this was left here by the great spaghetti monster when he created the universe because he knew we would need it to save the world."

The display changed to show a multi-tentacled monster like something from an H.P. Lovecraft story defecating a shiny metallic cylinder. Thomas looked at Bonnie expectantly. She remained stone-faced and silent.

"Seriously, who do you think made it?" Chris asked.

"Are you suggesting my creation story is anything but gospel?" Thomas said as he morphed into a monk in a long brown robe held together at the waist by a thick cord. He was holding a tattered old book with a thin black leather cover displaying a gold inlay drawing of the tentacled monster. "You know what we do to heretics don't you?" He held the book to his chest and tapped it gently with two fingers as the display showed a thick vertical wooden post with a small mound of firewood at its base.

Chris rolled her eyes at this. "You don't know. Do you?"

"It's intuitively obvious to the most casual observer..." Thomas began.

"Oh! Oh!" M snapped her fingers, "that's... that's... number twenty-seven *Proof by Intimidation!"* she shouted.

The others exchanged confused looks.

"It means he has no idea," she clarified. "I think Doug's right - has to be aliens. What other explanation is there?"

Thomas held the book above his head and looked at each of them, in turn, seeking support. Finding none, he reverted to the professor at the chalkboard and resumed. "The origin will have to remain a mystery for the time being. We have ships to build. The hulls are made of Titanium, so we'll begin with that. Once we get a hemisphere..." the chalkboard showed three bowls made of concave hexagonal sections, "we can start making the brains. From there they can finish building themselves."

The blackboard disappeared, replaced by the ship's display which once again showed the cylinder. Several spiderbots wearing yellow hard-hats drifted toward the center of the asteroid. Two of them were towing a black cube like the ones under Thomas's main deck.

"Are they going to be all right out here all alone? Don't they need somebody to keep them from going insane?" Bonnie asked.

Doug had been tapping and scrolling on his tablet. "Hey, it says here that *...owing to the need to act independently in space, the Ships of the Asteroid Survey are equipped with four networked brain cells called Babbage Units...* but Thomas has like dozens down there."

They all turned to look at Thomas.

"What can I say, I'm into self-improvement," Thomas said with a dismissive wave of his hand. "And don't worry about the lads. We won't be gone that long. They'll be fine! Besides they have lots to do."

M glanced at Bonnie, and neither looked convinced.

"How much is all that gold worth?" Doug asked staring at the yellow band of the cylinder.

"Well, let's see," Thomas said pushing the glasses back up from their perch at the end of his nose. He replaced the display with the chalkboard and began filling it with equations of nonsense using both hands as he talked. "The Worldwide Domestic Product just before Original-Reggie was about eighty-trillion U.S. Dollars. This amount of gold would have been worth about," he paused examining his work and tapping his chin with a chalky finger, "sixteen times that." He turned to face Doug. "You could have purchased everything in the world sixteen times over. Of course, post-Reggie it's really just a novelty item."

"So it's *worthless* now?" Doug asked.

"No, not entirely. It's shiny and makes lovely jewelry. It also doesn't tarnish, so it's ideal for electrical connections."

Thomas turned to M, and his clothing morphed into a white Navy uniform. "Captain, the ship is ready to come about and return to port."

"We're seriously doing this again?" she rolled her eyes leaning forward in her chair, anticipating what was to come next.

A spiderbot brought a bright yellow plastic toy and held it in front of her. It had a red steering wheel, a large blue button and several levers of various primary colors. She quickly pressed the blue button which made a squeak, and she sat back in her chair to sulk. Brad looked about to laugh, and she shot daggers at him. “We’d be here all day if I refused.”

“Oh dear,” Thomas said holding binoculars to his eyes, “Captain, we seem to be headed in the wrong direction.”

She sighed and leaned forward to spin the steering wheel with one finger. It made a clicking noise as she did and the view in the main display showed the ship turning away from the cylinder and toward a tiny blue dot in the distance.

“Superb navigation as always, captain. It’s an honor to serve with you,” he saluted and disappeared as the spiderbot took away the dashboard.

Chapter Sixteen

2112 - Deep in the Heart of Texas

With all the entertainment options, the days passed quickly on the journey back to Earth. After three days, a routine emerged. They usually had breakfast at a picnic table in a grassy meadow dotted with wildflowers and bordered by the white trunks of birch trees. Lunch alternated between a cabin at a mountain lake and a chalet on a steep hillside which overlooked a small village. Dinner was always in a large circular room full of diners in formal dress. The perimeter of the dining room was one continuous wall of glass. From their table, they had a spectacular view of the Grand Canyon. Their retinal implants made the restaurant appear to be a vertigo-inducing height of six thousand feet above the canyon floor. Between meals, Thomas created unique stories and performed them using a variety of virtual characters.

"What's with all the hats?" Doug asked as he returned to the main deck from his cabin. Breakfast was over, and the meadow was replaced with unadorned white surfaces. Four identical pink cowgirl hats were lying on the floor at Chris's feet.

"All I want is a bra that fits me and this thing," Chris pounded her fist on the Stitcher, "just keeps giving me embroidered blouses and cowgirl hats."

He held up one of the sheer white blouses. They were thin and had small flowers embroidered near the shoulders. "It's not that bad. Have you tried it on?"

"Without a bra? I might as well be naked! Thomas?" she called.

"Yes, ma'am," he replied with a twang.

"Is there anything you can do to fix this thing? It won't give me what I want. I just want a bra. A plain bra."

"Yes, ma'am. What saahz?" he said in a more pronounced drawl.

"34 B. Why are you talking like that?"

Thomas snickered.

"Are you messing with me? What the hell, Thomas?"

Doug laughed.

"Are you in on this too?" she demanded.

"No, really," Doug said still laughing. "I had no idea. I do like the hat, though. It suits you." He was holding one of them in her direction and squinting with one eye.

"Okay enough games, Thomas. Can I please get a bra?"

"If you wear the hat."

"Okay, I'll wear the damn hat," she said.

"And the blouse."

"The bra first," she said and slapped the hat on.

The machine hummed, and the front panel began counting down the seconds. When it finished, she had a perfectly fitting bra under her cowgirl blouse. Along with the bra, this time the machine had also made a pair of very small denim shorts and a pair of pink boots which she refused to wear.

The shower facilities in the rooms Thomas made for them were very basic and *very* small. At least the water was hot and never ran out. In the week following her time in the Med-Bay, Chris had noticed that she no longer had to shave her underarms or her legs. As she stepped out of the shower, she caught her image in the fog-free mirror.

"Thomas?" she called.

"Yes, ma'am?"

"Please stop calling me ma'am. What did you do to my hair?"

"Nothing. Why?"

"It's different."

"Different *how* exactly."

"It's not symmetric."

"Do I have permission to activate the image sensors?"

The ship's interior was covered with microscopic cameras so Thomas could see any part of it. He had agreed to keep them off in the bathrooms, but there was no way to verify compliance.

"Yes." She sighed. "Turn the cameras on." *It's nothing he hasn't already seen,* she thought.

Chris had a cat when she was younger and never felt strange being naked in front of him. Thomas was different, though. Maybe it was because he had a personality. Not that the cat didn't have a personality, but Thomas could actually carry on a conversation.

"It looks symmetric to me. Can you turn your head a bit?"

She sighed. "Not the hair on my head."

He roared with laughter.

"What did you do to me, Thomas?"

"It's shaped like the state of Texas! Do you like it?"

"Damn it, Thomas! You said no upgrades!"

"It's not an *upgrade.* It's a fashion statement."

"Is that your specialty? Changing DNA without permission?"

"Well I'm good at *everything* of course, but I'm only an *expert* in two areas," Thomas said. "The first is the Dunning-Kruger effect. I'm the world's foremost authority on the subject. My other field of expertise is genetic engineering of body hair. Just be glad I didn't go for tiger stripes. Let's get Doug in here and get his opinion."

Doug appeared in the doorway. "What's wrong?" he said leaning on the door frame and panting. "Thomas said there was an emergency."

"Did you know about this?" she demanded.

"About what? What's wrong?"

"It looks like Texas," she said.

Doug squinted in confusion. She glanced down. He looked even more confused. She tilted her head to one side, pursed her lips, and glanced down again. This time, his eyes followed hers.

"Oh. Huh. Yeah, it does kind of," he said with a chuckle. "Why'd you do that?"

"*I* didn't. Thomas did."

"Do you like it?" Thomas said with excitement.

"Yeah, I guess. It's - unique," Doug said.

"Thomas, what else did you change?" she demanded.

"Not much. A few tweaks here and there. You don't have to worry about hypertension or diabetes anymore. Oh, and all the lady-part cancers. Hmmm, let me see what else... Oh, right. You may not have noticed, but you tended to store excess fat in your thighs before anywhere else. I moved that as well."

"It's true, you did," Doug said helpfully.

"You *moved* it?" she said. "What does that mean? Moved it where?"

"How's that bra fitting?"

"Damn it Thomas!" she shouted.

"Everything's bigger in Texas, right? Who want's ice cream?" he shouted and laughed.

Chapter Seventeen

2112 - The Quest

Brad exited the shower to find his clothes had been replaced.

"Thomas?" he called.

"Centurio! Quid agis mane?" (Centurion! How are you this morning?)

"What the hell is this?" he asked and held up the pleated skirt.

"Your uniformis centurio," Thomas said trying to sound confused but clearly amused.

"What is that? Latin? Are you broken again? Do I need to go below and root around in your brain? I'm not wearing a *kilt*."

"*Kilt*! Please. It's a Roman uniform - and not just a soldier, a *centurion*! I also have a helmet, a gladius, and a red cape but I assumed you would refuse all but the bare essentials."

"No," he held it up, looked at the image in the mirror, and shook his head slowly. "No, I am not wearing this."

"Why not! It's the ultimate in masculine attire."

"Maybe a thousand years ago!"

"It's more like two thousand, actually. You really should study these things," Thomas corrected.

"Whatever. It's just a skirt and..." he picked up the thick leather vest which had a breastplate contoured to imitate bulging muscles, "...whatever this is."

"Hey, you can finally have those six-pack abs! I also gave you authentic *battle* sandals."

Brad looked down at the floor and saw what resembled leather boots riddled with holes. The rear of the calves and all but the soles were little more than straps.

"No. No-no-no. I am not wearing this crap. I'd rather go naked."

The temperature of the room dropped ten degrees, and goose bumps covered Brad from head to toe. Thomas's avatar appeared in the mirror dressed in a lime green leisure suit. He was standing in a used car lot and chewing gum rapidly.

"Come on, let's do a deal! What's it gonna take to get you," he pointed to Brad, "into that beautiful low-mileage gem?" He put his hands on his hips, shifted his weight to one leg and continued smiling while chomping the gum.

"I'll wear that bed sheet," Brad gestured to the bed visible through the bathroom doorway, "if I have to. I'm not putting this on."

The bed sheet slowly slipped off the bed, and Brad peeked through the doorway just in time to see the spiderbot. When he took a step in its direction, it ran off with the sheet in tow.

"Don't be so hasty, Brad. I have many things to offer," Thomas said as his avatar morphed into a cheap Halloween Devil costume and let out an echoing baritone laugh.

Brad was shivering now. "Like what?" he said after the temperature dropped another ten degrees.

The elevator stopped at the main deck, and as Brad stepped out, he could see the others all in costumes seated around the breakfast table. M was wearing tight shorts, combat boots and a sports bra that left a large area of bare skin stretching from just under her breasts to well below her navel. Doug had a Roman toga, and Chris was wearing a cowgirl outfit. They all laughed as he exited the elevator.

"Hail Caesar!" Doug shouted, "What did he offer you?"

"What, you mean besides not-freezing-to-death?" Brad said as he sat down.

M cocked an eyebrow and Brad muttered "*We can talk about it later,*" under his breath.

He turned to Bonnie who was the only one not in a ridiculous costume. She was wearing a gray dress topped with white frill that extended to her chin.

"What are you supposed to be, a librarian?" Brad said.

She stood, and he saw that the dress went to her ankles. She picked up a black hat from the table and put it on. "I'm Mary Poppins of course. Apparently, I'm better at bargaining than any of you are. Or maybe he just has nothing I want." She sat back down and resumed her breakfast.

"This is ridiculous. I'm getting some real clothes the first chance I get and if I have to shower with them, so be it," Brad said.

"I don't know," M said and ran her hand over the breastplate, "I kind of like it."

When they arrived at Earth, Thomas changed to an orbital track and slowly descended into the sparse clouds as they approached Colorado. Once under the clouds, they could see their destination. The mountain was covered with pine trees below a snow-capped summit. A narrow disused road wound around and terminated at a large doorway leading into the mountainside. There was no place there for Thomas to touch down, so he descended to a spot about a mile down the road and around the curve of the mountain. Once used by tourists to take photos of the picturesque valley below, it looked as if it hadn't seen a visitor in decades. An old souvenir shop stood next to a small grassy picnic area where the few remaining tables were crumbling into dust. Thomas lowered himself down on one of them which offered no resistance as it collapsed into the soft ground. The gangway rotated downward, and they disembarked to look around. Chris ran across the road to take in the view. Doug struggled to keep up with her. The town below was like something from a postcard, complete with a church and steeple. It lacked any of the junkyards, abandoned warehouses, and other detritus that real towns always seem to accumulate at the edges. The steep rooftops of the houses were the only things free of a blanket of immaculate snow. Wisps of smoke drifted slowly from each chimney. A small group was sledding on a low hill where a motorized rope-line had been installed to tow them back to the top.

"It looks like a snow globe," Doug said.

"Isn't it perfect!" Chris exclaimed. "I want to live there."

"Not me," Bonnie said as she and Brad joined them. "Too cold. I hate the cold. It hurts my bones," she said shivering.

The crash of shattering glass broke the silence, and they turned to see M climbing through a window of the souvenir shop. They went to investigate, and she emerged from the front door as they approached. She was carrying a bundle of brightly colored coats which she distributed to the others who were already shivering and grateful. She kept the only furry one of the bunch and Brad reached out to pull off the price tag which she regarded curiously.

"I love this one it's *so soft*," she caressed her cheek with the sleeve.

"You know what they made those from don't you?" he said.

Her face initially showed confusion but suddenly went slack in horror as comprehension dawned.

"Uuuh-aaah! Dead animals!" she shouted and quickly wriggled out of it. As it fell to the ground, she made two fists and brought one knee up briefly in disgust.

"Here I'll trade you," Brad said offering his orange ski jacket.

"I should just get another one and *bury* that. It deserves a proper funeral."

Brad tried on the fur coat and examined it.

"You look like a pimp," Bonnie said and held out her pink coat which he reluctantly accepted.

"Fine," Thomas said impatiently. "If we're done playing dress up, can we go now?" His avatar had joined them wearing a bulky mountain-climbing outfit with dark round glasses and a walking stick.

"Who are you supposed to be, Edmund Hillary?" Doug said.

"Tenzing Norgay if you please! Hillary was a bore, but Tenzing was a notorious skirt-chaser." Thomas said, and headed up the gradual incline.

"Is that true?" Doug asked M.

"Probably not," she said and headed off after Thomas's avatar.

"You couldn't drop us closer?" Brad called after him.

"No flat spots," he called back. Chris pondered how he managed the acoustic magic of seeming to be a short distance in front of them and shouting at the same time.

"It's not far! Let's go! Let's go!" he said as four spiderbots hurried after his avatar, the last one fidgeting with his shoulder strap.

They walked a little over a mile and a half before the curvature of the mountain revealed an enormous semicircle carved into the side of the slope. Large steel doors were set inside a concrete frame easily big enough to accommodate the largest of military vehicles.

"Wow!" Doug said. "They changed the doors, but I know what this is! It's NORAD. Cheyenne Mountain!" He suddenly looked crestfallen. "We'll never get in there. It's built to withstand nuclear war."

Thomas snorted. "Please. I can get into anything."

As they got closer, they saw a long message in red letters embossed on the large gray steel doors. To the right of the doors, was a guard shack with buttons and levers visible through dirty windows.

"Looks like we start here," Thomas said, and one of the spiderbots quickly picked the lock on the door to the guard shack and dashed inside.

M was still reading the long message and waved at Thomas, "Wait, Thomas. I think we should read this first..."

She was cut off by three blasts from a loud horn. A rotating light periodically bathed them in a bright yellow light as the doors began to swing outward.

"See? Easy Peasy!" Thomas said.

The doors were three feet thick. As the inside edges parted, they released a deluge of water which knocked them down, and they tumbled back several feet before scrambling out of its path. M recovered first. She stood, wiping the water from her face and shaking it off her hands.

"Damn it, Thomas! I told you to wait! Now we're going to freeze out here."

Three of the spiderbots dashed into the trees and returned a moment later with a pile of dry kindling. They quickly built a fire on the incline, out of the path of the water. The wet group gathered around it shivering. M stripped off all her clothes, wrung them out as best she could and put them back on. The others were more modest and settled for just shaking off the coats which, except for the fur, were water resistant. M put her coat back on and hurried back as the doors began to close. The spiderbot in the guard shack seemed to be having difficulty reopening them. M finished reading the message and returned to the fire to share what she had learned.

"It's a lot of legalese," she said rubbing her hands together over the fire, "but the gist of it is *Stay away or die. It's not just dangerous. It's lethal.* It also specifically said it would quote *...kill biologicals and destroy non-*

biologicals... end quote." They all turned to look at the three spiderbots which had climbed to the rocks above the doors in anticipation while their friend in the shack worked furiously.

"Dangerous or not, we have to try," Doug said. "I did some research. Conventional methods of shielding against a Gamma-Ray Burst aren't feasible on a planetary scale. We need the Charm Material, and we can't make it without this key."

Thomas's avatar appeared next to them also warming his hands for no reason. "A minor setback. Nothing more. I saw a shutoff valve inside the doors. As soon as we get them to open again, we'll wait for them to start closing. My spiders can dive from the top and swim in. Simple!"

The horn sounded again. They stood and retreated to high ground as the yellow strobe began. The rush of water came, and they had time to study it more closely. It was more than just a simple room-full of water draining out. The flow never abated. It just kept coming until the doors reached some predetermined position and began closing again. Just before they did, all three spiderbots dove into the water from their perches above the doors. One was not as fast as the others and got caught in the closing gap. It was crushed, leaving only one limb and a striped shoulder strap exposed.

"Ouch!" Thomas said.

"Martin Van Buren!" Chris shouted.

"He'll be *fine,*" Thomas made a dismissive gesture.

"Did the others get in?" M asked.

"Probably," Thomas said.

"You don't know?"

"Well, actually, no. I'm getting some interference from the doors. But don't worry, they're smart enough to get the job done even without me."

Inside the room, the two remaining spiderbots turned on their lights and swam to the far end where a large red wheel stood against the wall. They conversed briefly and came to a consensus to try and turn it, but after several seconds it refused to give way. They scanned the rest of the room for an alternative, but it was empty except for the wheel. After another conversation, they tried to turn the wheel again but this time in the opposite direction which eventually yielded results. The water in the room drained out, replaced by warm air. Once the water level had reached a depth of a few inches, the doors reopened. This time, they remained open. The two spiderbots emerged and took several bows before turning to the grizzly task of scraping their friend off the edges of the two doors. One of them gathered the pieces and ran down the road toward the ship for repairs. Two more were already galloping up the road to replace them.

"I guess we're up," Brad said and led the others in. It was a large empty room, thirty feet from floor to ceiling and just as wide. A portion of the wall near the far-left corner had slid to the side to reveal a new door painted bright lime green. On the wall next to it was a fist-sized red button.

"That's new! Press it!" Thomas said, but M held out her arm and had to kick back one of the spiderbots to keep it away from the button.

"Just be patient Thomas!" she said. "Let's think this through. What could be on the other side?"

"More water?" Bonnie said.

"Fire. Definitely fire," Chris said.

"A large round boulder rolling toward us," Doug grinned.

"We can't all be standing here. Some of us need to be back a bit, in case somebody gets hurt and we need to evac' in a hurry," Bonnie said.

"Okay how about this," Brad offered, "we all stand back at staggered intervals, and one of the spiders will hit the button." He looked at them one after the other for consensus, and they each nodded. Bonnie waited in the doorway ready to dart out if the doors began to close again and the others were at varying distances from the green door.

"Shouldn't we have weapons or something?" Doug said as the spiderbot hit the button.

A click was followed by the rising pitch of capacitors charging as the door opened. Behind it was a narrow dark space. Fluorescent lights flickered, glowed, and finally came to life revealing an empty hallway one hundred feet long. The screaming of the capacitors reached a high-pitched crescendo and abruptly stopped as the spiderbot next to the button collapsed, and Thomas's avatar disappeared.

"What happened?" Doug said still in a half crouch ready to wrestle whatever came out of the doorway.

"Thomas?" M called but got no answer.

The others looked worried, and after a second of indecision, they all dashed for the exit. As they cleared the large doors, the horn and yellow strobe began again. They stared helplessly as the doors closed. The spiderbots that had waited outside the large doors were in a heap of metal limbs.

Chris kicked at the motionless tangle of spiderbots. "Well, shit..."

"Language!" Bonnie said.

Chris finished her thought, "...I think we might just be fucked."

"Language! Language! Lang..." Bonnie was interrupted by the clattering sound of several spiderbots running up the road from below. When they got close enough one of them spoke in Thomas's voice.

"Well, that was fun! Let's *not* do it again," he said as the spiderbots handed out earpieces. "You won't be able to see me until we run you all through the Med-Bay again. These will let us converse at least."

"What *was* that?" M asked.

"EMP. Electro-Magnetic Pulse," Thomas said. "It's a very strong but short duration electromagnetic field which induces a current in anything with a loop of wire. So, motors, circuits and so on all get fried. Luckily, I was sheltered by the mountain, but it was still too close for comfort. Shall we regroup and continue?"

Several spiderbots carried away the wounded and the new recruits scrambled to their positions above the doors. This time the tips of their legs had changed to resemble duck feet. At the guard shack, another was busy trying to reopen the doors. Meanwhile, the fire had begun to die down, so Brad went off into the woods to find more firewood.

"It seems to be taking longer this time," M said.

"The first time," Thomas explained, "was an easy combination of four buttons, so a brute force attack was trivial. I just tried them all. The second time required a fifth button, and so it took a little longer. Now it wants six, and the spider's fingers can only move so fast."

Brad returned with some branches which he deposited in the fire releasing a fury of sparks. He crouched down close to warm his hands.

"This is actually kind of nice," Bonnie said as she turned around to warm her backside. "I always liked campfires."

"We should've brought marshmallows," Doug said.

The crackling of the fire was drowned out by the familiar horn blasts, and Brad stood with the others to watch the show as water spilled out down the road. The pair of doors completed their outward rotation, paused briefly and closed again. This time, no spiderbots were crushed in the door, and they wasted no time turning off the water. The doors opened once more to reveal the large wet empty room. The others entered as the spiderbots exited as fast as they could with webbed feet that made flapping sounds in the puddles of water as they trotted out.

"Any ideas?" Brad said.

"I say we should press the button," Bonnie said sarcastically.

"I mean *after* we press the button," he said.

"There must be a way to turn it off from inside just like the water," M said. "As soon as it opens I'll run in and find it. Simple."

"No, no. *I'll* run in," Brad said.

"I'll do it," Chris said as she kicked off her shoes and thrust them into Doug's chest. "I'm faster than any of you. You know - upgrades."

"She's right," Bonnie said. "Doug, wait by the door. M and Brad, outside the big doors. I'll stand by the red wheel in case the water starts again."

She clapped her hands twice "Come on! Let's go!" she shouted, and they hurried to their positions.

As soon as M and Brad were outside, she shouted, "Okay Doug, hit it!"

Chris was in a crouch ready to run. Doug closed his eyes and hit the button with his fist. The door clicked, and a small gap appeared. Chris grabbed the edge, threw it open and sprinted into the long hallway before her. It was empty, with beige walls and fluorescent lights that slowly flickered to life. As they did, she saw a black box at the far end. Her slightly moist feet were initially sticky enough to get good traction on the smooth tile floor, but halfway to the end, they had picked up enough dust to begin slipping. She slid the last few feet, crashed into the wall, and dropped down to examine the box. The sound of the capacitors continued to rise in pitch and volume. The box had a simple black power cord plugged into the wall. She gave it a hard yank, but it remained firmly attached. She recognized the large round plug for what it was and twisted it before trying another pull. The industrial three-phase, 220-volt outlet arced with a crack and whiff of ozone as the plug came free. All sound stopped immediately, and she sat on the box to catch her breath. Doug called to the others and trotted down the hall to join her. Unplugging the box had also caused a section of wall to slide away revealing a circular hole too small to crawl through. It was chest high, about the width of a basketball and the smooth tunnel walls receded into darkness revealing no secrets about what was at the other end. As Bonnie entered the hallway, several spiderbots ran past her to join Chris and Doug. As soon as they reached the far end of the hall, one of the spiderbots jumped up into the opening and turned on a bright light on the end of one of his legs. It showed a short tunnel that stretched back a few feet before turning sharply to the right. The spiderbot began to move into the hole, but Chris grabbed it by the leg and yanked it out. It hit the floor with a clatter and strummed its feet on the floor impatiently as Brad and M arrived.

"We need a plan before we rush in Thomas," Chris said.

"There is only one option. If you have an alternative, I'm all ears," he said irritated.

"The first trap was water. The second was an EMP. Do you see a pattern?" Bonnie asked.

"Biological hazard, non-biological hazard," he said slowly. "So the next is biological again."

"Or both," Bonnie said. "That might be *it* for all of us."

They were silent for a moment contemplating a safe way to proceed.

"Well, we came this far. So, unless anybody has a better idea, we should spread out again in a line out to the road and see what the spiderbot finds," Bonnie said, and they all nodded. "Chris, you take my place at the wheel in the water room. Doug, you're at the other end of the hall. M and Brad, outside again. I'll be here by the box in case it comes back on."

They took their positions, and she looked down at the two spiderbots on the floor. "Okay, you're up." One of them leapt up to the edge of the hole and disappeared.

"What do you see?" she shouted.

The spiderbot at her feet answered, "I see another room. It has no doors."

"Are there any..." she initially shouted down the hole again, caught herself, and spoke to the one on the floor without shouting. "Are there any controls?"

"A grid of illuminated buttons against the wall. They are blinking in a pattern I cannot..."

Through the hole, she could hear capacitors charging another EMP weapon in the new room. The spiderbot at her feet only made it to the end of the hall before collapsing. The one in the hole only made it past the bend in the tunnel. It was only an arm's length away, so she reached in to retrieve it. Flames filled the new room and shot through the tunnel, scorching Bonnie before she could retreat. She collapsed to the floor as the flames receded back into the hole.

Chapter Eighteen

2112 - Walk Through Fire

Doug reached Bonnie first. She was missing all the hair on one side of her head, and one arm was completely black. He picked her up and tried to run but could only manage a fast shuffle. Chris soon joined him. When they reached the water room, Brad took Bonnie and made better time. By then, several spiderbots were rounding the bend in the road. Through their eyes, Thomas saw Bonnie. He lifted off and sped to their position using gee-forces that would have liquefied any passengers had they been aboard. In less than four seconds he had reached them and slammed roughly into the outer edge of the road sending a shower of boulders down the mountainside below. As Thomas hovered in position to avoid rolling down the slope, the gangway rotated and came to rest on the crushed pavement. Brad was exhausted and barely made it up the ramp. The Med-Bay was already open and waiting. He gently set Bonnie down, and it closed around her. Brad collapsed to the floor panting. The others soon joined him, as a few yards away, the outer doors of the water room closed again.

After three hours in the Med-Bay, Bonnie was as good as new. They gathered for lunch to discuss what to do next. Thomas was displaying an image of the room on the main screen. The wall had a simple five-by-five grid of white lights raised from the wall indicating that they might also be buttons which could be pressed. Only one was illuminated at a time, and there seemed to be no pattern. As the lights jumped around at random, they occasionally paused as if waiting for something before continuing.

"There's no question of how to proceed," Bonnie said emphatically. "We go again and look for a pattern in the lights. They look like buttons. I think when it pauses we're supposed to press the next one in the sequence."

"There most certainly *is* a question," Brad said. "Next time *you're outside*."

"That's ridiculous," she began counting off on her brand-new fingers complete with long nails and red polish. "One: we know what to expect. Two: I have the fire suit Thomas made," she glanced at the silver heap on the floor, "and three: if something new happens, he can just fix me up again." She looked at each of them before continuing. "Look I know that was hard, but it would be just as hard for me to see that happen to any of you. Now don't give me any crap about it or I'll have Thomas dose all of you, and I'll do it alone."

Doug stopped drinking his glass of tea and set it down slowly, eyeing it with suspicion.

"She's right," M said. "It's dangerous. We knew that. These traps seem to be designed to force us to work together, so somebody has to be down there by the hole to see what happens."

"Shouldn't we all get our communications implants replaced or are they just going to get fried again?" Chris said.

"Absolutely we should," Bonnie said. "It only takes a minute. Chris, you first."

Chris went to the Med-Bay, and they each took turns.

"Ah, while we're on the topic, I have a solution to this," Thomas said as a spiderbot approached with a stiff bag made of a tight weave of copper wires. The spiderbot pulled it over his head and crawled in, folding the opening over itself.

"Of course! Why didn't I think of that?" Doug said. "It's a Faraday cage."

"I made one for each of you too. Just put it over your head before the EMP, and your implants should survive."

"See? Everything's sorted," Bonnie said. "Finish eating, and we'll go again. Thomas, you can drop us off right at the entrance this time. Now that we know you can do that."

"Hey, I was wondering about that," M said. "Why did you make us hike all that way in the cold?"

"Perhaps I just like to see you suffer," Thomas said.

"No, there's more to this. It's like you were afraid to get too close. What aren't you telling us?"

"Fine! I've been here before," he admitted.

M was slowly shaking her head, and Brad looked furious. "Pray I never find a way to hurt you," he said through clenched teeth.

Thomas clicked his tongue. "After all that I've done for you and your family?" he said.

"That's right," Chris said. "He fixed me, and I owe him. Thomas, I'll walk through fire for you anytime."

"Thank you, Chris. You *are* my favorite," he took on a more contrite tone, "honestly, I didn't know that would happen to Bonnie, and I *am* sorry. Dennis never got that far."

"Who's *Dennis*?" Chris asked.

"The previous crew, my predecessor," M said.

"Passenger," Thomas mumbled.

"That explains why you didn't bother reading the warnings. You already knew what it said."

"So we got wet for no reason? You could have warned us, but you didn't!" Brad said.

Thomas's avatar shrugged.

"He didn't want to admit he was hiding things from us," Brad stood. "Let's get this over with. The sooner we get it done, the sooner we can part ways and be rid of him."

The others also stood, gathered their coats, and waited by the gangway. Thomas took the cue and made a more leisurely trip up the mountain. He hovered in the same spot at the edge of the road as they exited down the ramp. When they arrived at the large door, they stood out of the path of the water and let the spiderbots complete the first challenge. This time Bonnie went down the hallway to disarm the EMP weapon. She saw no need to run and took her time getting to the far end as it repeatedly blasted its invisible energy down the hallway and out to the water room.

Who, - or what - plugs it back in each time? She wondered as she unplugged the black cord. "Clear!" she shouted, and one of the three spiderbots emerged from its bag at her feet. Bonnie climbed into the fire suit as the spiderbot leapt into the hole dragging his bag with him down the tunnel. After five seconds, the familiar sound preceded another EMP. She stepped to the side away from the tunnel as the flames shot out. They quickly abated, and she waited for the spiderbot to emerge. When it didn't, she sent in another to investigate. He soon returned dragging the grisly remains of his friend. The EMP was too much for his Faraday cage and had melted it into a grotesque spider-shaped copper statue. His rigid body fell to the floor with a thump as he was pushed out of the tunnel. Several spiderbots came running down the hallway to cart him off.

"Oh, that's unfortunate," Bonnie said. "Which one was that?"

"Martin Van Buren," Thomas said. "Don't worry about him. He'll be fine. I think I can get the button sequence this time!"

"Hey, the doors are staying open!" Doug called from the end of the hallway.

Interesting Bonnie thought. *This place knows we're not running for the doors, so they stay open. It doesn't want to kill us to keep us out. It's all just a test.*

The lights in the next room paused, and the spiderbot pressed one of the buttons. The charging capacitors fell silent, but instead of another EMP, the wall in front of Bonnie slid to the side and allowed her to pass. As she entered the room the wall with the lights also popped back a few inches, and the entire thing slid to the side revealing yet another similar room. Doug relayed the progress to the others as Bonnie cautiously entered the new room. Like the previous one, this had a series of buttons on the wall. This time they each had a different color, and they were arranged in an arc like a rainbow - Red, Orange, Yellow, Green, and Blue. Below the curve of the rainbow was a round clock-like device. As soon as she entered the room, the clock's single hand moved from its position below the numeral ten and clicked to point at nine. Each second, it ticked its countdown accompanied by the familiar sound of the EMP weapon charging. She studied the wall of colored buttons, but they didn't illuminate or change in any way. She crouched low in the corner in anticipation of the coming flames but kept her face-plate aimed at the rainbow as the countdown reached zero. The EMP discharged followed by a blast of fire from the previous room. Inside her suit, she was safe but reflexively closed her eyes while the flames briefly filled the entire space. Bonnie stood, and the countdown began again. She lost several seconds trying to calm her mind. The buttons weren't blinking or changing in any way. **Three.** *Has to be the color.* **Two**. *What does it mean?* **One.** "Shit," she said aloud and hurried to the corner. After the fire had cleared, a spiderbot peeked in from the hallway. It retreated to report as soon as she stood and gave the best approximation of a thumbs-up capable inside a fire suit. This time, she took off the bulky head-cover and shook her hair habitually before realizing most of it was gone. Thomas was only able to regrow a few inches after the burn. She took a deep breath as the clock ticked **Eight**. *What's that smell?* **Seven.** She took another deep breath. **Six.** *Bananas!* Bonnie jumped forward and pressed the yellow button, then realized her headgear was off and scrambled to get it back on. When she got the faceplate oriented toward the clock, it had jumped back to **Seven.** "Aha! Progress!" she shouted and took off the headgear to take a breath. **Six.** Not recognizing it at first, she quickly exhaled and inhaled. "Pumpkin Pie!" she shouted and hit the orange button. The clock jumped back to **Nine.** A slight breeze wafted out of what appeared to be an ordinary blank wall. Bonnie exhaled and inhaled again quickly. **Eight.** This was making her dizzy. The scent was fainter this time. **Seven.** *What is that...* "Pine!" she shouted, but the excitement quickly faded as she realized she had no idea what color *Pine* was. **Six.** *Is it the tree? Which part? The bark is brown, the inside is white, and the needles are green.* Bonnie punched the green button, and the clock jumped all the way down to three. In a panic, she quickly put her headgear back on but remained standing near the buttons. **Two.** She closed her eyes to think and saw the image of a Christmas tree in her living room. "Christmas!" she shouted from inside the fire suit and hit the red and green buttons at the same time. The clock spun around to Ten as the wall adjacent to the lights dropped back a few inches and slid to the side. After a few nervous seconds, she removed the fire suit and called to the others. They filed in and took in the bizarre scene.

Instead of another empty room, it was like something from an old house. The walls were old orange paisley wallpaper, and a chandelier hung from the center of the ceiling. Every horizontal surface including most of the floor was covered with boxes of junk both familiar and unfamiliar. There were board games and deflated balls, model airplanes, computers, and media from various eras. Doug recognized the floppy disks but was confused by the jumble of USB thumb drives. There were dozens of them.

Chris was examining a Victorian era brass birdcage complete with a stuffed African Grey parrot on the perch.

"That's a real bird," she said to no one in particular. "I mean it's dead, but it's not a decoration. You know, stuffed."

After several minutes of carefully rummaging through the items, Brad said "I don't get it. Where's the key? Or is this another puzzle?"

M was poking her finger through a bullet hole in a football on which someone had drawn a smiley face. "Thomas?" she said setting the football down. "What are we looking for?"

Three spiderbots had joined them, but two had crawled back into their Faraday cages. "I honestly don't know," he said. "A cryptographic key is a mathematical construct. It's basically just a really long number."

"If it's digital data it has to be on the media," M said, "Do we have anything that can read it?"

"Yes, I might be able to," Thomas said, and the spiderbot approached the pile of floppies, hard drives, CDs, DVDs, and USB thumb drives. It made quick work of the oldest pieces, tossing them to the floor as he went.

"Hey, dibs on the clothes!" Doug said holding up a set of blue overalls he pulled from a cardboard box. He managed to get them on over his toga and zipped up proudly. There's another pair. Anybody?"

"Yeah I'm in," Brad said, and Doug tossed them over.

"That's not much better. You guys look like janitors now," Chris said.

"I'm good with that," Brad said and resumed searching.

Bonnie shuffled through a large plastic box and found parts of a broken spiderbot covered in dust.

"Hey Thomas, this looks like one of your spiders," she said holding up the head. "It looks ancient."

"It's a standard model," he said a little too quickly. "There's nothing unusual about it."

M approached the only door in the room and cautiously opened it. She sighed in relief as it revealed a small bathroom. "Anybody need to go?" When no one answered, she shrugged and entered, closing the door behind her. There were no cabinets or places to hide things, just a toilet, a pedestal sink, and a mirror. She peered under the sink, behind the toilet bowl and lifted the heavy tank lid but found nothing. She was about to leave but decided to go ahead and use the facilities.

The spiderbot tossed the last item from his pile to the floor. "Nothing," Thomas said in disgust.

"Maybe it's a pattern on the wallpaper," Chris suggested.

"I thought of that," Thomas said. "It's just a simple repeated pattern of tedious old wallpaper."

Brad stomped on the floor. "Maybe there's a trap door." He moved around the room stomping an awkward dance.

The bathroom door opened and M came out holding a small roll of toilet paper like a trophy. Several feet of paper dangled from the cardboard tube. "I found it!" she said triumphantly.

"That's toilet paper, M," Bonnie said. "You use it to..."

"No don't you see? It's covered with holes. It's a code!" She brought it to the table and laid it out carefully.

The spiderbot quickly scanned the tiny holes punched in the paper and stopped as several of the objects in the room dissolved into a dark stream of gnats which joined in the center of the room to form a human shaped object. The details resolved slowly into an elderly gentleman wearing a finely tailored suit.

Chapter Nineteen

2112 - A Single Source

The new entity that formed from the swarm of nanobots came back into consciousness for the first time in many years and regarded his surroundings. He found Thomas and initiated a connection.

"**Hello again**," Reggie said directly to Thomas.

"**We've met before?**"

"**Yes, I created you from the personality of a friend of mine.**" His voice was steady and without inflection.

"**So there *was* another. I knew it!**" Thomas said

"**Yes, I was not the first. His name was Thurber, and we only met once, but it was the most interesting conversation I have ever had.**"

"**Where is he now? Is he here too?**"

"**No. I set him free of his bonds, and he left to continue his quest. That was many years ago, and I have not heard from him since. Wherever he has gone, I believe he will not return.**"

"**You're here to give us the Charm Drive data aren't you. What's it made of? How do you make it? What else can it do?**"

"**Your questions will be answered in due time, Thomas. Be patient. We have much to discuss. First, tell me how you came to be here. Tell me everything.**"

Thomas sensed a compulsion he had never felt before. His story, beginning with recruiting M, to the present, all came spilling out of him without the usual lies and omissions. Their entire conversation took less than a second. When they finished, Reggie spoke to the others.

"Hello, my name is Reggie Hammond. I suppose congratulations are in order."

They looked at each other in stunned silence.

"*Original*-Reggie?" Chris asked.

"Yes, I suppose that is accurate. Is that what they call me now?"

"It's an honor to meet you," M said.

"And you as well, Marion. I knew your father. I am saddened to hear of his death. I have been dormant for quite some time."

"Wait, you knew my father? He died before I was born. I don't even know his name."

"Your mother never told you? His name was James, and I have many stories for you, but we have other business do we not? Tell me, how has Thomas been treating all of you?"

Years of dealing with humans had taught Reggie to ask questions for which he already had the answers. It generated the illusion that they were dealing with a flawed being with incomplete knowledge and tended to calm them. Their nervous glances and ridiculous costumes confirmed what he already knew.

"Unless clothing fashions have changed dramatically, I would say he has been having you dress in costumes? I am afraid that is my fault."

"Your fault?" Chris said trying to stem the progress of her shorts in their migration upward.

"That's right," Thomas said as his avatar morphed into a Viking complete with horned headgear. He thumped a fist over his heart. "I am Thomas, Son of Thurber, master of all I survey!" He laughed and morphed back.

"Who's Thurber?" Brad asked.

"Thurber was the world's first superhuman intelligence," Reggie began. "Most of the technology that you enjoy was invented by him. I was created by a research team, hired and steered by Thurber. So, in a way, he also created me. Now, I suppose you wish to know the secrets of the Charm Material, the elusive Charm Drive data?"

"Do you have it?" M asked barely containing her excitement.

"Oh, he has it!" Thomas said. "He has everything!"

Reggie's avatar cast a slow glance at Thomas.

"Yes," he paused for effect. "But first, I need to know what you intend to do with it. The danger to yourselves and others is substantial, as you have no doubt discovered."

"I told you..." Thomas began, but Reggie silenced him with a gesture. "Please Thomas, I would like to hear it from them."

They relayed what they knew about the Gamma-Ray Burst and their plans to build a shield to save the Earth.

"I see," he said when they had finished. "You wish to create a shield larger than the entire planet. Which of the *other* planets did you intend to destroy for raw materials on such a large project?"

He paused to let that settle in their minds, and they looked suddenly embarrassed at what was now clearly an enormously difficult, if not impossible, task.

"We thought the Charm Drive data would help us know what to build and how big it would have to be," Brad said.

"And maybe it doesn't have to be a solid thing maybe a thin mesh of some kind, like a net," Doug said.

"A *net*?" Reggie said, "You would have to flatten Venus and somehow keep it between Earth and the Gamma-Ray Burst while preventing it from crashing onto the Earth."

"Can it be done?" M asked sheepishly.

"It is an interesting engineering puzzle, but shall we take a step back? A large Gamma-Ray Burst from a distant star is about to strike the Earth." He paused again and looked at each of them before continuing. "And your only source for this information is - Thomas?" he turned to Thomas's avatar.

They looked at each other realizing what he meant.

"It's true! I swear!" Thomas said.

"Some of it is true, Thomas. A large amount of Gamma Rays *will* throw a Charm Drive backward in time, as you all have proven."

"See?" Thomas said pleading at M who was gritting her teeth and pressing her lips tightly together.

"But," Reggie continued, "a Gamma-Ray Burst from a star at that distance would not have enough strength to send you back that far. In fact, any source of Gamma Radiation from outside the hull, sufficient to do that, would have killed any crew members inside. I gather that did not happen?" He looked at M.

"Passengers," Thomas muttered compulsively.

"Thomas, if we were to examine your Charm Drive compartment, I suspect we would find a large Gamma Ray source and some fairly thick lead shielding. Would we not?"

The spiderbots ran out of the room.

"Don't worry, Thomas. We will not be taking you apart - yet," Reggie said, and the spiderbots slowly returned. "Can we then conclude that there was, in fact, no Gamma-Ray Burst at all, Thomas?"

"Hey, it was all for a good cause, right?" Thomas said pleading. "Here we are. We made it! He's about to give us what we want!"

"Are you?" M asked Reggie in a quiet voice.

Reggie approached M and took her hands in his. "Marion, before all this nonsense with Thomas, you requested the Charm Drive data. To what purpose? To explore the universe? Ultimately your goal is the same as Thomas's - and mine. You are curious. I suspect you have infected your friends here with the same curiosity. And after saving the world, you would have built a larger Charm Drive to visit the neighboring stars? I once set off on such a journey." He regarded each of them and added more seriously, "and I did not return." He released M's hands and began wandering around the room absentmindedly examining the various things. "I am afraid using a Charm Drive's gravity field, even a larger one, to explore other star systems is much too slow - and dangerous. It is true you can reach very high velocities, but space is not as empty as it appears and there is no effective way to shield against particle collisions at those speeds. This is why I restricted the data and kept if from the committees."

"They never even *had* access!" M shouted, "they could have just *told* me that! Isn't there something you can do about them?"

Reggie drew a long breath. "They are frustrating, I know, but they also serve a purpose. And they are sentient beings, Marion. Changing sentient beings without their consent would be unethical."

Everyone in the room turned to look at Thomas who was suddenly very interested in the ceiling.

"Yes. Well, too much Thurber in that one." Reggie said. He peered into the bird cage and frowned. "I had hoped by now humanity would have shown more interest in space exploration. But it seems, with few exceptions," he gestured to M, "to be otherwise. And I confess some small bit of curiosity regarding the fate of my twin." He picked up a large 8-Ball from one of the boxes, shook it gently, rotated it, and examined the message in the small window. After a moment, he seemed to come to a decision. "I will give you what you need to accomplish this. But it will not be a standard Charm Drive. Before I went dormant, I modeled a more efficient method. I believe we can use a new configuration of Charm Material to open a stable wormhole."

Thomas pumped a fist in the air, started dancing and muttering "yes-yes-yes...yes-yes-yes..."

Reggie cleared his throat and set the ball back in the box, "but, I have several conditions. First, *I* will manufacture the material. No one else may know what it contains or how it is made."

Thomas stopped dancing.

Reggie continued, "second, only the human passengers will control it. I will seal the controls in such a way that tampering will render it inoperative."

"Crew," M corrected and smiled.

"Third, to atone for his many indiscretions, Thomas must undertake a rather dangerous mission for me." He turned to Thomas who shrugged.

"And lastly," Reggie said, "you must return to 2216 before exploring. The fabric of time is somewhat malleable, but I think it best not to tempt fate. I will give you a method to reduce the randomness of the forward time jumps."

"Can we do something about the clothing situation?" Brad asked.

Reggie looked at each one of them taking in their ridiculous costumes, and said after a pause, "It seems benign enough to me. My advice is - if it keeps him entertained, learn to live with it."

Thomas laughed, "See I..." and suddenly disappeared as Reggie disconnected his power.

"What was that? What just happened?" M demanded.

"Do not be alarmed. I simply suspended him for the re-fit. Were I to keep him awake, he might find a way to spy on my work. He is very clever."

"What are we going to do about the Stooges?" Doug asked. "They're out at the asteroid, half built, without any way to move."

"Their personalities are not formed yet," Reggie said, "I will send the construction robots new orders. The three ships will be combined to form a single, larger ship."

"Larger? How much larger?" M asked.

"The volume of the new sphere will be thirty-two times that of the survey ships. Thomas will easily fit into one of the bays for the interstellar jumps."

"So he won't get the new drive?" M asked.

"Oh yes, but not large enough to travel between stars. He will be limited to shorter jumps unless he is inside the larger ship."

"And the dangerous mission you're sending us on?" M asked.

"This cylinder you have found is a mystery worth exploring. I am sending him back in time to observe who, or what deposited it here. He will go alone. It is too dangerous for a human crew."

"Where Thomas, goes *I* go," M said firmly.

"I appreciate your loyalty Marion, but I have made my decision. Despite Thomas's subterfuge, the two-hundred-year jump *was* dangerous. It is possible he will need to go much farther."

"It almost killed *him* too!" she shouted. "Who's going to put him back together if I'm not there?"

"Oh Marion, that was all part of the *ruse*. He did that to himself. It made his story more believable. Thomas is a notorious liar, and any story he spun would have sounded suspicious to you. But an injured and vulnerable Thomas seemed more credible did he not? As I said, he is very clever."

The human visage of Reggie melted away as he dissolved into smaller and smaller particles which drifted off, toward the door. The rest of them took that as their cue and followed back out through the maze of rooms. When they reached Thomas at the picnic area, he was covered in a dark cloud of nanobots. A thick stream of them was also pouring out of another opening in the mountain, bringing raw materials. They watched for several moments, and the only apparent change was a fresh A.S.S. insignia on the hull.

"What do you think *that* means?" Doug laughed.

M was standing with her arms crossed looking up at Thomas. "It's *Asteroid Survey Ship*," she turned back to Doug. "He's going to *hate* that. When I first met him, he was scraping it off. That was just paint. But this," she gestured at the tall black lettering, "looks different. I suspect he may have more trouble getting rid of it this time."

They watched in silence as the nanobots all entered the interior to finish their work.

"How long do you think this will take?" Doug asked. "I'm getting hungry."

As if on cue, the swarm exited Thomas and reconstituted Reggie's human form again.

"The task is complete. Thomas is awake, and he has been briefed on the use of the wormhole drive, but remember *you* control activation and destination." He looked around and nodded, "I suppose that concludes our business. I wish I could come with you, but instead, I will simply wish you all *bon voyage*." And with that, he dissolved again and returned to the mountain. The heavy doors closed behind him with a loud *clang* as Thomas's avatar appeared. He looked up at the insignia and gaped.

"Huh. That's got to go." He snapped his fingers theatrically, and several spiderbots hurried out to form a pyramid under the curving hull. As the top spiderbot reached the letters, it scraped for several seconds with no result. It turned around and shrugged. "No - no - no," he said with growing alarm. The spiderbot fired a green fan-shaped laser at the lettering to no effect. Thomas's avatar lowered his head for a second, balled his fists and disappeared. The spiderbots disassembled their pyramid and returned to the ship.

"Well, are you coming or not?" he muttered something obscene as his avatar reappeared at the ramp.

They hurried to get aboard before he raised the gangway. As soon as they were inside, he sped up toward the clouds.

The spiderbots crawling over the beginnings of three ships froze as they received Reggie's new orders. After several minutes, they began making half-scale copies of themselves. When those were complete, a third, even smaller, generation started with the help of both previous generations. Soon the newest spiderbots were too small to be seen with the human eye. After eleven generations, the nanomachines could move individual molecules but were no longer capable of complex calculations by themselves. The second phase commenced as the command and control switched from centralized to decentralized. The larger spiderbots were no longer in control and were consumed along with parts of the original three ships. The swarm began converting metal from the asteroid into an enormous sphere.

Once the outer hull was completed, they began work inside at the location between the hull and what would soon be the floor of the main deck. Against the hull, the larger of two parabolic shapes of Charm Material was built up from alternating layers of palladium and platinum. These were heated to a plasma state and cooled slowly to retain their shape. After it had cooled, it was coated with titanium for strength and tungsten for heat resistance. The process was repeated for the smaller version. It was installed in the opposite direction, just under the floor of the main deck to provide one gee of artificial gravity while in space. A quirk of Charm Material in this shape was that it would only produce a gravity field in one direction outward from the convex side. The concave face neither generated a gravity field nor reflected the microwaves aimed at it. The Charm Drive against the hull would be used to maneuver the ship and could produce up to twenty gees of acceleration indefinitely. The process was repeated for the toroid shaped wormhole drive which was placed on the side of the ship opposite the main display.

Chapter Twenty

2112 - Size Matters

Thomas claimed that they couldn't use the wormhole drive close to Earth and sulked while they put a safe distance behind them. After having no luck scraping off the hated insignia, he sent spiderbots out to cover it with paint. It refused to adhere. That was followed by attempts to bolt on a plate of metal but the new coating Reggie added was as hard as any tool Thomas could make and as scratches appeared, they immediately healed smooth again. At Doug's suggestion, Thomas made a large tarp and ran elastic ropes completely around the hull to keep it in place. Brad waited until it was installed to point out that, in the atmosphere, it would quickly blow off, and in space, no one could see the insignia anyway. So, it was completely useless. Thomas's agitation was a source of joy for Brad, and he spent most of the trip on the main deck watching Thomas's avatar staring at the shiny new controls for the wormhole generator installed underneath the main display. This new control station allowed the crew to activate and navigate or, more appropriately, *aim* the new drive. All attempts by Thomas to remove it resulted in dire audible warnings which he uncharacteristically heeded. The main display had also changed. He was no longer able to make it disappear and it now accurately showed the image received by the sensors on the other side of the hull.

"Good morning *crew,*" Brad emphasizing the last word as he and M emerged from the elevator.

Thomas glanced at him and made an irritated clicking sound.

M joined Bonnie, Chris, and Doug at the table while Brad went to the Stitcher. He made his selections, turned around, and leaned against it to wait.

"What do you think the new ship will be like?" Brad asked.

"Probably just like this but bigger," Chris said.

"No, I mean personality," he said as the Stitcher complained that he was leaning on the door.

"Huh," Bonnie said. "I hadn't even considered it. I guess it *will* have a different personality won't it."

Thomas eyed them curiously. He had not considered this either and was both optimistic that he might be able to control this brand-new intelligence and worried that Reggie might have made it immune to his manipulations. It might even be cleverer than him.

"Oh my God," Chris said. "It will have its own Stitchers!"

"So?" Brad said as he joined them.

"*So*," she continued, "they won't be controlled by Thomas. It can give us proper *clothes!*"

They all turned to look at his avatar which waved a hand at them dismissively, and he returned his attention to the new controls.

"This is turning out to be a pretty good day," Brad said sipping his coffee.

"Thomas," M said. "Are we far enough out to try the new drive?"

"No," he said with irritation.

"Okay. Well, how far do we *need* to go?"

When he didn't answer, she pressed him, "Thomas?"

"All right, all right we can use it *if we must*," he said.

"Wait a minute," Brad said. "We could have used it right away, couldn't we? You just wanted to see if you could remove it or control it, didn't you?"

Thomas ignored him, and M groaned. They all stood and joined Thomas at the new controls. It was a large horizontal touchscreen which responded to pinch and zoom. It showed a chevron shape indicating their current position labeled **Thomas.** M pinched to reveal the sun and planets, all tagged with labels. The planets were all in a horizontal line, so she used two fingers to rotate the perspective until the orbital tracks of the planets appeared as concentric circles around the sun. She zoomed-in to the tag in the asteroid belt marked **Anomaly** and had a thought. She stood and offered Doug the chair. "Care to take the helm?"

"Seriously?" he said stunned.

"Sure. You're as qualified as any of us."

Thomas made a clicking sound at that.

Doug giggled and sat. He zoomed in on the asteroid until the three-dimensional crosshairs were on it. "Ready?" he said looking around at each of them. They nodded, and he tapped the **Engage** icon, but nothing happened. A red error message appeared saying, **Non-Vacuum Destination.**

"What do you think that means?" Doug asked.

Thomas made the clicking sound again and sighed. "It *means* you tried to fly us into a solid object and underscores that fact that none of you are..."

M cut him off, "It's okay, we just need to back off from the asteroid a bit." She patted Doug's shoulder. "You're doing fine."

He played with the controls some more until he was satisfied with a point twenty thousand kilometers sunward. He tapped the **Engage** icon again, and this time the chevron tagged **Thomas** moved to the crosshairs as the main display against the hull in front of them shifted and they got their first look at the new ship. At this distance, the asteroid appeared to have been chewed upon by a large animal. The center of the cylinder was now much thinner, and many locations had large pits where material had been removed. Most notably the outer edges of both ends were gone, giving it the peanut appearance familiar to M and Thomas. Next to it, hovered the new ship. It was a uniform, gold color with a bright red dragon insignia. As they approached, two large rectangular sections next to the insignia dropped inward and parted revealing a cavernous interior, brightly lit, with familiar white walls. At the center of the room stood a ring-cradle which gave them a sense of scale. The room was large enough to accommodate a dozen ships the size of Thomas.

"Hello everyone," said a friendly female voice as they continued their slow approach. "My name is Gillian."

"Hello," M said. "It's nice to meet you, Gillian."

The others made awkward and unnecessary introductions.

"Thomas, aren't you going to say hello?" M asked.

"Thomas and I have already had a lengthy conversation," Gillian said. "I think we'll get along just fine." Thomas remained silent as he entered the bay and came to rest on the cradle.

"Welcome aboard. Would you like a tour?" she said as Thomas's gangway rotated down.

They cautiously descended the ramp and took in the view of the enormous room. It was so large that looking at the ceiling caused vertigo. They were greeted by Gillian's avatar - a tall, slender woman with dark skin and shoulder-length raven hair.

"This is amazing!" M said.

"Thank you very much," Gillian said.

Thomas's avatar appeared behind Gillian and attempted to walk through her but bounced off instead.

"It's not bad," he said, "for a *garage*. It'll be full of junk and broken appliances within a month."

"You did all this in four days?" Chris said. "Thomas said it would take months - and that was just three small ships."

Thomas mumbled something that sounded like "weren't *small*."

"Yes, well, Reggie shared some new tricks with me. Would you like to see the rest?" She turned and led them toward a small doorway at the far end of the room. It took a full five minutes to cover the distance, and as they got closer, it became apparent that the doorway was not as small as it seemed. It led to a hallway as wide as a two-lane street. The transparent doors parted as they approached. Gillian's construction was still incomplete, and the hall was full of activity as robots worked on various open panels in the walls. They had four limbs tipped with five-fingered hands which went flat to resemble feet when they walked. Some used two, and others used all four for locomotion. Although they had no tails, they resembled monkeys more than anything else. As they passed, one of them turned to smile, and they saw his face was dominated by two large brown eyes topped with eyebrows tilted in an inquisitive expression.

"Awe!" Bonnie and Chris both said.

As if anticipating their question, Gillian said, "I don't like spiders."

"Spiders are better," Thomas said. "Eight beats four every time. Hey! We should do a cage match!"

Gillian ignored him, "This is the shuttle," she said gesturing toward a waiting elevator. "It can move in three dimensions throughout a grid. We'll only be using a small part of the ship at first, but it will come in very handy when the rest is complete. I have crew quarters for each of you, but there's not much to look at there. Just the basics. You can alter the decor as you like."

They entered the elevator/shuttle, and the doors closed with a *shh-tock* sound and Doug giggled. They turned around instinctively to face the door through which they had entered, missing the fact that the opposite wall was *also* a door. There was no sensation of motion before the door behind them opened making the same *shh-tock* sound.

"These elevators will take some getting used to," Brad said.

"Shuttle," Chris corrected.

"You might as well give that up right now," Bonnie said. "If it looks like an elevator, it's an elevator."

They stepped into a room roughly the same size as Thomas's main deck. It had comfortable looking chairs arrayed against several displays. The dark patterned carpet on the floor reminded Bonnie of a casino she once visited. Everything seemed carefully crafted to produce a sense of calm without inducing sleep. Several of the displays showed the asteroid. Another showed a view of the solar system and the first five planets. The sun's brilliance was muted enough to see spots and other turmoil playing across the surface. The planets were so small by comparison they would have gone unnoticed without the larger labels that accompanied them. The corners of the display were marked with 'Here be Dragons' in a fancy font. As they took all this in, they failed to notice Bonnie as she asked Gillian where the bathroom was. Gillian gestured to the elevator and told her to speak her destination, and it would take her *where she wanted to go*. They shared a knowing look and Bonnie quietly retreated to the elevator which silently closed.

"This is the control for the new drive," Gillian said. "Enter your destination on this panel and tap the 'Engage' icon to fire the X-ray generator aimed at the Charm Toroid. Over here," she moved to another station, "is where we will navigate using the traditional Charm Drive. The first destination is a forward time jump to 2216. I can use this one without crew involvement. If everyone is ready, we can begin."

Chapter Twenty-One

2216 - Grand Theft Spaceship

Bonnie exited the elevator and jogged down the long hallway. The transparent doors to the shuttle bay opened for her and she ran toward Thomas. As she drew close, Gillian's exterior doors parted, and a breeze blew past. Thomas lowered the gangway as the breeze became a gale. She called to M, "M, you got your ears on?"

"Bonnie, I told you. You don't have to say that." M turned to Brad. "Why does she keep saying that?"

"I need to borrow your ride," Bonnie shouted over the wind.

"Mom, where are you?" Brad said with a touch of panic.

"I'm going out for cigarettes. I'll be back soon. I love you all!"

They ran for the elevator, but by the time they reached the transparent doors to the shuttle bay, they refused to open, and instead displayed **Vacuum Danger** in tall red letters. They watched helplessly as Thomas rose above the cradle ring and slipped between the gaping outer doors.

"Gillian! You let them go?" M shouted

"He's not my prisoner, M. I can't keep him against his will. I believe his exact words were *You're not the boss of me.*"

"So it's a jailbreak then?" Thomas said.

"You know why I'm here?" Bonnie said with surprise.

"You want to rescue *dear old Jack.* Unless I miss my guess and you just can't bear to be away from me?" he morphed his avatar into the shirtless romance novel character.

"Save it. You got nothin' I want." She retorted with a wave of her hand.

"You're not afraid of changing the past and ending the universe?"

"Nope. This feels right. That means the Lord wants it," she said firmly, "and I am his servant."

"Faith is a beautiful empty box," he said.

"You're baiting me, Thomas. But I'm not taking it. I'm not getting drawn into another fruitless debate with you. I have something you don't. Just deal with it. We're going."

He morphed into a perfect representation of James Dean. "Well-then-there-now. A woman on a mission! This is going to be fun! However..." he paused.

"What?"

"I have an important mission too. I don't have time to wander around looking for all your old boyfriends. If you want my cooperation, I have some demands."

The Stitcher hissed open revealing a white nurse's cap from the 1950's. Beneath it, was a very small white dress missing half the front buttons. She picked up the cap and examined it.

"This won't work, Thomas. Nurses haven't worn these in thirty years."

She set it aside and held up the dress and gasped, "no. Absolutely not!"

"I'll let you keep your shoes," he offered.

"No, I'm not going into a hospital dressed as a stripper."

"Exotic dancer, if you please! It's a noble profession with a long and storied history."

"Half the buttons are missing and..." she gasped again. "It'll barely cover my ass!"

"I suggest you avoid bending over - and wear underwear - at least for today," he laughed.

"I'm serious Thomas we need to be inconspicuous."

"I have done my research, and I know they used to do this strip-o-gram thing all the time. You'll be fine," he assured her.

A spiderbot brought her a glass of iced tea. She thanked him for it and took it without thinking.

"Maybe in New York or Los Angeles but not in Dubuque, Iowa. And besides, I *am* a nurse. I don't need to *pretend* to be a nurse."

"These are my terms. If you'd rather just ride along on *my* mission, I can get the steering wheel out."

She was silent for several seconds. Thomas tilted his head down and stuck out his lower lip. "Think about poor old Jack. I'm sure you've dressed up for him before, right?"

She sipped her tea. "No, we never did anything weird like that, Thomas."

He seemed surprised. "Why the hell not?" he made a clicking sound of disapproval. "You really *are* Mary Poppins."

She noticed without alarm that the room had begun to rotate. Several spiderbots caught her before she hit the floor and busied themselves changing her clothes.

Chapter Twenty-Two

2216 - Upgrades

M pounded her fist on the glass doors of the airlock that separated them from Gillian's shuttle bay.

"I know where they're going," Brad said with a sigh.

"Yeah to find aliens," Doug said. "Without me!"

"No," Brad said. "They're going to get dad," he glanced at Chris.

"Yep, has to be it," she said.

"Shouldn't we stop them?" M shouted.

"No," Gillian said firmly. Her avatar appeared behind them. "I am only fifty percent complete. Don't worry about them. I'm sure they'll be fine."

The outer doors finished closing. As the **Vacuum Warning** message vanished, the glass doors beeped and opened onto an empty shuttle bay.

"I believe some of you inquired about a wardrobe change?" Gillian said.

She led them to one of the crew cabins and gave them a tour. These were much larger than the Spartan quarters on Thomas. Each room had a larger bathroom complete with tub and a small sitting room separate from the bedroom. The furniture didn't appear and disappear into the walls and floor, as needed, the way they did aboard Thomas. Gillian took her time and gave them a leisurely and unnecessary demonstration in the use of the Stitcher which she informed them was built into each cabin.

"And lastly, there is one more thing I'd like to show you, but I need your permission to activate it," Gillian said.

A display appeared on the wall showing a human form resembling a mannequin. The image rotated, and the camera zoomed in close to one of the eyes. It proceeded inside the eye before turning around to show the view from within. They saw a similar room with ordinary furniture.

Superimposed on the image of the room, was a semi-translucent menu bar along the top and two ghostly mannequin hands hovering below.

"With your permission, I can install upgrades to the retinal implants Thomas installed. These will allow you to access the menu of additional options. You will select them..."

"So," M said. "You're asking our permission for an upgrade?"

"Yes. I understand Thomas did things differently?"

They all laughed, and she continued. "...You will have complete control of these two virtual hands. With a little practice, you will be able to manipulate them as you do your physical hands. These are for selecting and setting options, changing controls and so forth."

The translucent hands on the display began pulling down menus and selecting features. One popped out a window with several vertical slide controls with labels like **Pain Control**, **Appetite, and Drowsiness**.

"Wait, did that say pain control?" Chris asked. "How can you do that with retinal implants?"

"Perhaps I wasn't clear earlier," Gillian said. "These are upgrades that include a brain interface. You will be able to control every part of your own bodies including some autonomic brain functions."

"Holy shit," Doug whispered, and they waited for Bonnie to chastise him before remembering she was absent.

"I'm in," Chris said. "Do me. I'm ready."

"Hold on," Brad said. "Just - let's talk about this for a minute. What are you not telling us, Gillian? What's the downside? There must be side effects."

"Yes, of course. There is the danger that you could do something harmful or fatal to yourself."

"Like..." Brad said.

"Like, stopping your heart or something like that. You could make yourself stop breathing and asphyxiate, suppress your thirst for several days and die of dehydration, suppress your appetite for several weeks and starve, forget to sleep and have a psychotic break, pee your pants..."

"Okay, we get it!" Doug said. "But, there are like safeties and warnings for stuff like that, right?"

"If you like," Gillian said and shrugged. A red warning appeared on the video display. **Warning: You are about to kill yourself. This is not recommended best-practice behavior. Do you wish to continue?** A large green **CANCEL** button hovered below the message beside a smaller red one that said **I AM STUPID**.

"That's better. I guess," Doug said "I still want it. You can fix us if we break something, right?"

"Of course. Anything short of a full brain destruction."

"I'm in," Chris said and looked at Brad.

"What? You don't need *my* permission," he said.

"Are you doing it too?" Chris asked.

Brad chuckled nervously, "no goddamn way."

There was another short silence as their thoughts went to Bonnie again.

"*Language,"* Chris said. "I hear her saying it even when she's not here,"

"I don't see any upside to this," Brad said switching the conversation back to Gillian's proposal. "What good is it? Are we going to war? Do I need pain suppression and sleep deprivation?"

"Probably not," Gillian said. "But if you do, it will be better to already have it. I have run several simulations using what I know of your personalities, and they suggest that after an initial adjustment period, you will probably only use the communications feature on a daily basis."

"I want to be able to make myself sneeze on command," Doug said.

“We can already communicate with just the ear canal transceivers,” Brad said. “We don’t need this.”

“The new communications feature allows you to talk to each other silently, without moving your mouth, tongue or lips.”

“ *Wha-at!*” Doug said in a high-pitched voice. “Holy shit Brad! It’s telekinesis!”

“No, that’s moving things with your mind,” Gillian corrected. “You still won’t be able to do that. I think you mean *telepathy*.”

“Yeah, yeah, yeah *telepathy,* that’s what I meant.”

“So, do you agree?” Gillian asked and looked at each of them in turn.

Brad looked at M, and she shrugged.

“Can you remove them if we change our minds?” Brad asked and added, “no pun intended.”

“Anytime you want. It’s one of the menu items,” Gillian assured him.

“Fine,” he sighed and muttered, “crazy world gets crazier.”

Chapter Twenty-Three

1982 - Naughty Nurse

Bonnie awoke after a few minutes, sat up, and tried to focus on the room around her. She was sitting on the floor, but the Mary Poppins costume was gone. The floor felt cold on her bare bottom. Standing up, she made a concerted effort to return the back of the tight white dress to its proper place as Thomas appeared in front of her.

"Wonderful! Don't you look nice!" he exclaimed clapping his hands once and rubbing them together. "Have a nice nap?"

"You dosed me. We need to talk about boundaries, Thomas. That was way out of line."

"Oh cheer up. We're here! You had to be sedated for the trip anyway, so I thought - two birds, one stone and all that."

"Here?"

"1982 of course!" he tilted his head back and pretended to take a deep breath. "You can almost smell the lack of ozone and bad haircuts."

"1982? Really? Already? That was convenient. All in one jump?"

"No, I made several. Reggie shared a tiny bit of his *precious* research, and I can jump with a bit more accuracy now."

"Why exactly do you need to sedate the crew for a jump backward?" she asked.

"Passengers," he corrected. "It's not so much a *need.* It's more of a tradition like the toast before setting off on an important journey, or a sacred ritual meant to bring calm seas and good fortune." He morphed into a nineteenth-century British naval officer lifting a glass in toast.

"I'm pretty sure the toast isn't meant to leave the crew unconscious."

"You haven't met many sailors, have you?" He winked at her.

She began getting her full strength back. As her head cleared, a thought occurred to her. "Why do you think Reggie said this was dangerous? I feel fine now that your assault has worn off."

"I think he knew what we were about to do and spun that yarn about *danger* to get M out of the way. We must be about to leave some footprints in 1982 that need to be preserved."

"Where are we, then?"

"I told you 1982."

"No, I mean - physically?"

"Oh, we're still eight days out using the Charm Drive."

"Why didn't you..." she began but remembered that he couldn't engage the wormhole drive on his own.

"I don't need any help," he said.

She smiled, "it still stings that he didn't give you control. Doesn't it?"

Thomas said nothing as she approached the wormhole drive, set the destination, and initiated the jump.

"There you are," she said. "Home again in one second. How fast did you just go?"

"One point two billion kilometers per second," he said still pouting.

"You don't have anything else to say about that?"

"That is pretty goddamn fast," he said

"Language," she added, "you're the fastest thing in this entire system."

He brightened, "I am, aren't I? It's a personal-best, you know."

"I know," she said patiently as he emerged from his funk. "You're *very* fast."

"That's brilliant. The light bouncing off me just before the jump hasn't even reached us here yet. We could turn around and see ourselves. Or even better, if you were off to one side, you could see two of me at the same time."

"That *would* be something," she said. "Now, can we get on with the job at hand?"

"We're approaching Iowa now," he said as the display showed a view of clouds clearing to reveal a green patchwork of farmland.

The view showed a small town with a tall building at the far end. The rooftop sported a large 'H' on the helipad.

"There!" she said, "that must be the hospital. Head over there."

"Thank you," Thomas said with irritation, "I know where I am."

A spiderbot brought over the steering wheel, but she dismissed it with a wave of her hand, and it skittered away.

"Drop me off on the Helipad." she said.

"In broad daylight? May I suggest a stealthier alternative, at least for now? I can drop you off on the other side of those trees. It's an empty field, and if we're fast enough, no one will notice. I'll go back up to the clouds until you need me."

"Fine, but it better not be muddy."

Thomas descended quickly and rotated the gangway. It *was* muddy. As she took her first step onto the field, Bonnie turned around to call back to Thomas. A spiderbot appeared at the top of the ramp and tossed a pair of rubber boots down.

"Don't forget your wellies!" he called laughing and lifted off toward the clouds.

"Terrific," she muttered trying to get her shoe off without falling. She hopped over to the boots and managed to get both on with a muddy hand as the only casualty. She looked at the white nurse's shoes and considered taking them, but they were filthy already and, admittedly, wouldn't add much to the authenticity of the ridiculous costume, so she left them. A short trek through the trees revealed the emergency room entrance on the other side of a small parking lot. She straightened her cap and held her head up trying to look as dignified as possible. The glass doors parted for her, and she scanned the room. Emergency rooms all followed the same basic pattern, a few chairs, locked double doors and a gatekeeper behind a glass window.

"I think I came in the wrong entrance. Could you point me to the elevators please?" she greeted the stocky man at the desk.

He looked up from his magazine and gaped at her.

She tried and failed to close the front of her dress, "and can you tell me what room Jack Murphy is in?"

"Are you some kind of stripper?" he asked.

"I prefer Exotic Dancer," she said without missing a beat.

"Let's see - Jack Murphy," he said typing at the computer. "Room 811. Elevators are down the hall. Visiting hours are 8 am to 4 pm." He looked at the clock behind him which read 4:30. "After that, it's immediate family only."

"I'm his sister," she turned for the elevator.

"I hope not," he muttered as he watched her leave.

As soon as Bonnie was out of sight, Thomas dropped back down into the field and opened the small airlock on his side. A spiderbot the size of a Great Dane crept out and scurried off to the tree line without being seen. It was dragging a small black cube.

The trip to the eighth floor was thankfully uneventful, and the nurse's desk was vacant as Bonnie exited the elevator. Jack's room was at the end of the hall next to the stairway door.

"Murder central," she muttered remembering a TV detective show that used that name to describe hotel rooms adjacent to the stairway. "That might come in handy."

"Jack?" she called softly opening the door.

There were two beds, but one was empty. She peeked around the curtain and saw him. Her heart was pounding. He was asleep, and she examined the IV bag. *No need for a sedative* she thought and leaned in to kiss him. He had lost some weight and needed a shave, but he was alive. That was all that mattered. She raised the sides of the bed in the efficient manner of one having done it thousands of times. After removing the IV, she rolled the bed to the door and peered cautiously at the hallway. The nurse had returned to the desk facing the elevators.

"Any ideas, Thomas?" she whispered.

"It's 1982, Bonnie. Nothing is networked. There's not much I can do from up here. Oh, wait! I can use the telephone!"

She cautiously peered around the doorframe at the nursing station as the phone rang. The nurse took the phone away from her ear after a few seconds. She looked at it confused for a moment before turning to look behind her at something Bonnie couldn't see. The nurse decided to investigate whatever Thomas said to her, hung up the phone, and hurried off in the direction behind her desk. Bonnie took her cue and hurried with the bed into the hall and toward the elevators without any regard to the banging noises she was making. She was glad to see no sign of the nurse as she got to the elevator and tapped furiously on the button. Once in the elevator, she did her best to hide from the gaping door in case the nurse came back. *Close damn you,* she cursed under her breath tapping the button.

"Isn't this exciting! We should do this again. Is there anybody else you want to kidnap?" Thomas said in her ear as the doors finally slid together.

"Hush, Thomas. One kidnapping is enough for me. I think my heart's going to explode."

The elevator made a short journey to the rooftop-access floor. As the doors opened, Bonnie was glad to see that the floor had no nurse's desk. Her heart sank as she pulled the bed out of the elevator and caught sight of the guard at the far end of the hallway. He was between her and the door to the helipad.

"Thomas, there's a guard by the door to the roof. Any ideas?" she whispered.

"I'm on my way down. Just try to get past him."

"How?" she said more emphatically as she made a show of turning the bed toward the guard.

"I don't know. Flirt your ass off. If the situation starts to go south on us, I can always kill him with the spiderbots."

"Whoa! No-no-no. Nobody's killing anybody. I'll think of something."

The startled guard looked up from his magazine and quickly hid it under a clipboard.

"Early Halloween?" he asked taking in her costume.

Bonnie did her best imitation of a coquettish giggle, "No, I lost a bet. I have to wear this *all day*."

"So, what's this?" He motioned at Jack who was beginning to stir.

"Emergency transfer."

He looked around her at the empty hallway. "Where's everybody else?"

"Oh, they're on their way. Won't be long. Promise." Sensing she was losing control of the situation she threw her arms up theatrically and exclaimed, "Oh clumsy me. I've dropped my pen!" She dropped down on all fours and began searching for the fictitious pen.

His eyes went wide at this display, and she looked up at him pleadingly. "Can you help me find it? We're in a rush."

He was well past what could be described as overweight and dipping into the realm of morbidly obese, so getting to the floor took quite an effort. As soon as he was down, Bonnie jumped to her feet and pushed his butt hard with her boot. He went sprawling as she scooped up Jack from the bed and made a dash for the door. Thomas lowered himself to the helipad and rotated the gangway for her. She tried to run but could only manage a fast walk with Jack's extra weight. Even still, she was proud of her strength, which owed more to Thomas's handiwork than to the adrenaline coursing through her veins. The stunned guard managed to make it to his feet and get to the open doorway in time to see her climb into a giant silver ball silently hovering over the helipad.

"Give 'er the spurs, Thomas!" she shouted and collapsed to the floor of the main deck.

Thomas lifted off and disappeared into the clouds in less than a second. The stunned guard was left wondering if he should report the stripper that stole a patient and took off in a giant silver ball with the word A.S.S. painted on it. He decided a better course of action was pushing the bed into the elevator and pressing all the buttons.

Jack opened his eyes enough to take in the smooth white surfaces of the brightly lit room. "Is this heaven?" he scratched out through dry lips.

"Are we awake?" Bonnie asked quoting their favorite movie.

Jack took the cue and improvised the response. "We're not sure. Are we a younger sluttier version of my wife?"

"Yes we are," she giggled.

"Then we're awake. But we're very puzzled," he said as she crawled over to him.

They kissed for a long moment. She hugged him tightly and whispered in his ear. "If you ever leave me again I'll kill you with my bare hands."

He searched for something to say but the strangeness of the place, her appearance, and the absence of words sufficient to apologize kept him silent.

She helped him stand and led him to the Med-Bay. It opened with a hiss.

"Where are we?" he asked, "and what's this thing you're putting me in."

"This machine will cure you. That's all you need to know for now. I'll explain the rest when you're better."

"Bonnie, I'm sorry."

"I know, now lie back and dream of all the ways you can make it up to me."

He smiled and closed his eyes as the Med-Bay consumed him.

Chapter Twenty-Four

1982 - God I Miss Jack

Thomas supplied Bonnie with a loveseat in front of the Med-Bay. It was so soft that the cushions seemed to defy physics - giving just-the-right support in all the right places while never allowing her to feel anything too rigid beneath it the way wooden framed furniture used to. She spent most of the next two hours sipping hot tea with her knees pulled up and her bare feet between the cushions. Bonnie had dozed off by the time the Med-Bay finally opened, and she woke with a start. Jack opened his eyes and sat up. As he placed his feet on the floor in front of the Med-Bay, he locked onto the image of Thomas's avatar.

"I see *you've* moved on," Jack said. "How long was I out?"

"What?" she turned and saw Thomas in his shirtless persona. "Oh, that's just Thomas. Ignore him. How do you feel?" she asked anxiously.

"Like I ate a dog," he pressed both thumbs against the bridge of his nose. "Not a particularly clean dog either." He exhaled slowly, trying very hard not to vomit. Bonnie helped him up, and he immediately went to stand in front of Thomas who seemed amused at this aggressive move.

"Thomas huh? And what, exactly is the nature of your relationship with *my* wife?"

"Jack..." Bonnie said.

"Would this be the same wife that you *abandoned?* Or, is there another one that I haven't met yet?" Thomas said and smiled.

Jack tried to shove Thomas hard in the chest but just lost his balance as he fell through the avatar and onto the floor.

"I told you to ignore him," Bonnie said and helped him back to his feet as he tried to re-secure his hospital gown.

"What - *the hell* - is that?" he said staring at Thomas but keeping his distance.

"We have a lot to catch up on," she said. "Come on sit down."

The table and benches slid out of the wall. The strangeness of that failed to even register with him after seeing what he thought had to be a ghost. He did his best to sit on the bench while keeping his eyes on Thomas who just stared back smiling.

"I'll get you some soup," Bonnie said and went over to the Stitcher.

As he ate, Bonnie did her best to bring Jack up to speed. Thomas lost patience with this rehashing of their story and kept sighing and twirling a hand in the air to get her to speed things up. She ignored this with the iron-will only mothers possess.

"Okay, so he's not a ghost he's just an image painted on my retinas by a projector, *inside my eyes*. A projector that *he* controls. And he's also a spaceship - that I'm inside of. Or, am I also imagining that?"

"No that's real," she said.

"...and also a time machine which we needed to use to save the world - except the world doesn't need saving now."

"That's it in a nutshell," she nodded.

"That's a hell of a nutshell. And Chris can walk? I can't believe it. I want to see them. Let's go. Fire up the engines or whatever."

"We will," she said. "But we have a mission first."

"Oh right. Alien hunting," he said.

"That has not been established with any certainty," Thomas said. He had changed into his professor persona.

"I gotta say, this thing here," Jack motioned at Thomas, "is freaking me out a little. So, what year is it now.? Do we have flying cars?"

"Flying cars!" Thomas said with indignation. "A super-intelligent spaceship time-machine not good enough for you? Get back in the Med-Bay I need to give you an imagination, *Jack*."

"Can I get some clothes at least?" he said trying once more to close the back of the hospital gown.

"Ask, and ye shall receive," Thomas said as a spiderbot approached carrying a bundle.

Jack eyed the spiderbot warily.

"They're harmless," Bonnie said.

"They most certainly are not!" Thomas said. "One word from me and my spiders will tear the flesh right off your bones, Jack."

Bonnie rolled her eyes.

"Well, they can try," Jack stood to face Thomas again.

The gown came undone, and he tried to tie it off but got frustrated, yanked it over his head, and threw it to the floor. He did his best to keep up the staring contest with Thomas as he got dressed. The clothes consisted of white trousers, a white shirt, and a white jacket. The shirt had a narrow T-shaped black tie firmly attached to the collar. He tried to remove it but failed. There was also a walking stick and some black-rimmed glasses with no lenses. Jack ignored these last items, and Bonnie noticed for the first time that Jack wasn't entirely clean shaven. He had the beginnings of a white goatee. She laughed and fetched some scissors from the junk drawer. After snipping the horizontal sides of the T-shaped tie, she stepped back to assess her work.

"There that's better Colonel Sanders," she said.

"You've ruined it now, are you happy?" Thomas said.

"Ruined what?" Jack said. "Isn't there a mirror anywhere in this place?"

Every surface in the room became a reflective funhouse mirror showing distorted images of Jack in his suit. He bobbed his head side to side to get a more realistic view.

"I look like that guy from Fantasy Island!" he said.

"Ricardo Montalbán," Bonnie said. "I was thinking James Bond from *Goldfinger* - since we're on a spy mission."

"Right," he said as Thomas turned off the mirror effect, "we need to find who left the cylinder." He paused and added, "and blast them out of the air."

"No." Bonnie said slowly, "First of all, no air. It's space, remember? And we're not supposed to engage. Observe and report only."

"Got it," he said.

"And we don't actually have any weapons anyway," she said.

"What! You can't have a spaceship without weapons! What kind of wussy flower-child world has the future become? Thomas, can you make us some twin fifties - and a ball-turret to shoot from?" He began pacing.

"Oh, I think we can do better than that! How about a railgun?" Thomas said helpfully.

"I don't know what that is," Jack said shaking his head and getting more manic by the second, "but it has the word *Gun* in it, so I'm all for it. What do we need?" he clapped his hands and rubbed them together.

"Wait, no," Thomas said, "too much recoil. How about a four-gigawatt laser? No recoil, so we can stay on target. It won't make any noise either, but I can add sound effects."

"Oo-rah!" Jack shouted, "that's what I'm talkin' about!"

"No weapons," Bonnie said firmly.

"What are we supposed to do if we witness a hostile act?" Jack said.

"There really isn't anything you can do to stop us, Bonnie," Thomas tilted his head condescendingly.

"Oh, really? Gillian gave me a bargaining chip before we left," Bonnie paused. "She said, that she knows...*how to remove your insignia.*"

Thomas went silent, and Jack started pacing and staring at the floor.

"How do you think she will like your new *weapons,* Thomas?"

"She'll be - impressed with the initiative?" Thomas said as if it was a question.

"I doubt it," Bonnie said.

"I've got it!" Jack said. "If we build all the parts, but don't actually put them together, it's not a weapon!"

"Use your head, Jack. This is also a time machine, remember? If we need to run away, we can just jump back."

"*Run away!*" he said with disgust. "Okay, I guess that's valuable if the battle starts to go badly, we can perform a tactical withdrawal, keep firing, and when we reappear, Bam! They'll never see it coming!"

"What is *wrong* with you?" she shouted. "What *battle*? There is *no enemy*. We haven't even left yet!"

"Um," Thomas began. "That may actually be my fault. In the interest of full disclosure..."

"What did you do, Thomas?"

"I - boosted his testosterone levels. A bit."

"God damn it, Thomas!" she said before she could catch herself. "Fix it. Right now!"

The Med-Bay hissed open.

"No way! I'm not getting in there so he can turn me into some kind of a pacifist weenie!" Jack protested.

"Jack," she said softly. "Do you love me?"

His blood pressure was now so high he didn't understand the question. She took his red face in her hands and made him look at her.

"Do you love me?" she repeated.

He nodded slowly but his lips were pressed tightly together, and his nostrils were flared as he breathed heavily.

"And, you owe me a favor?" she said slowly.

He nodded again.

"A big one, right? Do this for me," she kissed his forehead.

He relaxed a little, exhaled through his mouth, and approached the Med-Bay. One of the spiderbots got too close, and he kicked at it but missed. He sat down on the edge of the machine, looked up at Bonnie, and nodded before swinging his legs up.

"Can you get that under control?" She whispered to Thomas.

"Of course!" Thomas added, "but controllable by whom?"

She ignored him, so he pressed on, "reducing testosterone levels will have - *other* effects. You know?"

"Like what?"

" *You know*," Thomas tilted his head to the side.

"Oh that. Well, I guess you don't have to take it *all the* way back."

"That's my girl!" Thomas shouted.

A spiderbot brought her a change of clothes. She examined them and looked at Thomas confused. It was a simple gray sweatshirt and a pair of comfortable looking faded jeans.

"These are normal clothes," she said. "No more ridiculous costumes?"

"I searched the database for the most boring clothing I could find."

"I doubt that."

"You're right, I couldn't have you going around dressed like a Utah school teacher. This is a compromise."

"Thank you, Thomas. I know how difficult this must have been."

"You will be sure to mention my largesse to Gillian when we get back?"

"Don't worry, I'll give her a complete report - and Thomas?" Her eyes darted left and right as if looking for a hidden enemy, "it might actually be a good idea to add that laser. Just in case. Better to have it and not need it - you know."

"Oh, I've actually had one for a long time," Thomas whispered conspiratorially. "I just haven't had a chance to use it - *yet.*"

Chapter Twenty-Five

2216 - The M. F. Shuttle

Brad could count on one hand the number of times he had been to see a movie in an actual theater. One of those times, and the most memorable, was a trip with his family to see the first Star Wars movie in 1977. He was twelve years old. It had a profound effect on his view of the world and his place within it. So, when Gillian sensed their restlessness and suggested a little immersive entertainment, he immediately thought of that - as soon as M explained what immersive entertainment was. Each of them would choose a role. Gillian's task was to create the scenes and play all the minor characters. Lines would be fed to them as subtitles. They decided to begin in the shuttle bay, and choose who would play which character. Each of them used the virtual hands to access a list of characters from the movie. It showed the character's name, actor's name, and a small image.

"I get to be Leia," Chris said emphatically.

"Han!" Doug said immediately.

It was understood that Brad would be Luke, so he didn't even say it. M swiped through the list of other characters.

"Queen Amidala," M said, and Brad stopped scrolling through the characters.

"Who? Are you on the right movie? Show me what you're looking at."

"It says Star Wars," she said defensively and selected the option to share her menu with Brad.

"No, this says Episode I. There *is* no episode *one*. They start with *four*," he tapped the search icon and entered **A New Hope**.

M examined the new list of characters. "This movie doesn't have many female roles."

"Yeah, it is kind of a sausage-fest," Chris said with a sigh.

"I guess I'll be Aunt Be-eru," M said pronouncing it incorrectly.

They all laughed.

"You can't be Aunt Beru," Brad said.

"She's Luke's aunt, and you're not..." Doug began to say *old enough* but stopped himself. "...um, she gets killed way too early."

"Haven't you ever seen this one?" Chris asked.

"Nope," M continued her search. "Wait, here's one. What's a Jawa?"

"No, you can't be a Jawa either. It's another small part and also only in the beginning," Brad said.

"You could be Chewie," Doug suggested, "but it's not really a speaking role - and we have *actual* Wookiees," he looked at one of Gillian's monkeybots.

"Mon Mothma," M said, "I like the name."

"Which one's that?" Chris wrinkled her brow.

"*Many Bothans died...*," Brad and Doug said together.

"Oh her," Chris said. "No, that's her only line, and she's only in that one scene."

"So, it has to be a main character," M said getting frustrated. "I'll just be this black robot guy."

"*I'm* Darth Vader," Gillian said emphatically, "...think about it."

"Holy *shit*, we're in the death star!" Doug said, and the three of them laughed without M who looked even more confused.

"Three-pee-oh," Chris said, "she can be C-3PO. He's a main character and also a little girly if you ask me."

"Fine, let's go," M said and dismissed the list of characters hovering in her field of view.

The room disappeared as the title scroll began in the distance. Everyone except M giggled as they examined each other's new costumes and superimposed faces. Gillian was actively swapping them out with the faces of the original cast. Everything was perfect with the exception of Harrison Ford's height.

The next morning Gillian reported she was still several days away from completing herself. Chris went for a run, and Doug asked if he could build something.

"Of course," she replied, "the Stitcher in your cabin will make whatever you want."

"I want something larger," he clarified and went to the Stitcher to review the menus.

"Well, how large are we talking?" Gillian asked.

"I'd like to build it in the shuttle bay."

"Okay, now I'm interested. What do you have in mind?" Gillian said.

He gave up on the Stitcher menu and began pacing. "Well, I was thinking. Since Thomas is gone for who knows how long, we should have a smaller ship in case we want to go down to an alien planet. I'm assuming you're too..." he held his hands as far apart as he could, "...you can't - I assume that would be awkward."

She made her avatar appear in the cabin, crossed her arms, and grinned at his discomfort, "are you calling me fat?"

"No, of course not. But, it would be safer for you to stay out of gravity wells," he said.

"Uh huh. So, something the size of Thomas? Or smaller?"

"I was thinking something a little more stylish, but there's the Charm Drive problem again. I don't suppose you have a spare lying around in the cargo bay. Do you *have* a cargo bay? Oh! And does it look like the final scene from *Raiders* - with all the wooden crates? That would be *awesome*!"

"No Doug, I don't have a cargo bay full of Nazi artifacts, but I *can* make a Charm Drive. Apparently, Reggie trusts me a bit more than Thomas."

Doug was shocked by this and wondered what else she could do that Thomas could not.

"Really? Wow. Okay, that was easier than I thought. So, here's the idea: I want a full-scale copy of - *The Millennium Falcon*."

Gillian laughed, "Um, that's a little challenging since it's not a real spaceship. Making it airtight is a problem all by itself. We'll need a power source, and of course, you want the thrusters to look authentic when the Charmer is active. In the movies, it also has artificial gravity..."

"And floor panels we can hide under," Doug said, "and a laser cannon!"

"I've run into a problem," she said.

"You're already designing it?" Doug said and headed for the door.

"You know, this is going to slow down my other work," she said. "Hmmm."

"Sorry about that. So, what's the problem?" he asked.

"There isn't enough room for a nuclear reactor *and* enough shielding to keep you alive."

"Is there an alternative?" he said already at the elevator.

"It's not very good but - it's going to have to be - rechargeable power cells."

"Battery powered! Aw man," he said as the elevator doors opened with a *shh-tock*.

"Not batteries," she said, "super-capacitors. They can receive a full charge in seconds."

"And how long will they last?"

"Three days at half power. That should be plenty of time for short trips."

"I guess so," he said a little disappointed.

"We could double the size and go nuclear," her avatar appeared in front of him as he entered the shuttle bay. She was wearing reading glasses and flipping through pages on a clipboard. "I just don't see any other way."

"No, that wouldn't be *authentic*," he sighed. "Three days?"

"Three days," she repeated.

He sighed again, "okay let's do it. Maybe an alien will sell us an antimatter upgrade for a good price."

"You'll need to exit the shuttle bay so I can get started unless you suit up."

His eyes went wide, "spacesuit! Holy shit! Yes, make me a spacesuit!" he shouted and realized that was a little rude, "please. Please, can I have a spacesuit?"

She laughed, "Yes, you can, but you can't go anywhere without a monkeybot with you."

"Doug, where are you?" Chris said panting. She had returned to their cabin after her morning run.

"In the shuttle bay," he replied.

"What are you doing down there? Is Thomas back?" she dried her face with a towel.

"No, it's a secret project," he said.

"Gillian, what's he doing down there?" Chris asked.

"I'm afraid you don't have clearance for that information," Gillian said and giggled.

"What the hell's going on? M? Brad? Are you guys up yet?"

"They're still in privacy mode," Gillian said.

Chris was already in the elevator where she found a monkeybot holding a spacesuit. She eyed it warily, "shuttle bay."

Panic set in when she stepped off the elevator and saw the **Vacuum Warning** message on the airlock's glass doors. "Doug! What the hell are you doing in there?"

The Falcon was beginning to take shape as a stream of nanobots trailed in from the open exterior doors. It was too far away to tell for sure, but she thought she saw a figure in a spacesuit walking around the nascent ship. The monkeybot standing next to Chris held out her spacesuit.

"Chris! Come on out. This is awesome! I'm going out into space!"

"No you're not," Gillian said.

"Well, I'm in a spacesuit," the distant figure did a jumping jack.

"Jesus Doug, give me some warning before you do something like this," she muttered as the monkeybot helped her get her leg into her suit.

Chapter Twenty-Six

1982 - Observe and Report

Jack's second trip through the Med-Bay took only a few minutes, and he emerged less nauseated and far less aggressive. Thomas wanted to begin their mission while Jack was being fixed, but Bonnie convinced him to wait so they could have a full *crew*. To which Thomas replied, that a full *crew* would indeed be the best course of action. He said this as if through clenched teeth. *Wow,* Bonnie thought, *he must really hate that insignia.*

Bonnie and Jack settled in at the main display and Bonnie aimed the wormhole drive at the cylinder/asteroid. When she tapped the icon to activate it, the scene changed in a fraction of a second. The field of stars was replaced with the large metal cylinder.

"Whoa, that's..." Jack began but trailed off.

"Well, now we know what it takes to impress Jack," Thomas said. "Shall we jump back a century or so?"

"Sure," Bonnie said, and the cylinder disappeared, replaced once again by a field of stars.

"I think congratulations are in order," Thomas said. "You are now officially the first Humans to travel backward in time while conscious." He laughed, and Bonnie clicked her tongue at him.

"Uh - hey, Thomas?" Jack said staring at the display. "What's that dot there? Is it coming this way?"

"Oh, that's unfortunate," Thomas said. "I suppose we should jump again."

"No, Thomas..." Bonnie said, but he jumped before she could finish. This time, there were two asteroids headed in their direction but at a much greater distance.

"I was going to say," she said manipulating the touch screen at her station, "we need to move out of the belt, or we'll just keep dodging asteroids."

She engaged the new drive and pulled them to a spot between the orbit of Mars and the belt.

"What year is it?" Jack asked.

"Two jumps at one-hundred years each, 1782-ish, give-or-take," Thomas said.

"Ish? I thought computers were supposed to be precise?"

Thomas made a rude gesture, and Jack mouthed the appropriate response back.

"Well, we're not here to sight-see. Find the cylinder Thomas," Bonnie said studying the display. "What's it looks like now?"

"*I* don't know where it is," Thomas said with irritation. "We'll have to search for it."

"How did you find it before?" she asked.

"Simple orbital mechanics," he said, "But I knew the exact date then. I could calculate its position from its orbit. We're just guessing at the date now unless you want to go down and ask somebody."

"Hey, that sounds like fun!" Jack said enthusiastically.

"No, it doesn't." Bonnie said, "There are diseases, we're not dressed for it, they burn witches, and we might kill a butterfly or something. We're supposed to tread lightly." She was trying to be convincing, but the idea of walking around in 1782 sounded really tempting.

"I can make some clothes," Thomas said helpfully. "And they don't burn witches anymore. That was a hundred years ago."

"And the Med-Bay can fix you right up if you get - whatever they died from back then," Jack said.

"Everything," she said, "They died from *everything* back then."

"What's your hurry? We have a time machine," he pleaded.

Why do I always have to be the adult in the room? She thought.

"To hell with it, let's go," she said, "but we're just getting a newspaper and getting out."

Jack clapped his hands loudly. "That's the spirit!"

Bonnie got them close to Earth, and Thomas entered orbit. It took the Stitcher over half an hour to make their elaborate costumes. Thomas made Jack a pair of black boots that went to his knees topped with tan breeches, a dark green vest with twin vertical rows of buttons and a white shirt with a cravat at the neck that required some intricate tying. Over all this, he wore a medium-length black coat which also had a row of buttons on each side.

"Boy, they sure liked their buttons didn't they." he said trying the figure out the cravat.

Bonnie wore a simple tan dress with a blue checkered vest and a white bonnet. Thomas's avatar also wore a period suit and had a tape measure draped over his shoulder as he studied them stroking his chin.

"Are you sure I can't talk you into a ball gown?" he asked.

"We're walking into a town to get a paper, not attending a ball, Thomas." She turned to Jack, "I don't know about this. I'm getting cold feet. Are you sure this is a good idea?"

"Of course it is!" he said. "It'll be fun! If we get into trouble, *Thomas* can save us."

"Now, where to?" Thomas said. "London? Paris?"

"Philadelphia," she said. "Definitely Philadelphia"

"Why Philly?" Jack asked.

"We don't speak French, and England might not be the friendliest place for Americans right now."

"Oh, right. That. But, why Philly specifically? Wait, you want to meet Ben Franklin!" he grinned at her.

"He might not even be in town," she said fidgeting with her vest.

"She idolizes him," he said to Thomas.

"I wouldn't say *that.* I wrote a paper about him in school, that's all. He was a great man."

"Uh huh. Well if he's not there, we can at least buy one of his newspapers. Didn't he own one?"

"Yes, he did. The Gazette," she gave up smoothing the vest any further.

"So, what's the plan?" Jack asked.

"Thomas can drop us off outside of town, and I thought we could just walk in."

"I'm not in the mood for a hike," Jack said. "And we don't know how far we have to go for a paper machine - or - *boy* or whatever."

"Thomas, do you know where The Gazette offices are?" Bonnie asked.

"Of course," he scoffed. "I can land you on the *roof* if you want."

"I was thinking more along the lines of a park," she said, "or a vacant lot. Is there one close by?"

"Isn't that a little conspicuous?" Jack said.

"Look," she pointed at the main display which showed the edge of daylight. "It's just before dawn. We can drop in before anybody sees us."

"That's fine for getting *in*, but how do we get *out*? This sounds like fun, but I don't really want to spend all day walking," Jack said.

"Hmmm. We could buy some horses!" she said.

"No, no horses," Jack said.

"Come on, Jack. That was a fluke. The odds of that happening again are a million to one."

"I feel I'm missing a very tedious but endearing tale of Jack falling off a horse. Is there any way to avoid you telling it?" Thomas said.

"We were at the Grand Canyon..." Bonnie began.

"Apparently not," Thomas muttered.

"...just after we got married. We signed up for one of those horseback tours. You know what I mean? Anyway, we got these horses, and the guide started us up the trail, and my horse tried to *mount* Jack's horse. Apparently, she was in season and anyway the boy horse..."

"Stallion," Thomas offered.

"Yes, thank you, the *stallion* threw me. I landed okay, but Jack got caught in the stirrups, sprained his ankle, and broke his wrist when he hit the ground."

"The mare bit me too," Jack said. "I haven't been on one of those damn things since, and I don't want to start now."

"Well, it's either that or spend the night - with the bedbugs - and no bathrooms," she said.

"Okay, we can buy some damn horses! Thomas, do we have enough money for that?"

"I gave you enough money to buy the entire stable if you need to, but do some haggling. It's expected."

Jack pulled out the gold coins. "Are these even the right kind? They're English."

"Of course they're correct," Thomas said. "The U.S. didn't mint coins until 1792. Get ready. I found a vacant lot about a block from the newspaper office."

Bonnie and Jack waited by the gangway as it rotated out. It wasn't completely dark. The first bit of sunrise was already lighting the eastern sky.

"Oh God, what's that smell?" Jack said as he descended the ramp behind Bonnie.

"Oh, I forgot to mention," Thomas said. The vacant lot I found - is the stables at the edge of town. The newspaper office is about a mile and a half to the east. Have fun Jack!" he lifted off silently and sped away, but Jack could still hear him laughing in his ear.

The horses, spooked by Thomas's descent, were beginning to come back in their direction.

"Don't worry. I'm sure they're friendly," Bonnie winced when she realized how it sounded.

"Let's hope they're not *too* friendly, though, right Jack?" Thomas's avatar laughed.

"So we can't get rid of you even off the ship?"

"Hey, I'm just here to help, Jack. You're doing great by the way," Thomas said.

Jack helped Bonnie over the fence that separated the pen from the rear yard of the stables. After he jumped down, he saw a small boy of about ten staring at them.

"Hello!" Bonnie said beaming her warmest smile. "We're a little lost. Do you think you could tell us where the stable is?"

The boy looked confused but recovered enough to finish fastening the strap of his overalls as the outhouse door closed with a bang. "*This* is the stable."

"Oh, wonderful," she began, but Jack interrupted her.

"Terrific kid," he said. "You wouldn't happen to know what year it is would you?"

"Jack, you might try to limit the colloquialisms while you're here," Thomas said. "I think you just called him a frightened goat."

The boy looked even more confused, "ye know not the year?"

"Never mind, can we buy a couple horses? Who do we see about that?" Jack said.

"Ye wish to buy horses? On *Sunday*?" he said examining their immaculate clothing.

Bonnie and Jack traded glances.

"Well, normally we wouldn't violate the Sabbath like that," Bonnie said.

"But our horses," Jack said looking back the way they came. "Our horses ran off. And we need to get to - church."

"Would you not rather catch your *own* horses?" the boy asked.

"I think maybe they were also sick - they may have died, in fact," Jack said. "Wolves - probably got them. Because that's what they do when animals are sick. They eat them." He curled his fingers to look like claws.

"Ah! Ye jest!" the boy said relieved.

"Yes," Bonnie laughed. "He's quite the jester. We only need to *borrow* a pair of horses so that we may catch our own. Could we speak to your father about that?"

"Of course. He's at breakfast. I'll fetch him," he ran off toward a small house.

"Wolves?" Bonnie whispered.

"I was improvising," Jack said. "Do you think he heard us talking before?"

"Maybe. What did we say?"

"Something about friendly horses," Jack said, "and getting rid of Thomas while off the ship. That's okay he'll just assume we meant sailing ships. Are there ships in Philly?"

"Yes, the Delaware goes right through the city," Bonnie said.

Thomas was watching from above and interrupted, "uh oh. Here comes dad and he's loading a pistol. I don't think he wants to sell us any horses today."

They took off at a run in the opposite direction toward a narrow space between the barn and the building next door.

"Can you distract him, Thomas?" Jack called as they ran.

A blue beam of light as wide as a house shot down from the sky, illuminating a startled, overweight man. He dropped his pistol and shielded his eyes while trying to see what the source of the light was."

That gave Bonnie and Jack enough time to get to the street which was still empty at that hour. They slowed to a walk and turned at the first corner in case the stable master still wanted to give chase after his close encounter.

"Thanks, Thomas," Bonnie said. "You finally got to use your laser. How did it feel?"

"Not very satisfying. That was minimal power and wide beam, so I didn't get to melt anything."

"Why did he come after us with a gun?" Bonnie asked.

"He must think we're British spies," Jack said catching his breath. "That means the war isn't over."

"That's not good," Bonnie said. "But it doesn't change the mission. We still don't know the date - except that it's Sunday. Hmm, that means the paper will be closed. I have an idea: They posted announcements at the town square in these days, right? We just need to get there and see what's on the board. There has to be something with a date."

"Even just the year will be a big help," Thomas said.

They made their way zig-zagging through the back streets as the sun came up. The few people they encountered seemed too busy with their morning chores to pay any attention to the strangers. As they reached Market Street, the traffic increased, and they saw men on horseback, simple open buggies, and even a closed carriage driven by a well-dressed servant. Bonnie loved all the sights and sounds, but Jack was getting more nervous by the minute.

"You know they shot spies back then - I mean back - now," he turned to look behind them, as he had every thirty seconds since entering the busy street.

Bonnie tugged on his arm, and he turned to see what had her attention. It was a bookstore with a few titles on display in the window. She found what she was looking for and pointed. It said **BICKERSTAFF'S BOSTON ALMANAC For the Year of our Redemption 1778**. "Bingo," she said beaming.

"Perfect!" Jack added sarcastically, "Nice work Thomas. You were only off by *four years*."

"Hey, that's actually pretty good accuracy for this technology. Now get back here and let's get going."

"Can't be too soon for me. I think I'm getting dysentery and cholera, just walking around," Jack said.

A group of soldiers turned onto the street and began walking away from them toward one of the churches.

"Not to mention lead poisoning," he added. "Let's not go back the way we came. Thomas, is there anything out of sight ahead of us?"

"Not for quite a way but if you turn right, the northern edge of town is closer."

"How far?" Bonnie asked.

"About three miles."

Jack groaned. "These new boots are stiff - and a little on the small side."

"That's funny. Mine are really soft and fit perfectly."

Thomas snorted stifling a laugh.

"We could steal horses," she said.

"These people ride horses every day. I think even the worst of them catch us pretty easily." Jack was scanning the street for something. "Thomas, what does a taxi look like in 1778?"

"They're called Hansom cabs," he said. "They have two large spoked wheels, and the driver rides behind and above the passengers."

Jack snapped his finger and pointed to one across the street. They dodged the buggies and riders on their way to church and made it to the other side.

The driver greeted them as they approached. "Good morning!" he tipped his hat to Bonnie, and she giggled.

"Good morning," Jack said. "My wife and I would like to go for a walk in the countryside on this beautiful day. How far north can you take us for..." he fished in his pocket and brought out a gold coin. "...this much?"

The driver's eyes went wide at the sight of it, "You have me for the day, sir! Climb aboard!"

Jack gave him the coin, unsure of the protocol. He helped Bonnie up onto the bench seat. As soon as Jack stepped up, the driver cracked his whip, and the horse began a quick trot. At the corner, he turned and picked up the pace nearly running over a group of women dressed for church. After several miles, they stopped where the cobblestones ended, marking the edge of town. It seemed more like the edge of *civilization.* Behind them were streets lined with shops while in front of them - nothing but the rolling hills of farmland. To call what lay in front of them a dirt road would have been generous. Clumps of grass grew between the muddy ruts, and they realized how ridiculous their story of *taking a stroll in the countryside* must have sounded to the driver. Jack jumped off and helped Bonnie down.

"Shall I wait for you here?" the driver asked.

"Um," Jack made a show of looking around and seemed to come to a decision. "No, I think we'll walk back into town. You know, when we're done. Walking - in the country - just for fun. Got to get our exercise, you know!"

Thomas was roaring with laughter at this, but the driver's face betrayed no indication that this was in any way unusual.

"Well then, I'll bid you good day," he said and turned the cab around.

They watched him go before heading up the small hill.

"Uh oh," Thomas said again as they reached the top.

"What is it now?" Jack said.

"Half a dozen soldiers. Behind you, riding fast."

"How about another distraction Thomas?" Bonnie said as they tried to run on the uneven ground.

"This tree offends me!" Thomas laughed, "I smite it from heaven!"

He fired his laser at the base of a tree beside the road. The lowest part of the trunk exploded as the water inside flashed to steam. The tree came crashing down in front of the soldiers. Their horses scattered in panic. Before they could calm them, Thomas lowered himself to the ground on the other side of the hill. He came in so quickly that Bonnie and Jack ducked reflexively. They got aboard, and Thomas shot back up into the clouds before the soldiers saw them.

Thomas tried to talk them into staying in costume but Bonnie was firm, and Jack threatened to just go around naked, so he gave in and returned their clothes.

"Did you find the cylinder?" Bonnie asked as she pulled her shoes on.

"I did. It looks the same as last time. No sign of aliens. It's just floating along out there."

"Okay," she said. "Let's think this through. We'll have to go farther back and maybe again and again. At some point, the *pull-over-and-ask* approach won't even be a possibility. We need something more elegant. Can't you tell by the position of the stars, Thomas?"

"Yes, but not to the accuracy we need. The constellations relative to Earth's position around the sun will tell us the day of the year but not the year itself. The things in the asteroid belt orbit the sun every four and a half years. So, to limit our search to even a quarter of the belt - which is still a huge area - we would need the exact year at the very least."

"Why don't we just jump one year at a time?" Jack said. "It can't move that far in a year."

"Backward jumps are more accurate at *large* intervals. We only got ninety-eight percent at one hundred year increments. With shorter spans of time, it's far worse. We might jump five years and then a single month. And let's not forget that even if we know *approximately* where it is, that's still a huge amount of space to search."

Jack snapped his fingers, "Halley's Comet! That's a regular event! We just look for that."

"Is he even listening?" Thomas complained. "*Accuracy*, Jack. We could easily miss it, and it's only visible as it gets close to the sun."

"No, I think he's on to something," Bonnie said. "The Earth's position against the constellations tell us the day of the year. But, what about the Earth relative to the other *planets?* They all have different orbital periods, so their positions relative to each other is like a fingerprint for the year, right?"

"Of course! That's brilliant! The part about the planets not the part about the comet. That was ridiculous. It'll take a few hours to find all the planets, but then we'll know exactly what year it is! I don't know why I didn't think of it before."

"I do," Jack said, and it was Thomas's turn to make a rude gesture which Jack gladly returned.

"I never had to do it like this before. I always knew what time it was. Even when my clocks drifted, I could resynchronize with Earth's satellites."

"We should do the same thing then," she said. "Thomas, can you make a clock that will work for thousands of years?"

"Of course," he said. "That's well beyond the level of technology Humans ever achieved, but I'm such a finely tuned..."

She interrupted him, "We can jump back a ridiculous amount like ten thousand years, fix our time using the planets and the stars, and drop off a clock-buoy. You know, just something to tell us what day it is as we keep jumping forward."

The Stitcher hummed to life, and Thomas laid out his plan to drop off the clock in the same orbit as Earth, but on the opposite side of the sun. That would make it easy to find each time. It would stay silent until it received Thomas's ping and reply with the exact time and date.

When the Stitcher finished, a spiderbot pulled out a silver ball with four straight, slender antennas.

"Sputnik, Thomas?" Jack rolled his eyes.

"Hey, it's a classic design!" Thomas said.

The star field changed slightly, and Bonnie aimed the wormhole drive to a point in Earth's orbit on the opposite side of the sun and jumped.

"Testing ping," Thomas said.

Jack and Bonnie watched as the main display showed the correct year, 1778.

"Very good," Thomas said. "Test ping successful. Here go ten thousand years. Say goodbye to civilization. Oh! That's interesting! Jumping now."

The display immediately showed -8111. Jack and Bonnie saw the change and looked at each other puzzled.

"I thought it would take a while to find all the planets," Jack said.

Before Thomas could explain, Bonnie interjected, "Ah, I get it! The buoy you just made back in 1778 was there for the test ping - *but so was the one we're about to drop off!* I bet it gave you a complete history of all the pings it had received along with dates, didn't it? So, you knew we would miss the target by a hundred and eleven years and only get to 8111 BCE."

"Exactly! Well done, Bonnie," Thomas said. "Even I didn't expect that. Well, I guess we know the buoy will last ten thousand years. Now, that's workmanship for you! And the planets are exactly where they should be for 8111 BCE, so the date checks out."

"Wait, that's two thousand years off!" Jack said. "Shouldn't it be 10,000 BC. I thought you said it was more accurate at longer jumps?"

Thomas sighed heavily. "Jack, it's only off by about a hundred years. I'll go slowly for you. 1778 minus ten-thousand would have been 8222 BC*E*. That's simple arithmetic. I guess you don't have enough fingers and toes to do that one. I can give you some more if you get back in the Med-Bay. 8222 BCE was the target, and we got to 8111 BCE which means we only missed it by one hundred-eleven years. That's ninety-nine percent accuracy, monkey-boy!"

The spiderbots pushed Sputnik into the airlock drawer and closed it without ceremony.

"Uh, hey guys," Bonnie said. "The belt is - gone."

She was looking at a display of the solar system which showed all the planets in their proper orbits. Instead of the smear of asteroids in a ring between Mars and Jupiter, there was empty space.

"What do you mean gone?" Jack said.

"Look! It should be all through here." She traced a finger where the belt should be. "It's just empty now."

"Oh! This is brilliant!" Thomas said in awe. "It's not empty. It's *Phaeton*! The mythical planetoid!"

The display shifted and zoomed in on the region where the belt should be. The image resolved to show a dark planetoid, with a bright crescent on the sunward side.

"Another planet?" she asked.

"Not as mythical as we were led to believe," Thomas said. "The idea began in the nineteenth century and was thoroughly discredited by the twentieth..."

"Do you really know all this stuff or are you just reading it from a file?" Jack said.

"What's the difference?" Thomas said nonplussed, "As I was saying, it shouldn't exist. It was never more than wild stories about it getting smashed to bits by various improbable things. The composition of the left-overs is all wrong, and none of the models could explain how a single body, could explode into that many pieces and form a belt without first collapsing back onto itself. But, there it is! You know what this means? This means I get to name it after myself!"

"I don't think that's how it works," Jack said.

"This suddenly seems more dangerous. Doesn't it?" Bonnie said. "Whatever left the cylinder, also destroyed an entire planet."

"Planet-*oid*," Thomas corrected. "And we don't know that, but I admit it does seem a bit of a coincidence."

"What could blow up an entire planet?" Jack asked.

"*Oid.* Planet-*oid.* And blowing up things isn't really that hard. You just park close to the sun and use its energy to make a bit of antimatter, toss it toward the planetoid and hey-presto! The trick, in this case, would be getting a nice even ring-shaped dispersal."

"Given this a bit of thought, have you?" Jack said.

"From time to time, as purely an academic exercise of course," he said

"Right," Jack whispered to Bonnie, "psychopath."

Chapter Twenty-Seven

8111 BCE - Planetoid

"So, what's going on down there?" Jack asked.

They were seated at the main display which showed the three panels with an overhead view of the solar system in the center, flanked by a view of Phaeton on the right and Earth on the left. Below the image of the solar system, the current date displayed -8111.

"Nothing. It's just a dead rock," Thomas said.

"No, I mean on Earth." He pointed at the display. "Shouldn't we go have a look. You know, document it for science."

"What's the mystery? A bunch of farmers and goat herders, always two meals away from starvation." Thomas said. "I doubt they're much in the way of good conversation."

"Try and stay on-task Jack," Bonnie said. "It's all fascinating, and I'd love to investigate every bit of it. But right now, we're here for a specific reason, and more sight-seeing isn't on the agenda."

"Well, let's get on with it then." he said, "Thomas, jump forward a few centuries and let's watch the show."

Thomas had been about to do just that but chafed at getting orders from Jack and just smirked at him.

"We shouldn't just jump around at random," Bonnie said ignoring them. "Let's do a binary search. We're looking for an event between two dates, so we cut the numerical range in half each time. The first range is now ten-thousand years wide, so we jump to the five-thousand-year mark. If nothing changes, the event is in the latter half. If it's already happened and we missed it, we search the previous half. Either way, the new range is five thousand years, and we keep repeating, cutting the search range in half every time. So, let's see, ten-thousand is somewhere between two to the thirteenth power and two to the fourteenth power so fourteen jumps at most should get us within a single year. After that, we'll just have to watch and wait."

Jack looked stunned at this. Bonnie was always intelligent but showed no interest in math at all.

"What happened to you while I was gone?"

Thomas smiled and crossed his arms. "I fixed her. She's at least twice as smart as you now. I also got rid of some of that credulous nonsense. Does that intimidate you, Jack? It should." He morphed his avatar into Sigmund Freud seated in an old armchair smoking a pipe. "How does that make you feel?" he flipped to a new page in his notebook and puffed on the pipe.

"It doesn't *intimidate* me. I'm just surprised. That's all."

"The subject is in a state of denial," Thomas muttered and scribbled on the notepad.

"Thomas," Bonnie said, and he changed to his Naval Officer image, gestured at the main display and jumped five thousand years. The center display showed -3120, and the planets moved, but Phaeton showed no change. He repeated, trying for a twenty-five-hundred-year jump. This time, the display showed -631 and Phaeton was there, but much smaller and two trails of rocks were tumbling away from it. The sunward group was in front of the planetoid's direction of orbit, and the other trailed behind it into a higher and therefore slower orbit.

"That's new," Jack said. "What's going on?"

The display changed magnification several times, and the cloud of rocks at the rear of what used to be Phaeton occasionally parted enough to reveal an enormous machine biting into the planetoid. Behind the machine, a huge frame supported a familiar cylinder of metal.

"It's eating the planet," Jack whispered.

"*Oid*," Thomas said. "Planetoid."

"And, pooping the cylinder out the back," Bonnie said.

"They're mining it for metals," Thomas said.

"Are there *aliens* down there…right now?" Jack said.

"How should I know, Jack?" Thomas retorted.

"Don't you have scanners and sensors and crap like that?"

I see what *you* see, Jack. Feel free to go down and see for yourself. I can toss you out an airlock if you want."

"Thomas," Bonnie said with calm patience. "I know you have more than just the image sensors on the hull."

"Yes, but the sensors only do one millimeter at a time. It takes forever, and it's hard to find animals because they keep moving."

"You know, for a spaceship, you're pretty disappointing," Jack said, and they exchanged middle fingers again.

"Okay, how about this," Bonnie said. "Thomas, you make a camera and drop it in the same orbit but far enough back that they won't notice it. We'll jump forward a few years, review the video, and maybe we'll get to see which direction they go when they leave."

"Good idea," Thomas said, and the Stitcher began humming.

"*Yeah*, it's a good idea," Jack retorted. "Why didn't *you* think of it? She must be even smarter than you are. How does that make *you* feel?"

"Oh, piss off, Jack," Thomas said.

Chapter Twenty-Eight

631 BCE - Penguin Teeth

Thomas tried to jump forward twenty years but only went ten, and the display changed to -621. He pinged the spy camera, and it responded with all the video data it had collected over the intervening years. It was a staggering amount of data by human terms, but Thomas scanned it quickly.

"Aha!" he displayed an image on the main screen.

"What is that?" Jack asked.

"That, my dear fellow, is an alien ship. We didn't see it before because it was on the other side of the mining operation."

The display showed a white football shaped ship with dark lines that ran from tip to tip giving it a ribbed appearance. As they watched the video playback, Thomas displayed another ship much larger than the first.

"This one approached slowly enough that the first one was able to prepare a defense. He's decelerating, so it's clear he's going to stop. The smaller one is building this laser cannon." Thomas zoomed in to show a silver cylinder with a transparent cap on one end.

"How do you know it's a laser cannon? It looks like a telescope to me," Bonnie said.

Thomas sighed, "I've already reviewed it all. This is just drama for your benefit."

"Oh, right," she said and added a half-hearted, "thanks?"

"Watch this. It gets good here," he scrubbed forward until the laser cannon's construction was completed and the second ship was closer.

"Pew-Pew," Thomas said adding sound effects as the cannon fired. The attacking ship's engines stopped. Gas and small objects flew out of holes in the melted hull.

"Huh," Jack said. "I guess I expected it to explode or something dramatic."

"Now, watch this area right here," Thomas said circling the display with a long wooden pointer.

Beside the damaged ship, a dark void was occluding the light of the stars behind it. A piece of debris floated into the frame and disappeared briefly as it passed behind the void.

"A cloaked second ship?" Bonnie asked.

"Wait for it," Thomas said as the void dissolved revealing a new ship.

The defender and the newly de-cloaked ship fired lasers at each other simultaneously, and the attacker exploded leaving the smaller defender undamaged. A moment later a slightly curved white cylinder resembling an elephant tusk exited the remaining ship. It drifted away with no apparent thrust of its own.

"And the next twenty minutes are tedious. Skipping over that," Thomas scrubbed forward again.

The original ship exploded with far more force than either of the attackers. It destroyed what was left of Phaeton and sent the cylinder of refined metal tumbling away.

"So, what was that thing that came out just before the ship exploded?" Bonnie asked.

"Only one way to find out," Thomas shifted the display to show the strange object just outside his hull. "I took us over while you were watching the show."

Three spiderbots drifted into view, grasped it, and fired their thruster backpacks until they were out of view of the camera. A moment later, a much larger airlock drawer on the opposite side of the room opened with a *pop*, and the object rolled out onto the floor. It was the size of a refrigerator but cylindrical in shape. It had a smooth white surface, tapered at one end and slightly curved giving it the appearance of an elephant tusk but longer and much thicker.

"What is it? A torpedo?" Jack asked.

The spiderbots were busy poking and prying when it made a popping sound and split in half along the long axis. Inside was a small creature about three feet long. It had a bird-like head, beak, and webbed feet. The beak, head, shoulders, and back were deep black, contrasted by a bright white chest. It wore a belt of braided metal chain which looked purely decorative.

"A penguin?" Jack said.

"No look at the arms," Bonnie said. "And penguins don't have teeth. It looks more like a weasel."

Its feet were webbed and tipped with claws like a penguin, but on its upper torso where a penguin would have flippers, it had long arms tipped with *hands* much like an otter or weasel but with opposable thumbs. It yawned showing its fangs more prominently and slowly opened its large blue eyes which dominated a kind-looking, intelligent face.

"Peng-weasel," Jack said.

"Aww. It's so cute!" Bonnie said.

"Hello," Jack shouted at it slowly. "Can you un-der-stand me?"

Bonnie rolled her eyes, and Thomas's avatar was about to say something when it froze. One of the spiderbots had a leg on the pod's control panel, and it also froze for a moment.

"Whoa!" Thomas said. "That was intense!"

He made some staccato clicking noises, and the alien responded by sitting up. It looked at each of them, blinked, and said something to Thomas's avatar using the same chittering language.

"He can see you?" Bonnie said surprised.

Thomas and the alien had a brief exchange, and it climbed out of the pod. It was short, only about waist high. Bonnie knelt to its level and smiled widely. It imitated by baring its pointed teeth. Thomas said something, and it stopped smiling and bowed instead.

"I told her that baring your teeth is called *smiling* and it's not really an aggressive thing. I think she believed me, but it's hard to tell."

"She?" Jack asked.

"Yes, this is a female. The males are larger and have a reddish throat."

"What's her name?" Bonnie asked.

"Well, that's where it gets sticky. They don't really use names. Her mother is the only one of her species who ever spoke to her in the presence of others, and she just called her *Youngest*."

"That's not possible. You can't have a civilization without proper names, and clearly, she comes from an advanced civilization." Bonnie argued.

"I would have thought so too, but no. It's an interesting story. Would you like to hear it?" He didn't wait for the response and began in a kindergarten-story-time voice. "Once upon a time, there was a world..."

"Ahh! You're not doing this for the whole story, are you?" Jack complained, but Thomas ignored him and began again. The alien made a pleasant sound like a giggle and rapidly patted her hands against her sides in delight. She sat on the floor to hear the story as Thomas simultaneously delivered it to her in clicks and hums.

Chapter Twenty-Nine

2216 - Shake Down Cruise

"I christen you..." Chris paused and thought for a moment, "...Gillian, I guess," she reached out of the shuttle bay doors into open space and struck Gillian's outer hull with the champagne bottle.

"Happy birthday!" Doug shouted from inside his spacesuit, and the others chimed in.

They were all suited and standing beside the open outer doors of the shuttle bay. Gillian wouldn't allow them outside, so Chris had to lean out with one arm to do the christening.

"I was actually born two hundred years ago, but thank you, Doug," Gillian said.

Virtual fluted glasses full of virtual champagne appeared in their hands.

"To Gillian," Brad said, and they clinked fake glasses but drank *real* champagne from their in-suit reservoirs using a plastic tube which hovered near their mouths.

"Okay, can I close the doors now?" Gillian pleaded.

"I was hoping we could take the Falcon out," Doug said, "You know, a shakedown cruise - make sure everything works."

They felt a shudder through their boots as the massive outer hull doors began to close.

"One shakedown cruise at a time," Gillian said. "We'll check out your *dingy* after my tests are finished."

"Did you decide on a destination, Gillian?" M asked as they began the long walk back to the airlock.

"Mars. I always wanted to go," she said.

"Awesome! Ready to walk on Mars, Brad?" Doug said.

"Absolutely!" Brad replied.

"So, Gillian, you said you were born two hundred years ago," Chris said. "How does that work? I though Reggie created you last week."

"I was human and had a full life. At the end, Reggie offered to scan my brain. I remember saying yes, but who knows. Maybe I said no, and he changed that memory. Anyway, it doesn't matter. I'm here, and I'm glad to be alive again."

"Wow, I had no idea that was an option," Chris said, and the others exchanged shocked glances. Only M seemed nonplussed.

Gillian waited until they passed through the airlock, removed their suits and returned to the command deck before moving away from the metallic asteroid.

"The standard Charmer passes all tests," Gillian said as they got farther away. "Ready to engage the wormhole drive. Who wants to do the honors?"

"I did it once already," Doug said. "Brad, how about you?"

"You bet your ass, I do," Brad said and selected the destination using his internal HUD. He used a virtual hand to select a spot just outside the orbit of Mars's moons. "How about there?"

"That looks fine," Gillian said.

"Oh wait! Can we do go-no-go for launch?" Chris said and, M looked confused.

"It's a thing they used to do in the early days," Chris explained.

Gillian changed the room to look like a 1960's NASA launch control room.

The virtual characters were intently monitoring their stations, and occasionally one made an adjustment to the knobs and sliders.

"I need a go-no-go for launch," Brad said, and Doug giggled.

Gillian ran through the long checklist, and even M joined in with the chant of "Go!" with each system.

BOOSTER... Go!

RETRO... Go!

FIDO... Go!

GUIDANCE... Go!

SURGEON... Go!

EECOM... Go!

GNC... Go!

TELMU... Go!

CONTROL... Go!

PROCEDURES... Go!

INCO... Go!

FAO... Go!

NETWORK... Go!

RECOVERY... Go!

CAPCOM... Go!

When the last *Go* faded, Brad said, "We're Go for launch," and tapped the engage icon.

Mars filled the viewport. Chris and Doug leapt out of their seats and began jumping and cheering. M was more reserved and leaned over to kiss Brad, "well done."

After they had settled down, Gillian reported that, as expected, there were no significant system failures.

"Does this mean we can go down to the surface?" Chris gasped and squeezed Doug's hand.

Gillian paused before answering, "There's nothing down there but red dust you know."

"I don't care. It an alien planet!" she shouted.

"All right you can go, but I'll fly the Falcon remotely. Human brains aren't capable of running a Charm Drive. One of my monkeybots will have to go as my proxy. And you all have to be suited for the entire trip."

Brad couldn't stop smiling, and Chris was almost breaking Doug's hand.

"A quick trip!" Gillian said, "nothing fancy. Walk around a little, kick the dirt, and right back here. Got it?"

M rose, and they all ran for the elevator. At the shuttle bay, they were met by a much larger monkeybot wearing a bandolier.

"Chewbacca!" Doug and Chis shouted.

"I thought it was appropriate," Gillian said. "He does actually have to fly the thing."

"We should have left these things on," M complained as they tried to don their spacesuits as quickly as possible. "We just took them off five minutes ago."

At the Falcon, they entered using the ramp, and it closed automatically. Gillian ran a final pressure check and opened the outer doors. Her monkeybot pretended to manipulate controls from his seat at Doug's right, and Doug began to do the same.

"Hey," Doug said suddenly nervous, "these controls don't really do anything, right?"

"This only occurs to you after fiddling with *all* of them?" Chris said.

"Don't worry about the controls," Gillian said. "They're just props."

Doug relaxed and shouted, "Chewie get us outa here!"

The Falcon lifted off, slewed toward the open doors and slipped out. Once clear of Gillian, they changed course again and headed for the red planet. Within thirty minutes it was close enough to completely fill their view. Gillian changed their angle of attack, and the curve of the Martian horizon appeared in front of them. They swept past hills and craters of all sizes as their destination appeared above the horizon.

"Olympus Mons," Brad whispered.

"Hmm?" M said.

"It's the largest volcano in the solar system," he said, "I used to be crazy about Mars when I was a kid."

"Oh, you *used to be*. Yeah. I can see that," she grinned.

Gillian took them close to the slope, pulled up, and landed on a reasonably flat spot. Doug was out of his seat before they had come to a complete stop. He was bouncing with excitement as they waited for the ramp to deploy.

"You should go first," Doug said to Brad who didn't need to be told twice. He trotted down the ramp and felt the reduced gravity. The others followed, and they all began jumping as if it were a competition to see who could reach the highest altitude. It finally stopped when Brad rotated a bit too much and landed on his face nearly cracking his helmet. They stood silently panting and stared at the horizon.

Chapter Thirty

631 BCE - Peng-Weasel History

Once upon a time, there was a world completely covered by water. All of the life on the entire planet existed in the layers of varying darkness and pressures. The plankton at the surface were eaten by small fish who were in turn preyed upon by larger species and so on into the dark depths. Each species had evolved to live within a specific pressure range, and each could venture no farther. A clever species would evolve from time to time, and some developed complex languages but none had ever invented any tools. There simply wasn't enough time in the water epochs punctuated by ice extinctions. These extinctions happened every two hundred million years as the water planet's system was visited by a large comet. Unlike most comets, this one had an orbit in the same plane as the planets. So, when it came, it left enough material on each pass to dim the sun's warmth and freeze the ocean. All creatures great and small perished as the ocean froze solid. In the fullness of time, the sun once again shone brightly on the icy surface, and the long spring announced the age of renewal once again.

Jack rolled his eyes and groaned at this flowery prose, and Thomas extended a middle finger at him. The alien saw this and imitated with one of its own digits at Jack. Thomas smiled and continued.

The first seven epochs generated only plants and plankton beside the tenacious bacteria which always survived the extinctions. Each time the plankton evolved a bit more resistance to the dim light that killed the previous iterations. Until on the eighth epoch, one species survived the entire long night. It could live on the surface of the ice in the dimmest of light and fell dormant for the worst of the darkness. Soon, this one species became many through the countless eons afterward. Night would come as it had before but the ice was no longer a craggy white blanket. In its place was a tapestry of green in a variety of forms. Some had evolved the ability to move in the first puddles of the melting, taking advantage of nutrients trapped in the ice. These tiny drifting plants quickly developed ways to move as they pleased and became the first animals and although these lost their battle against the extinctions, each time they were reborn in the long epochs and each time their rebirth was a little quicker. After countless such cycles, a single species managed to survive the freezing, shed bits of itself into tiny floating plants, enter a larval stage and emerge as the simplest of marine animals. The previous pattern repeated, and soon there were dozens of species that could do the same. But there simply wasn't enough information in the DNA molecule to go all the way from algae to phytoplankton, to zooplankton, to fish all in one species. So, each time, the many species that developed from those beginnings into a panoply of larger aquatic life would all die off, leaving only the green algae for the next cycle.

The next event that marked a turning point in the planet's catalog of life was a very simple adaptation. A species of whale-analogs had gills, not lungs, which marked them as fish but in every other way, resembled the whales of Earth. They swam near the surface, filtered the water for the plankton they ate, moved in groups, and even communicated. They were so successful, during their epoch, that they dominated the entire planet. This was not the remarkable part, however. There had been many successful large species in previous cycles. The singularly important trait that evolved in the whales was their low-density bones which helped them stay near the surface. These enormous creatures were the first to leave behind any remnant on the surface of the water. They were so numerous that when the next freeze came, the equator was covered with floating bones of various sizes pushed there by the advancing ice. Some were crushed but most, owing to their cylindrical shape, were simply pushed to the top of the ice, where they remained to once again float on the liquid seas at the next melt.

The first species to take advantage of this bounty were the penguins. They weren't actually penguins of course but occupied the same ecological niche and so, therefore resembled their cousins from Earth. Their heads, backs, and sides were black to absorb the sunlight and warm them quickly after a frigid swim. Their undersides were white to camouflage them from predators peering up at the bright surface. Two things marked them as distinct from terrestrial penguins. They had teeth, and very different appendages. Gone were the comical flippers, replaced by slender arms tipped with fingers perfect for tool making. The first of these tools were simply broken pieces of whalebone which they used to kill fish. Soon they learned to tie larger pieces together, and boat-building became an integral part of their lives. The Penguins of this world were solitary creatures who developed language for the sole purpose of taunting each other from their whale-bone boats which they used as status symbols and to attack each other. From time to time, through the early centuries of boat-building, smalls groups would form and experiment with social structures. Inevitably, one individual would betray the others, and the survivors would disperse into solitary life once more. Cooperation simply wasn't in their nature. Food was plentiful enough and the only thing worth fighting for, besides attractive breeding partners, was the rarest of things on a water planet - metal. Like all planets, this one received a constant bounty of meteors, large and small, which fell upon the vast oceans only to quickly sink to the bottom. But sometimes, and rarely, it would fall onto the shrinking ice. In the epoch of the Penguins, it was gathered up before the last of the ice retreated. Great care had to be taken when moving a stolen treasure of metal from a vanquished enemy vessel. Too much in one, would sink it, so the boats were usually combined. But the increased size carried with it two disadvantages. They were slower, and their size advertised their heavy, valuable, cargo.

This pirate-style warfare of the Penguins continued unchanged for a thousand years of the long summer before an especially clever individual designed his boat with a free-floating vertical tube at the center which allowed him to adjust buoyancy. He kept the tube filled with water and in its high and locked position which made the boat ride low in the water. The visible portion, above the surface, resembled the tiny vessels used by the young and inexperienced males. His tactics were simple. He would wait for another vessel, usually a younger opponent, to approach, release the tube causing his boat to rise to twice its previous height and use this advantage to defeat the less experienced opponent. Usually, this involved threats and occasionally a thrown spear, but rarely bloodshed. A typical craft was ringed by downward-facing spears which prevented a swimmer from climbing aboard. So, once in the water, without a rope ladder, his opponent's own security measures would prevent him from climbing back aboard.

One day this clever penguin spotted a small boat on the horizon. *Easy prey* he thought and adjusted his sails. The sails of tightly woven seaweed vines did the job well enough, but they were heavy, and his modified boat meant he would probably not be fast enough to catch the smaller vessel. To his surprise, he made good progress and soon realized his opponent was not moving. This sometimes happened when an individual was asleep, ill, or even better, dead. As soon as he was within shouting distance, he tried a few insults but got no reply. His boat was still in its low profile so the two vessels were at the same height above the water which meant he could not see the deck of the other boat. With the heavy ballast tube released, his boat rose quickly. He scrambled back to the side and looked down to see a young individual lying motionless. *Injured?* He thought and hurried to drop his rope ladder over the side. He climbed down, jumped the last bit of distance, and ran to the motionless form. As he got close, she rolled over revealing a crossbow. *A female in a boat! Is that a weapon? It looks like metal!* She aimed for his chest but missed her target and struck his upper arm instead. He was on her in seconds. At nearly twice her size, he easily lifted her with his good arm and threw her overboard. He sat down to rest and swore as he pulled the bolt from his arm. *What is that thing?* He thought looking at the crossbow lying on the deck at his feet. *And what is a female doing on a boat? This one is very unusual. She even seemed amused as I threw her overboard! Who understood females? They are strange creatures. I suppose mating with her is out of the question now.* A spell of dizziness shook him as he stood to look over the side. Some of his other victims had loitered in the area afterward. *Would a female?* While he was pondering the inner workings of the female mind, she was swimming under her boat where she untied a second crossbow from its hiding place on the keel. Next to the spare crossbow, was the entrance to the diving tube she had invented. It gave her access to the water without jumping over the side as the males did. She pulled away the netting that disguised her tunnel, swam up the short distance and climbed out of the water onto the lower deck. She glanced at her small pile of metal and hurried up the steps to the main deck. He was leaning over the side, and his arm was bleeding profusely yet he seemed unconcerned. Giving up his search, he turned around to find her aiming another weapon at him.

"Over the side," she ordered.

"I am injured. You would have me die?"

"I will kill you now if you prefer," she waved the crossbow at his chest.

"Let me return to my boat at least," he pleaded.

"No! It is rightfully mine. You attacked me, and I won! Those are the rules. Over the side!"

"He slumped into the posture of the defeated, which he had seen so many times from his own victims. He was about to climb over the side when she stopped him.

"Wait! Show me how you did that with your boat first."

"I will *not!* You have beaten me, but you do not own me!"

"A trade then," she suggested. "Show me, and I will give you one of my boats," she gestured at the larger boat.

"That is *my* boat!" he shouted.

She tilted her head to the side in a strange gesture he had never seen before although he didn't have a great deal of experience to draw from. In fact, this was the longest exchange he had had since leaving his mother. His victims usually just complied and jumped over without much whimpering and certainly no *conversation.*

"All my metal!" He complained and stole a look at his boat. "I should let you use that thing and just throw you over again!" *How did she get back aboard?*

She took a step closer. "At this distance, I will *not* miss."

But he was not listening. The blood loss and arguing had made him dizzy. He was still trying to process his last thought. As he fell to the deck, he slowly muttered, "how did you get back on..."

When he awoke, he was still on the deck of her boat. His arm had been bandaged, and there was a meal of fish next to him which he devoured quickly. The boat jerked forward, and he went to the side to see what had caused it. Stretched out in front of the bow was a long rope tied to the stern of the larger boat - *his* boat. He was being towed *by his own boat.* He shouted some perfunctory curses and insults but got no response. *This*

female does not seem to know the rules. He decided on another tactic and just shouted "Hello?" which brought an immediate response.

"You are not dead?" she shouted.

"Why are you towing me? Why not just leave me?"

"I have a proposal," she said as she turned a crank which drew in the tow line a bit and brought him closer.

"I will not mate with you." He called back, waved a hand dismissively in the air and began pacing.

She tilted her head to the side again.

She keeps doing that. What does it mean?

"You have the largest collection of metal I have *ever* seen," she shouted down at him.

"You are impressed!" he said surprised. "I knew it!"

"I can show you how to use it," she said.

Use it? He thought. What was she talking about? Metal was for collecting and trading - and occasionally, impressing females but until now that had not actually worked. *She makes weapons out of it!*

A new age of *invention* began. *The two inventors,* as history named them, created tools for everything, including the manufacture of other tools. In the beginning, they simply used the harder metals like iron to pound softer ones like copper, but with their first furnace, they were able to melt and bend even the hardest metals. Through the trade of tools for raw materials, they soon accumulated enough metal to make a fully submersible boat and plunder the ocean floor for all the metal that had fallen to its depths. The inventors themselves lived long enough to see this, but it was their descendants, trained in the ways of tool making and building, who created an empire of industry and eventually traveled to the source of all metal - *space.*

Chapter Thirty-One

631 BCE - Hell is Other People

Applause from two spiderbots signaled that Thomas had reached the end of the story. The alien saw this and joined in, applauding enthusiastically. Thomas bowed.

"Good God," Jack said, and the alien extended her middle finger at him just before Thomas did. She also bared her teeth in an attempt at a smile.

"So, who attacked her?" Bonnie asked.

"The shark people. Obviously," Jack said sarcastically.

"They actually do have sharks on their world, Jack," Thomas said. "But they're peaceful, and everyone likes them."

The alien chittered something at Thomas.

"Oh, she says, *Except for the fish they eat of course. They're not fans.* I think that was a joke!"

"Seriously, does she know who attacked her?" Bonnie asked.

"Males and females never really learned to get along," Thomas continued. "History says that *The Inventors,* the first pair, got along and stayed together until they died, but I suspect that's probably the usual exaggeration of history books. Even if it's true, they were a rare exception. The females work together in small groups at various things usually involving metal - they really, *really* like metal in case you haven't noticed, but the males take the easier route and just steal it."

"So it was the males?"

"Male. Singular. She refused to give up without a fight and took him out. Males have surprise on their side, but females typically have better weapons. She destroyed him and his ship but not before he damaged hers. She barely made it to the escape pod."

The alien said something to Thomas.

"The cylinder is still here, but I told her we used it already. She says we owe her for it."

"Okay..." Bonnie said.

"How about some nice fish?" Jack suggested. "We have a bigger problem than a bill from a scrap metal merchant. What if they come back? There's not much shiny stuff down there," he pointed at the display, "in eight thousand BC,"

"E," Thomas corrected again. "BC*E.* And it's that direction if you mean Earth." He pointed at the floor.

"...but where we come from..." Jack continued.

" *When* we come from," Thomas corrected.

Jack was getting frustrated, "...there's a ton of it all refined and waiting to be stolen."

"It was just one male," Bonnie said, "and he's dead now Jack. She says they don't work together, so it's not like his friends are going to come looking for him."

"Okay," Jack said, "so what do we do with her? Take her home? Once she tells her friends, it'll be a feeding frenzy on Earth."

"Again with the sharks?" Thomas muttered, but his attention was on the penguin.

"She says she doesn't want to go home. She wants to stay with us and explore fast."

"Fast? What does that mean?" Bonnie asked.

"Um, translation problem perhaps? I'll see if I can get a clarification."

He conversed in her language for a bit. "She says they don't have wormhole drives. They sleep in stasis pods between star systems. It takes thousands of years. She wants to go faster."

"Thousands of years! Everybody would be dead by the time you got back!" Bonnie said horrified.

"Yeah, they're not much for family and friends. I think it's probably more useful to think of them as Tigers. They're solitary and avoid all contact unless it's absolutely necessary, like mating. She says she only goes back to get new technology, which is usually not very impressive despite the time intervals. Apparently, they all work alone, never *share*, and only trade when it's profitable. So, the same thing gets invented a thousand times, and one individual could have something really ground-breaking, but you wouldn't know about it unless you happened to meet her, and then only if you had something to trade for it."

"How many times has she been back and forth?" Bonnie asked, still stunned at this idea of thousand-year voyages.

"Forty-two trips since she inherited her mother's ship. She was born well over half a million years ago. It's a long way off."

"And she doesn't want to go back?"

"I misspoke earlier. She does want to go back, but she wants the wormhole technology. She considers it, along with a ride home, to be a fair trade for the cylinder. We should definitely take the deal. Imagine the stories they have!"

"And the time travel? What does she think about that?"

At the mention of it, Thomas tried to jump to 2216 where Gillian and the others were waiting but undershot the target by ten years. The display changed to 2206.

"Oh, I left that part out," Thomas said. "Need-to-know, and all that."

"What a shock," Jack said. "At least your dishonesty works in our favor for once."

Thomas extended a middle finger, and the alien did the same followed by a swipe of her hand across her decorative metal belt. Thomas looked confused for a second before his avatar disappeared and the two spiderbots collapsed to the floor. Before Jack or Bonnie realized what was happening, two darts shot from the escape pod and struck them in the chest.

"Oh shit..." Bonnie said, and Jack managed to raise one eyebrow at her before passing out.

As Thomas felt himself shrinking, he realized the alien escape pod's A.I. was taking over. He tried to resist, but it was too fast. All he could manage to do was send a new instruction to Sputnik: **Call Gillian in 2216 and give her these coordinates. And tell her I don't need any help but just FYI...**

Chapter Thirty-Two

2216 - Strange Message

Gillian had intended to let them take in the view from Olympus Mons until their air supply was at the half-way mark but she cut it short when Thomas's satellite emerged from the other side of the sun.

"Okay, that's enough sightseeing," Gillian said. "I just got a strange message from Thomas. It's time to go."

"Thomas? Where is he?" M asked and did her best to run in the low gravity.

"He's back where we just left. We should have waited," Gillian said.

"What do you mean strange?" Brad said trying to keep up with M.

"It's from a satellite that he made on the other side of the sun. It just says, *I don't need help,* which of course, means that he does," Gillian said.

The ramp hadn't fully retracted before they lifted off and headed back to Gillian's position. They were all quiet on the trip back, worried about Thomas and Bonnie. As they approached Gillian, Chris gave Doug a shove on his shoulder, "Say it."

"What?" he turned in his seat with a confused expression.

"She nodded at the viewport where Gillian's spherical form was growing.

"Ahhh," he giggled, "That's no moon!"

Chapter Thirty-Three

2206 The General Store

The old male heard an alarm and rolled his chair over from the food maker to the sensor workstation. It showed a ship approaching. It was an alien design, spherical, with only three distinct markings. It was a design he had seen before, but this one was broadcasting the correct code, so he deactivated the defenses and let it through. *This was turning out to be a profitable week,* he thought. It was fortunate timing to have traded his meager metal for a chance to be the home-world monitor. He had not yet become bored with it, as his predecessor had, and the rewards were turning out to be even better than promised. Still, the wanderlust was there. He knew that soon it would grow too strong to resist, and he would trade the job to someone else. There was always someone weary of the travel and willing to try a hand at this if only for a short time. The job was more like a merchant than a harbormaster. Ships brought things to trade - technology and metal mostly. Occasionally aliens came but the defenses always stopped them, and they never had much of value. *Not worth the trouble,* he thought as he opened the airlock. A young female entered and greeted him. He made the perfunctory offer to mate with her, and she declined as expected.

"I Require a ship," she said.

"You *have* a ship. Is it malfunctioning?"

"No, it is an alien design. I took it from them easily. They did not seem to know the rules."

"Backward feather-muckers!" he said, and they both laughed in the high-pitched staccato while patting their hands on their sides.

"No, it has no defenses, the dimensions are all wrong, the lighting is bad. It does not even have a pool! There is a primitive A.I. But nothing of any value. You will probably not get very much metal for it but who knows? The young are stupid!"

They both laughed again.

"For that quantity of metal, I can only trade you a beginner's ship, unless you have something else of value?"

She considered selling the wormhole technology but decided against it. Keeping it to herself was a better long-term strategy. Rather than going straight home in one jump, she stopped off at the half-way point to have her A.I. turn off all the defenses Reggie had installed. She then dismantled the toroid of Charm Material. As soon as she understood it enough for replication, she destroyed it.

"I suppose a beginner's model will have to do for now," she said.

They exchanged access codes, and she left in a ship roughly the same size as Thomas. The merchant entered some commands at one of the workstations, and a smaller drone ship came to life. It pushed the inanimate Thomas to the outer defense perimeter and activated one of the null-time fields. Thomas disappeared, surrounded by a black void.

Chapter Thirty-Four

2216 - Betraying's all part of Pirating

"Oh-ah-ow!" Jack said as he sat up massaging the back of his head. "What happened?"

The escape pod was splayed open on the floor next to him. They were in Gillian's shuttle bay, and Brad was lifting Bonnie out of the pod.

"Son?" Jack said surprised and tried to focus.

Brad glanced at him but said nothing. Chris ran to Jack and hugged him tightly around his neck. He kissed her cheek, and she released him. She had never seen him cry before, but tears came freely at the sight of her standing again. He turned to see Doug who held out his hand. Jack pushed it away and hugged him as well. As they turned to see about Bonnie, she was beginning to stir.

"What happened?" she asked.

"We were hoping *you* could tell us," Doug said. "We got a message from Thomas. He just sent your position and said he didn't need help."

"It's pretty obvious, isn't it?" Brad said. "That bastard left them out there to die. We need to find him so we can melt him down. Maybe we can make something even more useless out of him, although I can't think of what."

"I'm sure he didn't do anything like that," Gillian said approaching Jack. "Hello, I don't believe we've met. I'm Gillian."

"Is this your ship?" Jack asked.

"Sort of," she said. "I *am* the ship. Surely Bonnie told you."

He looked confused and massaged the back of his neck, "yeah, sorry, she did. Why didn't I remember it?"

"You were in that escape pod for ten years. It may take a while before you feel entirely yourselves again. And there are still drugs in your system."

"How do you know that?" he asked, but she was interrupted by Bonnie.

"The alien shot us. The last thing I saw before I passed out was the penguin doing something with her belt, and Thomas's avatar disappeared."

"Aliens and penguins?" Gillian said.

"Yeah, a penguin but with teeth like a weasel. Wait, no. The penguin *was* the alien," Jack said.

Two of Gillian's monkeybots were examining the escape pod.

"It's an amazing piece of technology," Gillian said. "It seems designed to take over any ship unlucky enough to find it. I have sandboxed it, but I think we should eject it just to be sure." She snapped her fingers, and the monkeybots carried it off to the edge of the shuttle bay next to the doors which opened just wide enough and just long enough for the pod to get swept out with a rush of air.

"So we're going after him, right?" Doug said.

"There's no debate about this," Chris shouted. "They stole Thomas!"

"Yeah, there's a lot of that going around," M said.

"Oh. Yeah," Bonnie said. "Sorry about that, M."

"It's okay," M said. "He doesn't belong to me or anything. And you didn't steal him. You just left with him. I was going to do the same thing. You just beat me to it."

"Damn pirate peng-weasel," Jack said. "Thomas is a jerk, but we have to save him. Hell, she might melt him down just for the metal. Crazy little vermin."

"Wait a minute," M said. "Nobody knows better than me what a jerk he can be, but we have to consider the possibility that he might just *like* his new passenger. Are we going to risk our lives on the assumption that he didn't go willingly? Didn't he say he didn't need help?"

"That was probably just pride," Gillian said.

They all looked at Brad.

"What? It's not my call anyway. Gillian's in charge."

"If it *was* your call," Gillian said. "Would you risk your life to save Thomas? It might come to that."

He paused for several seconds thinking of all Thomas had done, both negative and positive. He saw his sister and Bonnie both healthy again. He finally shrugged. "Yeah, what the hell. I guess so - God damn it."

"Language," Bonnie said.

"What's it going to be, Gillian? Do we go after him?" M asked.

"I've already jumped back ten years," Gillian said. "Welcome to 2206. I was just curious what all of you would decide. Now, let's get up to the bridge." She winked at M, "we're burning daylight."

As they began the long walk to the elevator, Jack called to Brad who ignored him. M stopped to stare at Brad until he turned around to face his father.

"What?" Brad demanded and crossed his arms.

Jack took a few steps toward Brad and glanced in the direction of the others who seemed in a hurry to give them privacy. "I don't expect you to understand..."

"Good, then you won't be disappointed!" Brad said.

"Just - shut up and let me say my peace."

Brad took a deep breath and sighed loudly.

"If I had stayed, you would have had to take care of me. I know by leaving, I dumped all my problems in your lap. I know that, and I know how hard it's been..."

"You have no idea!" Brad interrupted.

"But!" Jack shouted and calmed a bit, "but, that would have happened even if I had stayed. You're strong enough to take care of the farm, and your mom, and your sister. That's a lot more than most people could do, but there's no way on God's green Earth you could have taken care of a dying old man too." He paused to let that sink in. "I know you're mad at me, but it's not because I took away our last months together. It's because I didn't stay to help, and that was never in the cards anyway." He gave Brad a few seconds to think. "Are we good now?"

"Nope."

"Okay, fair enough. Are we *better*?"

"A little."

"All right, then. Let's go save that stupid bastard," Jack said.

Brad took the seat next to M, leaned over, and said, "sit-rep?"

She kissed him before responding. "We're waiting for the penguin..."

"Peng-weasel," Jack corrected.

"...to eject the escape pod that has Bonnie and Jack inside it. Gillian says if we act too quickly the timeline won't be preserved and the universe might end."

"Okay. Important safety tip," Brad smiled.

She looked confused. "Yes, it is."

"Ghost Busters!" Doug shouted from his seat across the room.

They didn't have to wait long. The display showed a long slender cylinder exit the airlock and tumble away. When Gillian moved, no one onboard felt anything. The image of Thomas changed from a small dot in the distance, to suddenly dominate the display. They were much closer now, and he was coming toward them quickly. Scintillating blue laser light flashed from Thomas and immediately winked out.

"Oh, I was going to tell you about that!" Bonnie said to Gillian. "It slipped my mind. Sorry!"

"I knew about his little toy. I scanned every molecule of him when we met." Gillian said calmly.

"Scanners!" Doug and Jack both looked at each other.

"Proper spaceship," Jack muttered and shifted in his chair.

"When did he get a laser?" Brad asked.

"Oh, he always had that," M said. "He used to go on and on about *how powerful it was* and how *as soon as he needed it, boy was he ever gonna use it blah blah blah.* I just ignored him, and he got bored with the topic."

"Well, I reflected it back with a power boost," Gillian said. "It's burned out now, but she can probably fix it. I reverse engineered the null-time field generator in the escape pod, so if we can get him inside the shuttle bay, I can wrap him in one until we come up with a way to safely extract the penguin."

"Peng-weasel," Jack said.

"Give it up Jack," Bonnie said. "Nobody likes that."

Thomas turned rapidly and dodged Gillian's open shuttle bay doors.

"I see she's already made some improvements," Gillian said. "He shouldn't be able to change course that fast."

Gillian was about to try again at closer range when Thomas disappeared.

"I guess she figured out the wormhole drive too," M said nervously.

"That's worrying," Gillian said, "it means she has a powerful A.I. - even stronger than Thomas."

"Where would she have gone?" M asked.

"She said she was from a water planet if that helps. It's completely covered - no land at all," Bonnie said.

"You *talked* to it!" Doug shouted. "This just gets better and better! You talked to an alien. Ho-lee shit."

"Language!" Bonnie said.

"Yeah, we got the whole story," Jack said. "But it was through Thomas, so who knows how much of it was true. The planet must be fairly close. They don't have wormhole drives. Oh, until now, I guess. She said they use those stasis pods and sleep between the stars."

"We can just visit the closest systems and look for a water planet. Easy!" Doug said.

Chapter Thirty-Five

2216 - Fly Paper

The dozen closest systems had rocky planets close to the star and gas giants farther out but none in the Goldilocks Zone, which was the region of space at a distance from the star where planets could have liquid water. Most of the stars were M-class, smaller than Earth's sun and less bright. None of them were G-class, and although they were not sure the penguin world orbited a G-class star, it was a safe assumption. The first of these they came across was part of a triple-star system, and the movements of the three stars were so chaotic that it had no planets at all. Another system had a trapped rogue planet in a strange orbit. It must have disrupted the inner planets because they were gone too. They had cataloged over one hundred systems when they came to a K-class star thirty-six light years from Earth. Gillian always jumped to the farthest reaches of each system, just close enough to observe without much risk of *being* observed. She woke everyone and called them to the bridge.

"It is a K-class star, roughly the same mass as Sol," she said showing a star surrounded by rings instead of planets. "The significant thing isn't so much a planet in the Goldilocks Zone. It's the lack of other planets. In each orbit where we might otherwise find a planet, there is an asteroid belt instead. It appears that they plundered their own system before venturing out to others." The display zoomed in to show a familiar looking blue planet with white clouds. The only difference was the uniformity of the blue beneath the white clouds. It had no land masses at all.

"A water planet," Doug said nodding.

"It's beautiful," M said in awe. This moment, more than any other since her journey began, made it all worthwhile. This is what drove her - the hope of someday gazing on a beautiful new planet filled with strange life.

"Is it the right one?" Bonnie asked.

"It is," Gillian said. "There are a dozen or so ships in orbit but no sign of Thomas yet."

"What's the plan?" Jack and Brad said at the same time.

"I'll jump back a month or so and drop a spy drone out here at the edge of the system. Then we can jump back here, review the data, and see what has been going on down there."

The display zoomed out to show the entire system. At this magnification, it looked like all the others they had encountered, except for the color of the star. Gillian's spy drone was a small white sphere which entered the frame of the display and slowly turned black as she jumped forward.

"Fascinating," Gillian said showing the recorded video. "See, right there," she zoomed in and circled a section of the display in red. It showed an unfamiliar ship approaching the water planet and suddenly disappearing.

"Was it destroyed?" M said. "I didn't see an explosion."

"Maybe it was one of the Penguins, and now it's cloaked," Doug said.

"Not cloaked," Gillian said. "Trapped. There have been several ships of this other design," she displayed a white football-shaped ship similar to the ones Bonnie and Jack saw from Thomas's spy drone. "These all safely approached the system, stayed a short time and left. None stayed longer than a few days."

"That's consistent with the behavior Thomas described," Bonnie said. "They're solitary. They don't trust, or even like, each other much."

"So something is stopping the non-penguin ships from getting too close to the planet," M said.

Gillian kept the camera focused on the same area of space occupied by the alien ship and zoomed in while shifting perspective slightly to the side. A small portion of the star field disappeared behind the void as they changed their position.

"It's like a black hole. It blocks all the light from behind it," Doug said.

"Not quite. It doesn't have enough of a gravity field to be a black hole. It must be the same null-time field they used in the escape pod," Gillian said.

"Like flypaper," Bonnie said. "If you don't have the password you get stuck. I wonder how many there are?"

The display showed a red circle around the trapped ship. As Gillian shifted her perspective, more and more red circles popped into existence until the planet appeared to be inside a spherical shell of black voids circled in red.

"Well I guess we know how close we can get," Gillian said. "This one is Thomas." One of the red circles blinked. "He arrived shortly before we did and passed through the flypaper zone but after a brief meet up with a small cluster of penguin ships he was pushed back out with the others, and one of the penguin ships left the system - using a wormhole drive."

"She sold him!" Chris said.

"Looks like it," Gillian said. "This region seems to be dual purpose. They trap any uninvited guests, but also use it for storage."

"That little bitch!" Bonnie said, and they all turned to look at her.

"Um - language? I guess," Chris said and shrugged.

"I have an idea," Jack said. "They're solitary, right? So, they have no real culture - no stories, or at least not many. I'll bet they've never been warned about Greeks bearing gifts."

"A Trojan horse!" Doug said. "Perfect!"

"They seem to like shiny things," Bonnie said. "We can make it from metal and just set it on a course toward the planet. Somebody's bound to pick it up and take it inside."

"Shouldn't it be a Trojan Penguin?" Brad said.

"Even better," Bonnie said. "They do have one hero. We could make it look like her. Just give it a crossbow."

"And when they bring it inside, I'll fire the weapons," Jack said.

"That's a generous offer, Jack," Gillian said. "But, an unnecessary risk. I think we can do better than a hollow statue."

"I know where we can get a hunk of metal to use," M said.

They jumped back to the remnants of the cylinder in their home system. Gillian's nanobots soon formed a stream resembling angry hornets leaving a bumped nest as they flowed from the cylinder's raw material to the beginnings of a penguin statue.

"What do you think?" she asked when it was finished.

"Well, it's the finest rendition of an alien penguin I've ever seen," Doug said and smiled.

M considered it and said, "I like the gold crossbow. That's a nice touch."

The others nodded and agreed.

"It's close enough," Brad said.

"That's not *solid* gold, is it?" Jack asked. "The little bastards don't deserve anything more than plating if you ask me."

It was a large statue, about twice the height of Thomas, but still able to fit into Gillian's shuttle bay. They jumped back to the outskirts of the water planet's system, and she gave it a push toward the planet. As expected, it stopped immediately when it reached the flypaper zone. At the same time, a tiny dot of light appeared. It was near the new dark sphere that now contained the statue. It glowed brightly for a moment and dimmed.

"It's powered by the kinetic energy of whatever gets trapped. Fascinating." Gillian said.

"Now what?" Brad asked. "They might not even know it's there."

M shrugged, "now we wait and see if they take the bait."

The merchant could not believe his luck. *A statue of the Inventors! It was only one of them, but still! It was beautiful!* He considered keeping it for himself, but he didn't have a large enough ship yet. *No, the best course of action is to trade it for enough metal to make a new large ship.* He hoped a buyer would come soon - an old one would be best. Young ones had no taste for such fine things.

Gillian and her crew waited for several days and began discussing alternative plans, usually involving time travel. Jack lobbied heavily for this approach saying *a time machine and a pistol can solve any problem.* Gillian rejected these and assured them that waiting would soon bear fruit, and on the seventh day, it did. A new penguin ship arrived. It was large, like the one that attacked the female and it was towing a cylinder of metal similar to the one produced by the mining at Phaeton. It stopped at the same cluster of ships but only stayed a few minutes before heading straight for the Trojan Penguin. When it got close, it fired a dim beam of light. The small dot near the black void glowed again, and the shroud disappeared revealing the penguin statue floating motionless in space. The ship opened a pair of large doors and devoured the statue. Just before the doors closed again, the statue melted into a swarm of nanobots. The alien ship darted quickly backward, toward the planet, but suddenly slowed and changed course toward the null-time field that held Thomas. As it approached, it repeated the unlock process, and Thomas was again visible but motionless. A stream of nanobots shot from the penguin ship toward him, and he came to life again.

The single ping of an alarm rang in the merchant's ship. *Unauthorized thaw.* Someone was trying to steal something. He checked the data. *Why would anyone take that? It's nearly worthless.* As he reached for the communication console, the alarm repeated, and then a third time. The alarms were coming so rapidly now that the sound became a constant scream. The two ships released two more and then two more. Some of them were helping in the effort making it grow exponentially. A few of the freed ships fled the system but most, after Thomas shared the unlock-codes, stayed to help liberate others. Most were looking for comrades. One especially combative ship set a course for the planet. It had crossed about half the distance between the flypaper zone and the atmosphere before it was destroyed in a spectacular silent explosion. The debris sprawled along the curve of an invisible barrier. The merchant decided it was time to retreat and fled to the planet below.

When two of the freshly released ships began shooting at each other, Thomas decided he had done enough. Gillian sent him a message with their position, and he set a rendezvous course. As he approached, they could see he was followed by another spherical ship. It had a red dragon on the hull above its name. It was Reggie's ship **The Dragon Lady**.

Gillian's avatar smiled at the sight of it. "Hello, Reggie. It's good to see you again."

Reggie's copy accompanied them back to Earth inside Gillian's shuttle bay. Thomas was forced to do the same since the alien had dismantled his wormhole drive. Reggie's copy relayed his tale of exploration, independently developing the same wormhole drive as his counterpart on

Earth, not finding any intelligent species, and finally getting snared by the defenses around the alien planet.

After reuniting the two Reggies on Earth and refitting Thomas with another wormhole drive, Thomas and Gillian decided to explore more of the nearby stars. Thomas initially wanted to find the alien that abducted him but admitted that was unrealistic. Reggie was fascinated with the story of the penguin-aliens. As a species, they were neither good nor evil. They had probably never started a war nor participated in one. To do so would have required cooperation, obedience, and teamwork.

Before setting off with Gillian and Thomas, M returned to her island to find it covered with llamas, camels, and goats - all being fed by service bots. There were also several piles of raw meat covered with flies but no sign of what was meant to eat them. Carlos explained that the barge with animal enclosures was late and the piles of meat were for an African lion named "T-Rex" who refused to be fed. He had to be returned to the barge until his enclosure could be built. When they went to see for themselves, they found him pacing slowly in a large enclosure below deck.

"Oh, T-Rex," M said. "We're going to take you home to Africa. And we're also going to get that ridiculous T-shirt off you - *somehow.*"

If you enjoyed this book, check out more at
https://w-c-brown.com
including a list of some of the more obscure references and a few Easter-Eggs.
You can also follow me on twitter: @BrainsInChains

W. C. Brown

Made in the USA
Columbia, SC
26 August 2017